Unearthed
Volume 1
By Marc Mulero

D1736206

Contents

Chapter 1

"Blague, how do you plan on clearing out the wreckage? The Hiezers have eyes on us," Eugene warned while surveying the area.

Blague had a habit of thinking a few steps ahead of his opponents, at the cost of time that no one had to spare. Blague looked at Eugene with a half smirk and hopped onto the first layer of what seemed to be endless debris blocking their path.

"We're going to dig a hole under the midpoint of the wreckage and plant six pounds of C-4. The heaviest portion of this pile of junk seems to be the foundation, so once we weaken it, I expect the dam to cave inward," Blague explained calmly, dangling on the second layer of filth with one fist firmly grasped around a stray pole.

Eugene noticed Blague's blue, distorted tattoo on his arm shining in the moonlight. Blague released his grasp on the pole and fell about eleven feet without bending his knees upon landing. He walked a few paces, analyzing the structure of the heaping pile of junk blocking their path. After a moment of thought, he turned from the wall and placed his muscular arms on Eugene's shoulders.

"I want the Hiezers to see this. Senation hasn't had a gleam of hope in nearly a decade. Things are about to change. Are you with me, Eu?" Blague questioned.

Eugene nodded and sighed.

"Good," Blague said in a calm voice, "now inform our people to set up camp a quarter mile behind the wreckage and call in two diggers. We make our first move at sunrise." Eugene jogged off, while Blague remained there to reflect.

A calculated gamble, but not with terrible odds. A quarter mile should be more than enough space to avoid casualties, but should leave our people close enough to obtain favorable positioning upon breaching the blown wreckage as the Hiezer reinforcements interfere. If the Hiezers notice the smoke, that means the people of Senation will as well. We need to stir up some optimism. Hope is important. It is the cornerstone of ambition and is a virtue that is lacking on this continent. If we can spark hope in the people of Senation, we can disrupt the social class system that keeps these people in chains. This suffering has dragged on for far too long now. What's the point of carrying out a lifetime if there is no joy in it?

Moments later, Jerris and Gense jogged up to Blague, lugging shovels. Each pounded their chest once, giving their leader a salute, one which communicates strength and loyalty. A cloud of dust puffed into the air from pounding their dirt encrusted clothes. Blague stared at them with wide eyes for about thirty seconds, although not at all acknowledging the sight of them. Instead, his mind raced, contemplating how to proceed once they reach their destination. Finally, he snapped back.

"Gentlemen, dig three feet deep at the midpoint coordinate I marked off over there," he said, pointing to the mark and locking eyes with both men.

Blague's deep, brooding voice did not match his

intense stare and muscular physique. With his deep set green eyes, pushed-back wavy black hair, and an above average size nose that he would jokingly say commands respect, Blague had the look and demeanor of a confident commander in the Special Forces. Over the phone, however, he could be mistaken for a middle-aged college professor. His tan skin made his blue, glowing tattoo stand out immensely.

Blague stared up into the moonlight, as the diggers flipped their shovels off from their shoulders and got to work.

Back at the camp, Eugene and the other top commanders led both the civilians and fighters a quarter mile away from the mountain of wreckage. Patrol fighters assisted the commanders by positioning themselves on the outer rim of the group, armed with assault rifles and keeping watch for suspicious activity. The ground they trekked across was dusty, a mix of sand and pebble that stretched for miles, with piles of garbage and flimsy huts decorating the view.

"Eugene," a mysterious woman beckoned with a slightly raspy voice, "I have a feeling our target destination is guarded, and if it is, we don't have the means to push forward head on. I've decided to scout ahead and scale the wreckage before sunrise."

Eugene looked down and shook his head. "Lesh," he said with a disapproving tone, "that's unnecessarily risky. If we lose one commander before we breach the wreckage, we will undoubtedly fail to reach the mansion."

"Nonsense," Lesh said dismissively, "I'm heading out. Inform Blague once I'm fifteen layers high. And don't be a fucking moron and try to stop me."

They smirked at each other. Eugene remained silent, watching her stealthily sprint ahead, knowing it was senseless to argue any further. Her shoulder length brown hair was surprisingly clean and flowy for the conditions the group was subjected to. The eight sizable, bloodstained knives strapped to her back in a circular fashion were certainly the mark of Lesh. She fought countless times alongside Eugene and Blague and had yet to lose a throwing knife.

As the group decided upon the most favorable spot to set up camp and enjoy a meal before the mission, the matriarch of the group, Cherris, was surrounded by the younger followers. As always, she served as a human questionnaire to the generations that weren't alive before the global catastrophe.

"Cherris!" shrieked an excited boy with black hair straggled over his face, "How did you survive the Global Quake? And how was Senation created? My mama says it was the will of God!"

Cherris warmly smiled at the boy. The crowd of faces was dimly lit from the light of a small roasting fire, small enough that the smoke fizzled out just above their heads. The dancing flame shifted the light to different parts of their faces.

"To answer your first question," she said as she held up her index finger, "I was located in Kansas, smack dab in the middle of the United States on November 1st, 2022, and although the Global Quake was felt around the world, only certain areas toward the edges of continents were completely upheaved. So, although my house was torn in two, I managed to escape with my family relatively unscathed." Cherris looked around the fire to see many sets of engaged eyes. "Senation was created by that quake; it represents most of Old California, little one. No one on this earth knows why for sure, but we all have our beliefs, such as your mama." Cherris mussed the boy's hair, "Your family must be new to the group. What's your name?" she asked, looking down at the boy.

"I'm Milos, the Conqueror!" the boy shouted proudly.

"That's one hell of a name," Cherris said as she sat back in her make-shift chair.

All of the other kids crowding around listened intently. Their collective attention was strong when listening to Cherris speak about the Global Quake, no matter how many times they've heard it before.

If the Hiezers heard a boy boasting that he had an addendum to his first and only name, even he would be made an example of. He would be beaten bloody during such a crucial developmental stage of his life. Even so, I don't think I could bring myself to crush his pride and imagination at this moment. The fate of tomorrow is uncertain. I have to maintain some sense of serenity and let these kids live in this moment while it lasts.

Cherris sat forward with her mind made up, "Milos

the Conqueror, how do you plan on taking over the other exiled continents? With your bare hands?" Cherris smiled while looking the boy in the eyes.

He looked down, breaking eye contact for a moment. "No," Milos said as he looked back up at her and pointed to his head, "with my mind!" All of the other younger followers laughed. Milos blushed for a moment, then stood confidently and faced the crowd, "And maybe a few guns," he finished with a smile. The other kids morphed their laughter into cheers. Cherris was impressed.

To so easily overcome such potential embarrassment, this kid has courage. He may survive this journey that all of these kids were forced to take part in because of the views of their parents. One thing is for sure, their innocence will be lost.

"Ok, kids," Cherris raised her voice, "that's enough for tonight. Go eat your dinner and get some rest. Tomorrow is expected to be an important day."

"Goodnight Cherris!" the kids exclaimed unharmoniously.

As Milos ran to his pleasantly smiling mother, the mother looked over at Cherris and nodded to her graciously. Cherris smiled and nodded back. She looked around to note the guards patrolling around the chosen camp.

We would be overrun if we were caught. Seven guards to protect about one hundred and fifty civilians against any number of threats. I hope Blague calculated correctly.

The moonlit rocks reflected a bluish glow, creating a compelling silhouette of the speaker, who stood confidently on the second layer of wreckage at the midpoint. Blague had his head slightly tilted, inspecting his frosted, deep blue Desert Eagle; it was his only gun of choice. Directly behind him to his right stood Eugene, head tilted back and cigarette lit, dimly illuminating his dirty blonde hair as he mentally prepared for the unexpected morning. His sniper rifle was firmly strapped to his back. Directly behind Blague to his left stood Briggs, a six foot eight top commander whose talents extended from weapons to communications. He stood with a bold, yet humble expression; his confidence was backed by two sub-machine guns pointed down at either of his sides. Briggs was responsible for the secure line that the group had successfully communicated through for the past six months. Standing below on the first layer stood the remaining four commanders. Facing them was a sea of eyes, about one hundred fighters eager for a chance at a decent life. Their identical tattoos glowed blue, a half circle at the base of their shoulders, morphing to a sharp point ending on their biceps.

"Fellow Sins," Blague's voice echoed as he took his eyes off his gun, "I implore you all to reflect with the remaining hours we have left before sunrise. We have battled the Hiezers from the shadows up until now. Starting tomorrow, we will no longer hide as a group. Starting tomorrow, we will rally with the Sins of the other exiled continents. Starting tomorrow, we will bleed for a chance to pave our own path. Tomorrow, we will claim our first victory!" The fighters cheered. Blague put his hand up for silence, "But don't let your eagerness drown out the reality, brothers and sisters. I need your all if we're going to survive this. Reflect deeply. I won't hold it against you if any of you decide to walk away, but make your choice tonight." The fighters looked solemn, but no less dedicated. "My instinct tells me that not even one of you will turn away and that's how I know this can work. Sins, beyond this wreckage stands a mansion," he said while pointing to the backdrop in the distance. "This mansion is a base for the Hiezers, like many others on the exiled continents. Not only do I expect it to contain research revealing advanced human engineering secrets, but I expect it will also hold truths that you may not want to accept. Lesh has been gone for over four hours. I expected her back here thirty minutes ago. I fought alongside her long enough to know that she has a reason for not showing up to this meeting. The mansion must be heavily guarded. So get ready fighters, I expect you to give them hell!" The fighters pounded their chests once each. Blague gave an old fashioned salute with his Desert Eagle.

We have about an hour before the break-bomb is detonated.
Eugene stood slightly hunched, cleaning his rifle. It was jet black with one thin red stripe wrapping around the gun's exterior. His exhaustion began to subside as the adrenaline started to kick in. He was about to lay his life on the line, again. Something he's not expecting he could ever get used to.

Briggs walked up to Eugene and slapped him on the back, "What's up, little bitch?" Briggs said with a wide smile.

Eugene looked back and sighed, "Why don't you go say that to Lesh and see how that goes?" Eugene said with a slight grin.

Briggs hesitated, "Uhhh, n...no," he said with a comically fearful look on his face.

They both laughed. After a short pause, Eugene's concerns started to pour out. "Have the hidden Sin scouts reported any Hiezer activity? They're our lifeline after all. If even one screws u-"

"I know, I know," Briggs interrupted, "Blague has been asking for hourly reports. We're under control. If a Hiezer assassin happens to slip through to the civilians, we will act immediately. They are guarded after all."

Eugene looked up at Briggs, unconvinced. He sighed and proceeded to continue cleaning his rifle.

"So," Briggs said as he placed his weapon down next to Eugene's and poked around the table for spare tools, "did you notice Blague's Cryos tattoo glowing like that? It was far brighter than ours or any of the other fighters."

Eugene looked at Briggs curiously, "Yes, I've noticed that on multiple occasions. I doubt it means anything though. The Cryos chemical has always had strange effects on our bodies."

Briggs leaned on the table and folded his arms. "It's just so odd," Briggs said, "It's not a stamp like ours."

Eugene put his gun down and looked over at Briggs, "I asked him about it a few months back, after the TERRA mission. Blague paused for a long while before answering me, but there was no lying in him. He told me that it was 'Undeniably a Cryos mark and it was meant to label me as a Sin the same as you, Eugene. The only difference is, I resisted every step of the way.'"

Briggs looked impressed, "That's why he's our leader, right bud?" Briggs playfully punched Eugene's arm, causing him to stumble and drop one of his tools.

Eugene sighed and whispered, "What the fuck is wrong with this guy?"

Briggs put his hand to his ear and leaned in, "Say what?" Eugene smiled.

Lito, one of the ten commanders, called out to them, "It's time, guys. Let's get into position."

Eugene and Briggs looked at each other seriously. Eugene flipped his rifle on to his back and gave Briggs a pound.

"Be safe," Eugene said before they went their separate ways, "Guard your son, Briggs."

They both hastily split, heading toward their positions.

Tomorrow is going to be the start of Blague's grand scheme. That bastard better know what he's doing. There are a lot of lives on the line here. Eugene whipped his gun around as he stationed to kill from afar. *I don't want to be labeled as a Sin forever. I'll continue sniping for the day my Cryos tattoo symbolizes an act of heroism, instead of this disgraceful low grade criminal exile bullshit.*

Chapter 2

Blague stood at the tip of the triangular-formed group. His commanders stood directly behind him, followed by nearly one hundred Sin fighters, and one hundred and fifty civilians. Blague held up his fist. His blue tattoo was stifling; the heat emanating from it was similar to heat rising from the sand in a desert. The dust twirled around them. "Alright everyone, this will be a simple mission with profound results. Take over the mansion. I expect there will be more than enough room for everyone once we do. Once the mansion is clear, strip all cameras after Briggs pops our EMP. Then, escort the civilians and their supply crates to the ground level. We will reconvene from there. Understood?" Blague turned to face the mountain of wreckage in the distance. He heard the echo of about two hundred and sixty salutes. "Lito!" he shouted, "Detonate the break-bomb!" Blague drew his Desert Eagle. An echo of weapons being drawn followed.

Lito pressed his finger down heavily on the detonator. Moments later, the sound of an explosion resonated. The wreckage began to ripple and then quickly caved inward to the center. The ground trembled beneath the Sins' feet. The fighters tensed up.

"Brace yourselves, everyone," Lito shouted as his black and green mohawk quivered in unison with the ground. "We will have company soon, once the Hiezers realize there's been a breach."

The midpoint of the wreckage resembled a tidal wave crashing down. The screams of children could barely be heard amongst the overwhelming clattering of metal scraps bouncing off of the dusty ground, thrown in random directions. Eugene began to notice the pattern of falling debris and where the breach point would be, so he quickly found high ground for sniping visibility. Briggs looked at his heat sensing radar for signs of human activity ahead. At this point, there was none. The trembling ceased. A piece of scrap metal rolled and stopped about thirty feet away from them. A dangerous path of debris paved the way to the mansion ahead, which was now visible from where they stood.

Blague turned his head and shouted to the group behind him, "Advance slowly! Use the debris as cover! Move!"

Briggs looked down for a moment to check his radar again. He immediately felt goosebumps and the heat of blood rushing to his head. His eyes grew wide before he could speak. "Blague!" Briggs yelled. The advancing commanders turned to him. "Heavy activity incoming!"

The commanders quickly shifted their focus forward and took refuge behind the fallen debris. Through the huge haze of dust and smoke that was rising above like a mushroom cloud, Blague spotted the silhouette of a Hiezer patrolman with an assault rifle. He motioned for his people to advance as he led the way. The patrolman pointed at the crowd of people he thought he saw, but as his finger went up, his head jerked back; a bullet from Eugene's rifle ripped through his skull.

Moments later, Hiezer guards flooded the scene as the smoke began to clear simultaneously. Gun fire erupted from both sides. The sound of bullets ricocheting off of metal and intense battle-cries polluted the scene. The unnerving sounds provoked anxiety in the distance, as the civilians took cover near where they had set up camp. Kids were shaking with a mix of fear and curiosity as their families held them tight. The battle became too heavy for the civilians to advance at this point. Blague stood from cover and fired two shots from his Desert Eagle, one head shot and one chest shot, causing two guards to stumble down into the jagged debris. Twenty feet away, Briggs hoisted Lito into the air from a trench. While airborne, Lito pulled a short-fuse dynamite from his back pack, lit it and threw it. Four guards were tossed into the air from the explosion. About forty guards rushed through the breach to take their place. Bullets whizzed in both directions as the Sin fighters continued to fire their weapons. The battle ensued for about ten minutes. The Sins outnumbered the Hiezers, allowing them to lead a successful assault. The commanders ordered the fighters back to prepare for the next wave of enemy fire. Blague gasped as he saw a gunner soldier emerge from the breach. The soldier held a massive machine gun, while another soldier ducked down and held the chain of bullets.

"Take cover!" Blague shouted from the front lines as

the gunner opened fire.

Lito was exposed, remaining close to the breach from his flight. He sped in front of the bullet trail following him and dove behind some wreckage. Briggs stood up as a distraction, drawing his two sub machine guns and opening fire. He clipped the soldier's ammo feeder, but the gunner turned to where Briggs stood. Blood splashed in the air and landed on a Sin fighter's face. Briggs plopped down and dropped his guns, holding his wounded arm, wincing in pain.

"That better be a flesh wound," the fighter said. The gunner continued his assault, aiming at Blague, when all of a sudden the gunner fire stopped. Blague emerged from cover with his arm held out stiff, ready to retaliate. To his surprise, the gunner was already dead, lying face down with a knife in the back of his head. Lesh flipped down from a section of the wreckage, stepped on the dead gunner's head, and took back what belonged to her. Blague focused his attention to a Hiezer guard who appeared behind Lesh. He quickly shifted his aim and fired. The bullet whizzed by her, making its stop in the advancing guard's heart. Amongst the chaos, Lesh leapt to a piece of stray debris while pulling a knife out of the ring on her back. She tossed it as she grabbed onto the jagged edge of a metal scrap. The knife shot through a guard's throat. Without skipping a beat, she took another knife and flung it while flipping herself off the debris. Dust was kicked up as her feet hit the ground. She took a glance of her surrounding area and sprinted toward her impaled victims, eyeing the exposed knives. She artfully recovered her weapons, appearing only as a shadow for the brief moment she was exposed at the breach. Another guard leapt out as Lesh dashed back toward Lito and Blague. As she weaved around the wreckage, she caught a glimpse of Lito waving his hands for her to get down. As the guard was about to open fire, a sniper bullet ran through his chest and threw him backward.

Briggs' arm was limp, wrapped tightly with his tank top. His bicep veins bulged as he tried to focus on the heat radar. "We're clear for now," he said to Blague through his radio.

Blague then quickly turned to the fighter closest to him, "Get the civilians moving!" he commanded, knowing there was no time to waste. "Report our casualties in four minutes," he demanded from another fighter. The fighter nodded. Blague hopped over some debris to get to Briggs. He moved the makeshift bandage and inspected the wound for a moment. "I see an exit wound," Blague said. "The good news is you're going to be ok. The bad news is the pain is going to become more apparent within the next few minutes, when the adrenaline wears off. Go see a medic and sit the second wave out."

Briggs barely had the energy to acknowledge the request, but he began to move toward the civilians. Lesh and Lito rummaged through debris to get to Blague.

Blague put an arm around Lesh, "You saved our asses back there, Lesh."

"Maybe," she said in a whisper, "but I scouted a second wave of guards. We slaughtered the outdoor patrol, but there's also a patrol within the mansion. About one hundred strong," her raspy voice cracked.

Blague turned around to the fighter with a casualty report. "Yes?" he said.

The fighter looked solemn, "Eleven casualties and fourteen injured, including Commander Briggs. All were fighters."

Blague, too, looked solemn. "Have the civilians gather the dead and tend to the wounded. We will address the situation as a whole once we settle into the mansion."

Briggs looked at his radar while walking towards the civilians, who were slowly advancing toward the breach. In shock, he saw bodies quickly approaching from the back way, heading straight for the civilians. The wreckage breach was also becoming populated. Briggs desperately grabbed onto a fighter, showed her the radar and said, "Inform Blague, immediately!" The fighter shared Briggs' angst after a peek at the growing heat signatures on the radar. She quickly ran to Blague to give him the warning as Briggs dashed toward the civilians, holding his limp arm in place. He heard a scream in the distance, panic ensued through the crowd. Briggs stopped a frightened man in his tracks by putting his huge arm in his way. "What's going on?" Briggs asked with intensity.

"Two people were attacked from behind by Hiezer guards," the man said.

That means a scout in one of the outer cities either betrayed us or was found out. Either way, this wasn't anticipated. I have to find Kentin. Briggs nodded to the man and raced off to find his son in the chaos.

Cherris had a front row seat to the attack. She gathered a few kids and told them to hide in her supply wagon, which she would guard. Ten Hiezer guards stormed from the back of the camp, where seven Sin patrolmen were strategically placed at the back entrance to protect the civilians from an ambush. All seven perished in gunfire, but so did eight of the Hiezer guards. The remaining two spread out and ran into the civilian crowd. Cherris spotted one of them not so far off, but she couldn't leave the kids. She screamed for help, but the sound was drowned out by the panic. Tears streamed down her face as she witnessed one of the guards draw his pistol and point at a woman's head. A man jumped out in an attempt to tackle the guard, but he was swatted away. Cherris felt her breath shorten when she realized that the woman was Milos' mother.

Not a moment later, Milos ran to the scene with determination in his eyes and a knife in his hands. Without flinching, the guard opened fire point blank. Cherris abandoned her post out of instinct, but was nowhere near close enough to stop him. Time slowed in that instant, as Milos stabbed the guard in the calf at the exact moment he saw his mother's life brutally taken from her. The bullet hole in her head, mixed with blood and tears streaming down her face was inconceivable. Milos' eyes became painstakingly bloodshot; his body wasn't equipped to handle the anguish. The guard screamed in pain, pivoted, and pointed his gun to the kid's head. Milos looked up without fear of his own imminent death.

The split-second the guard's finger began to flex was the moment a knife pierced his skull. His body went limp immediately. Lesh, rarely showing compassion, hugged the boy with one arm and ripped her bloody knife out of the guard's head with the other, whipping the knife back into her knife ring.

"Child," Lesh said, "you will never be the same. Go to Cherris to soothe the pain, but come to me when you're ready to inflict it."

She let go and pushed him into Cherris' arms. Lesh looked at Cherris with a straight face.

Cherris stared back in despair, "There's still one out there."

Lesh shook her head and pointed behind her. There Briggs was, with his son, and a dead guard over his shoulder. Briggs walked over and shrugged his shoulder to release the corpse, letting it fall onto the other guard's body.

"Is that all of them?" Cherris asked.

"From the back way, it seems all ten are accounted for. The fighters are clearing the breach as we speak. Blague sent me back to account for this situation," Briggs said while glancing over at the dead woman a few feet away.

"What happened, Briggs? I thought we were protected from this side?" Lesh questioned, tilting her head slightly.

Briggs frowned, "I suspect a mole."

"How unfortunate," Lesh said, "that mole cost eleven lives so far. That person better hope we never cross paths."

Briggs stared at one of his devices. "All I have to do is find out which lookout isn't accounted for. If he isn't alive, he was found out. If he's still breathing, we have a traitor."

Nearby, Milos looked shell-shocked as Cherris held on to him tight. They both had tears flowing down their faces. Cherris sobbed, but Milos' face looked as though it were made of stone.

Back at the breach, the Sin fighters were spread out, firing at the second group of Hiezer guards that Lesh had warned about. The guards were seeping past the breach and taking cover behind debris. As Blague hid behind a stray piece of cement, a haunting memory rushed to the front of his mind; a memory of his late wife screaming in pain as she was drained of her life force.

She was attached to a circular metal contraption that shackled her spread out limbs. Blague's recollection of the memory stirred a stress in his heart that rendered him helpless and desperate, as he remembered the eight men holding him down, preventing him from saving her. His blood vessels were popping all around his green eyes and his veins jolted from his neck. "Elaina!" he screamed, as uncontrollable tears dripped down his face.

After her last desperate cry of pain, her limbs went limp. For a moment, time stood still.

She looked up at Blague calmly and said, "It's alright love, there's no more pain now. I'll miss you." Her head slumped to the side, lifeless.

As his senses returned to him, his feeling of

desperation from the memory of Elaina morphed into rage. The sound of bullets clanking against the debris around him slapped him back to the present. His senses became heightened and his body grew tense. His Cryos mark was glowing in bright blue and his muscular arms had defined veins running through his skin's surface. He heard a Hiezer guard stumble right above from where he was taking cover. Blague stood up and whipped his arm around, cracking the guard's black, full coverage helmet with his elbow, dazing him. Blague quickly spun in the other direction and swung his three-foot black carbon blade, slashing the guard's throat. Wasting no time, he jumped out from cover and grabbed the dying guard by the collar and hoisted him as a shield.

"Lito!" Blague shouted in a chilling tone. "Give me cover, I'm charging in."

Lito looked frightened, as Blague's appearance and demeanor shifted from his usual calm, deep thinker persona to an enraged beast. Blague sprinted easily as if he wasn't hauling a two hundred pound armored soldier as a shield. He charged the breach and Lito sprinted to catch up to him.

"Toss two 'nades and then gather everyone to head to the mansion. I'm not risking anymore casualties from the rear," Blague said.

Lito nodded and sprung two grenades from his backpack, bit off both pins in one bite and hurled them toward the breach. He then spun around and headed to carry out the rest of the order. Eight Hiezer guards remained at the breach point. The grenades blew debris in every direction and Blague sprinted even harder to get in range before the smoke cleared. As it cleared, Blague took a shot and strafed to his right. A guard's helmet popped as the bullet seared through his head. The remaining seven opened fire, but Blague was too quick. Very few bullets hit his human shield. His Desert Eagle was unique in that it held twelve bullets per round instead of seven. He opened rapid fire at lightning speed. The spray took out four guards, who dropped to the floor, shouting in agony. Blague decided to advance forward, now in close range fighting distance. He let out a deep chilling roar as he hurled the shield at one of the guards, spun, and popped another in the forehead. He then kicked to his right, fracturing a guard's shin. As the guard toppled forward, Blague whipped him with his pistol. The last guard opened fire. Blague strafed, twirled his gun back into firing position and took a shot, which penetrated the guard's chest. Blague was breathing heavily, staring straight faced as every visible muscle was bulging. Blague's rage had only been seen a number of times in battle by his closest commanders; no one ever approached him about it. Blague's deep seeded haunting memories shot to the front of his mind at opportune times, almost as if it were a survival mechanism.

A few seconds later, his rage lessoned, recognizing that the mansion was in plain sight. Up close, the mansion appeared to be the size of a small school that would easily fit the entire lot of Sins. Its unique architecture reflected a regal presence.

Eugene sprinted up to Blague, "You know that grenade idea made it impossible to get a clear shot."

Blague flashed him a dirty look. They both turned

their attention to the sky as they heard the sound of a helicopter fly by, both following it with their eyes.

"It's headed for the roof of the mansion," Blague said, "There must be Hiezers inside trying to flee. Eugene, take it out."

Eugene flipped his rifle into position and took aim. His first shot poked a hole in the gas line of the helicopter. The pilot realized if he landed, his life would be over, so he jutted the helicopter forward, trying to get out of the sniper's line of site. One of the passengers threw down a rope ladder. Eugene started running backward, trying to get a clear shot. Finally, the helicopter began to peek into sight. He backed up a bit more and saw two men with knee length black leather cloaks trying to escape from the mansion. Eugene took aim once more and fired toward the front glass of the helicopter, piercing it but missing the intended target. The pilot stumbled for a moment as the helicopter tilted awkwardly. One of the two men in robe lost balance and fell off the rope ladder. The helicopter took off, the pilot raced to their destination before the punctured fuel tank depleted. Blague and Eugene looked at each other and then ran toward the mansion.

Blague pulled out a small radio. "Lito, Briggs, pick up speed and get everyone in the mansion now. Pop the EMP as soon as you're in range. Eu and I are storming the front. We suspect a Hiezer was left behind. Have Lesh and Sabin scout the higher floors while you populate the ground level, copy?"

"Copy," two voices responded slightly out of sync.

Blague and Eugene marveled at the twenty foot high front door that was left open by the panicked Hiezer protectors of the mansion. They both confidently entered, knowing that the eerie silence and the desperate attempted helicopter escape meant that the mansion was clear. All except for the robed man that was left behind.

"What exactly do you hope to find in here, Blague?" Eugene wondered as they advanced with their weapons drawn.

"I'll explain later, but in short, a home for the Sins that risk their lives for this cause, a rare chemical, and important research materials," Blague responded.

"Won't the Hiezers just bomb the location and write it off?" Eugene continued to probe.

"No," Blague said, "not if the chemical I'm looking for is here. The research can be transferred in milliseconds, but the chemical is invaluable."

One of Eugene's eyebrows went up. "I'm very curious to hear more. You never disappoint. Things always seem to get a bit more interesting as we move forward."

Blague remained silent as they hastily ascended up four flights of stairs, each with uniquely carved, intricate patterns and made from notably rich marble. The entire mansion was completely out of place in Senation, considering the next best shelter was a fifteen foot dusty hut.

"Eugene," Blague said, "I know how the Hiezers operate. Expect the coming months to pique your interest. Stay sharp."

After climbing to the fourth floor, they heard a voice. "Ok, ok boys. I know when I'm cornered," a man said as he approached from the darkness with his hands up.

He had black gloves on with a golden pattern that matched his armored shoulders. His pauldrons were slightly raised with black ornate orbs at the center of each piece, surrounded by a sleek golden pattern. The armor was connected to his knee length black cloak. The getup looked as if it were intended for status.

"I'm Jeck Stone," the man said in a firm tone. "I'm assuming this is another rebel uprising?" Blague and Eugene looked at him with guns pointed his way. "Well," Jeck said, "I've never seen a Hiezer mansion successfully stormed," he said as he began to pace, maintaining eye contact with the two of them. "You know this will disrupt our communications and our progress." Jeck gave a smug look to both of them.

"Shackle him," Blague said.

"You know, boys, you may think this charade is justified, but nonetheless, it's a crime that will just add to your Sin reputation. This fight will fizzle out, like all the rest, and you will be left fewer in numbers and viewed as a tad more violent than the other social classes already perceive you."

"That's enough," Blague said, "Contrary to your thoughts, I am going to let you preach your side of the story, if you cooperate. Judging by your demeanor, you think we aren't going to kill you. My response to that thought is not to be so sure."

Jeck's face changed from smug to serious. All three of them heard the crowd entering the mansion.

"Take him to Lito, Eu. Then help everyone get settled with their supplies. I have to consult with Cherris. We have a lot of future steps to sort out. Feel free to join when you're ready."

Eugene nodded as he pushed Jeck forward.

Chapter 3

Blague walked slowly through the crowd on the ground level of the mansion, observing the mixed emotions among the Sin civilians. He made it a point to stop and attempt to console the families who lost loved ones. On his way through, he saw a woman crying over the corpse of a dead fighter. He knelt down on the opposite side of the body. While doing so, he allowed himself a moment to notice the dust and dirt that covered her face and much of her hair. He then realized everyone had similar filth all over them, including himself.

The woman looked up with tears, turning the dirt into mud as they dripped down her face. Desperation was evident in her expression. "Blague," she cried, "he was all I had in this world."

"I know," Blague said as he reached over and put his hand on her shoulder. He leaned back, thinking of the fallen soldier, "Peke fought for you, so you could have a better life. We're all fighting for a better life for the Sins. His death is not in vain," he said in a deep, pained voice.

The woman cried harder and looked down, grasping for the lifeless hand of her fallen husband. "I lived waiting for him and waiting for all of you to do something for us. I think I'm done waiting now. Peke's death just proves that it does no good," she said in between sobs.

"Chella," Blague said "don't give up on us."

She shook her head, "I'm thinking just the opposite. No longer will I stand here as a civilian, waiting for someone to save me. I'm joining the Sin fighters."

Blague looked surprised. "I won't stop you, I hope that's what you want. We would be honored to have you." Blague stood up and solemnly said, "I'm truly sorry for your loss. Peke was a zealous man." He placed a comforting hand on her shoulder, and continued on his way.

Making his way through the crowd, he looked up and noticed that all of the camera's lights were dead, some of which gave off a sporadic spark.

Briggs must have successfully carried out his job in detonating the EMP. Considering how fast information travels, my hunch that the Ayelan chemical is within this facility is probably correct. Otherwise, this place would have been wiped clean already. Chances are we aren't being overrun because the Hiezers are confident that we wouldn't know what to do with the chemical even if we found it.

As Blague continued walking, a kid ran straight into his leg. He felt the pressure of something knocking into him and bouncing off. A mix of confusion and surprise washed across his face for a moment before looking down.

The kid rubbed his head and looked up, winking one eye painfully. "That hurt, mister," the kid said.

Blague smirked "Sorry bud."

"Hey," the kid said with a flash of recognition in his eyes, "my mom says you're the leader of our group."

Blague looked at him and nodded.

"Ok, Mr. Leader, is this our new home?"

Blague nodded again.

"Is it going to be safe for my mom?"

Blague paused for a moment, "I'm going to do my best to make it safe. What's your name?"

"Sigan," the boy said.

"I'm Blague, nice to meet you," he said, extending his hand outward.

The boy slapped him five and scratched the back of his head, causing Blague to chuckle. "Ok, bye Mr. Blague," the boy said as he ran away.

"Farewell for now, Sigan."

As Blague continued on, he admired the architecture of the mansion. Elegantly designed pillars shot up from the ground level to the fourth floor. The structure was semi-open, similar to the inside of a prison. Only instead of cells, the living quarters resembled up-scale hotel rooms that stretched as far as Blague could see. It was at that moment he realized that a public debate between him and Jeck was going to be a crucial experience for all.

The Hiezers are not black and white tyrants. There are many shades of grey from all perspectives.

Blague heard his name being called and a bark followed. A man appeared with a half cape draped over his shoulder. He had a trim black beard with white streaks that mirrored his wolf's coat. He strutted confidently with his golden eyes and his short black hair that connected to his beard. A path cleared as he walked and all eyes were on his pet wolf. Sins were not allowed to have pets, so original Sins had never seen a tamed animal. Mars was the only exception. Stray animals on the exiled continents resembled vicious beasts rather than approachable companions.

"Sabin and Mars, my favorite duo," Blague said.

Sabin winked, "The third floor is clear my friend."

"Excellent," Blague said.

When they approached each other, instead of a handshake, they slapped each other's forearms and gripped firmly. The commanders knew why Sabin wore a half ripped cape that completely covered one arm; it was to hide the fact that he had no Cryos tattoo marking him as a Sin. This would make the Sins skeptical of him.

Blague spoke to his commanders eight months ago about Sabin, letting them know that he was to be trusted. He explained that Sabin is technically a Templos, which is four social ranks above the Sins. In order to make his way to Senation, Sabin posed as an anthropologist, which is a qualified profession for the Templos; that's how he boarded a cleared aircraft en route to Senation. "His cause is our cause," Blague enforced. "He heeded my call that I dispersed through aging network connections. So if you trust me," Blague said to his commanders, "trust Sabin." At that meeting, Eugene had his arms folded and was abnormally quiet. What's worse is that he didn't make any suggestions or make a peep for that matter. Blague was keen to Eu's skepticism, which was one of the main reasons he chose him as his first in command.

Blague walked alongside Sabin and Mars as he searched for Cherris.

"Can we hold this fort, Blague?" Sabin questioned.

"There are two exits on the main floor, a landing pad on the roof, and at least three hundred feet between us and the breach. I believe Lito can plant enough explosives to guard the walkway from invasion, but we have to be careful not to use trip mines. Remote detonators should be planted to prevent from killing our own. There needs to be patrol guarding the three entrances at all times. I believe it's manageable," Blague responded.

Sabin nodded and thought for a second, "Hah, we're not already dead because there's the Ayelan chemical within this mansion, probably in the underground shoot."

"Undoubtedly so, old friend," Blague replied with a half smirk.

"Do the other commanders know?" Sabin asked.

"In due time," Blague said.

"This was a bold takeover. Everyone in Senation must be buzzing about the explosion and the dust cloud that lingered in the sky," Sabin said excitedly. "Do you believe Briggs' scattered scouts are spreading our story to the citizens?"

"Hopefully," Blague said, recalling his protocols. "I expect intel on their feedback within a day."

"Ah," Sabin said loudly, as he pulled a piece of meat out of Mars' mouth. A little girl with long blonde hair sat there on the floor with an empty plate and tears in her eyes. Sabin looked at her with a nervous smile, "Sorry, sweetheart." He dropped the half chewed meat back on her plate. The girl looked confused. Sabin waved awkwardly and continued on. Blague held in his laughter. Sabin turned back to look at Blague and laughed. "It looks like there's no shortage of food," Sabin said as he took a look around the enormous room.

"That's one area that we are very fortunate," Blague

responded. "We have very little room for technological or economic advancement in Senation, but we do still have excellent irrigation and a wealth of food supply. Our fighters remain strong and healthy as a result," Blague explained.

Sabin nodded, "The exiled continents are peculiar that way. The powers that be do what they can to keep the Sins from progressing intellectually. In some sense, it's a more brutal form of punishment than being sent to jail."

"Agreed," Blague replied with a nod, "Our movement will continue to strive to alleviate this class system from the horror it creates." As soon as he finished his sentence, he saw Cherris seated at a table, speaking to a teenage boy and girl. Blague and Sabin walked up to her while she finished answering the teens' question.

"Maran, there are three ways you can become a Sin. Either through accumulated misdemeanor crimes, which now includes every crime except rape and murder, refusal to carry out an assigned job of which the choices are limited amongst the lower social classes, or you're born into this world from Sin parents. The latter is the case for you two. You were both born into Senation and received your Cryos marks when you were kids. That's why your marks are smaller than the adult marks." The teenagers looked at each other and then thanked Cherris for the information. All three of them looked up at the unique looking gentlemen that were glancing over at them and smiling. Blague's green eyes were piercing even when he meant to be at ease. Cherris smiled at the teenagers, "Okay Maran and Kleina, I'll be glad to tell you more later on," she said as she politely waved them away. The kids got up and walked off, discussing their thoughts about what was just revealed to them. Blague and Sabin took a seat near Cherris.

"Cherris, I'm relieved to see that you're alright," Blague said sincerely.

Cherris faintly smiled. "I am, but my heart continues to break. We lost good men, most of whom were husbands and fathers. Right in front of my eyes I witnessed a boy become an orphan. This life sounds full of meaning when you speak to us, Blague, but the painful day to day journey is numbing," she said, unable to mask the staggering pain in her voice. Blague and Sabin shared her pained expression, offering comfort. "I knew this would be the case going in. I was fully aware of the dangers surrounding us, but you can never prepare yourself for the death of friends and family," Cherris continued, letting tears trickle down her face.

Blague reached over and put his hand over hers, "I share your pain. We all knew the hardships that we signed up for. This is a pain that we will continue to endure. You've both known me for a long time," Blague broke eye contact with Cherris to give Sabin a brief look, "And I'm confident that you trust my judgement. I'm not a man that fights blindly, nor am I a man who will fight for a petty cause. All three of us have seen the deteriorating treatment of the Sins. The punishment no longer fits the crime. As future generations continue to grow without hope or a chance at a decent life, the idea of this rigid social class system becomes prominently more horrifying. An obvious example of this is the Hiezer guards you witnessed attacking the civilians. Cherris, I need you to suffer with me while we make our strides." Blague waved his hand, displaying the hundreds of sheltered Sins settling into the mansion. "Our suffering is not in vain. We made a leap today. Look around you. We have taken a base and now we will hold that base and learn to exist as a community before we expand our goals further."

Cherris nodded periodically as Blague spoke. Her eyes were slightly sunken due to the horror she saw earlier that day. Her hair was long with a blonde and grey mixture. She had some wrinkles, but had a glow about her that seemed to drown out her age. "I trust you, Blague, as I always have. My struggle comes from my lack of strength I suppose. Just pour your spirit in my direction to pull me back up from time to time," she said, feeling a bit of relief.

Blague smirked, "Of course, anytime."

Sabin leaned back in his chair with his arms folded, looking impressed. "Ok, darling," Sabin said to Cherris. "Now that we're pumped up again, shall we begin strategizing?"

Cherris nodded and smiled at Sabin. Blague motioned for Sabin to take the lead.

Sabin leaned forward and began to lay out the facts. "So, we have a Hiezer, but I don't believe he's a highlord."

"He's not," a somber voice interrupted. Sabin was startled for a moment since the voice came from behind him.

"Eugene," Blague said, "have a seat." Blague motioned to the chair next to Sabin.

Sabin turned around and looked at Eugene with

squinted eyes, somewhat playfully, mocking Eugene's mistrust. Eugene looked at Sabin with a serious face and one eyebrow raised as he took his seat.

Sabin turned back and continued. "As I was saying, we have a lower ranking Hiezer, a group of Sin fighters, civilians committed to the cause, and a newly found base that we're confident we can hold. From here, what steps should be carried out and in what order?"

Cherris spoke up, "First, we should inform and comfort our people by establishing protective guard duty."

The others agreed with Cherris.

Eugene interrupted, "Do we have intel on whether the Hiezers will seek to rescue Jeck and reclaim the mansion?"

Blague shook his head, "In one hour, I'm going to meet with Briggs to discuss the rallying of Senation as well as any impending attacks. For now, I have fifty percent of the fighters actively guarding the entrances on two hour rotations."

Eugene nodded and put his head down to think. Sabin put an arm on Eugene's shoulder.

"Cheer up bud, that's a good thing," Sabin said with a smile.

Eugene sighed and shrugged Sabin's arm off his shoulder. Mars barked, as if offended.

"Hah," Sabin scoffed, "you'll warm up to me eventually. Wonder how many times I have to save your ass in battle before you do though." Sabin's smile grew ear to ear awaiting Eugene's reaction.

Eugene just looked at him and rolled his eyes,

"You're a delusional jackass."

"C'mon gentlemen," Blague said as Cherris laughed in the background, "Let's focus for just a few minutes."

"Alright," Sabin said, "what do you intend to do with Jeck?"

"I intend to let him speak his views to the new residents of the mansion," Blague said. His audience reacted with a bit of shock.

"That could cause civil conflict," Cherris said.

"It could," Blague replied with his head held high, "but I'm confident it won't. These people deserve to be educated with all sides of the story. How else will we topple the class structure if not with informed followers?"

"But some of the followers are very intelligent," Eugene said, "We have civilians that were doctors and scientists in their former lives."

"Yes, but many of them haven't been able to make a free decision for years now. We have to hand that ability back to these people if we're to prosper. Besides, I will speak as Jeck's opponent. I intend to address the grey areas of this world. We won't drag out the arguments either. We will both present our views in one speech each. The Sins are already devoted to the cause, but now we need them to fully understand our enemy," Blague said.

Eugene sighed, "More risks Blague, I swear, you like to stir shit up."

"No, Eu, but I appreciate your consistent oppositional viewpoints. It keeps me in check."

Sabin glanced at them both, "You two are like an old married couple." Blague laughed and Eugene nearly smiled. "Ok," Sabin said, while smacking the table, "so we hold the mini debate after primary intel is gathered and we can declare the base protected and stable?"

"Yes," Blague confirmed.

"Alright," Sabin said, "now are we to discuss the reason that we're all still alive?"

Blague nodded and leaned forward. "Do either of you know the full story about the chemical Ayelan?" Blague engaged both Cherris and Eugene.

Eugene looked up, "Only that it's an extremely rare chemical. Sins that are crazy enough to believe that it exists spend their lives searching for it in hopes to be automatically bumped three social classes if they submit it to the proper Hiezer channels."

Cherris shifted eyes from Eugene to the middle of the table, "Rumor has it that this chemical is used for very unnatural experiments with the goal of preserving human life."

"Both of you have the right idea," Blague explained, "but they aren't rumors." Sabin sat back with his hands behind his head, as if he knew what Blague was going to say. "As all of you know, the first generation of Hiezers represented the top one percent of wealth after the Global Quake in 2022. Once the chaos ensued after the continents cracked in half or split from its edges, countries were in disarray economically, politically, socially, and morally. The damage on November 1st, 2022 was seemingly irreparable. That was until a group of people banded together to create a powerful network, which served to preserve civilized life. The wealthiest people in the world at that time communicated with each other to create order out of the chaos. One of the Hiezers, Orin Grenich, was smart enough to act while the currencies of the world prior to the Global Quake were still acceptable. The Hiezers began building fortresses around the world and reestablishing global communication." Blague paused for a moment, recognizing that he needed to make his point, "I'll curtail the history lesson of the Hiezers here, but know that this group brought about the social class system we all know. However, what's more notable is they dedicated most of their time and effort to research, hence why they wear long black robes that somewhat resemble the old world's lab coats. The Hiezers discovered two new chemicals that were revealed to the world upon the devastation of the quake. Scientists were not able to pick up traces of these chemicals sooner because their attributes are very similar to chemicals that had already existed. These chemicals can bind themselves to any object and once you see these elements, it is apparent that they are unique. Cryos, as we all know it, gives off a blue hue that tends to glow periodically. That is the more common of the two chemicals. On the other hand, Ayelan is an extremely rare chemical that can be identified by looking at it; if an object is two completely different colors when viewing it from one angle to the next, similar to a hologram, then you know it may contain Ayelan. After a year of research, the Hiezers discovered that human life can be preserved by administering a shot that includes the right combination of chemicals, one of which is Ayelan. I believe that a small amount of Ayelan is located in this mansion, which was to be used for testing by the Hiezers. That is the reason this mansion hasn't been bombed yet. The Hiezers may pull the plug on utilities once we've extracted the chemical. They're probably only keeping the building live to maintain their experiments. I'll have to make arrangements to stockpile generators and develop a long-term solution."

Cherris nodded. Eugene lit a cigarette and sighed.

Blague pointed to Eugene and Sabin and said, "I want the both of you to work with the scientists we currently have in our group to locate and secure the Ayelan." Eugene massaged his temples with one hand, as he felt the stress of the situation.

Sabin folded his arms and looked at Eugene with a smile. "No problem, boss," Sabin said.

"Cherris," Blague locked eyes, "I need you to inform the people of what I just explained. More details will come once I feel we are more secure."

"Of course," Cherris said, "Just one question though. How did you stumble upon all of this knowledge?"

Blague paused for a moment before answering, "My past is colorful, as I'm sure you've realized. But that is definitely a story for another day."

Chapter 4

Lito and Jeck sat in one of the lavish hotel-like rooms within the mansion. The room was empty, except for two chairs in opposite corners, Lito's gadgets, and Jeck's shackles. Lito worked on his remote explosive traps that were to be placed on the pathway to the mansion, starting at the breach point. He had goggles on that served as both magnifiers and protection against the sparks from welding flames. He bobbed his head to music, but he didn't have headphones on. His black and green mohawk bounced with him. Jeck stared at Lito very curiously.

♫ *Keep staring at me, yeah yeah, keep staring at me… and I'm… gonna… kill 'em kill 'em. Keep staring at me… and I'm gonna kill 'em kill 'em* ♫.

After about one hour of Lito working in his own world and Jeck staring, Jeck finally broke the silence.

"Lito is it?" Jeck sneered. Lito's head stopped bobbing. "This may end badly for your group. The Hiezers do not forgive nor do they take lightly attempted takeovers," Jeck said.

Lito put down his contraption, lifted his goggles, stood up, and lifted his chair above his head with one lean arm. He walked over to Jeck's corner and slammed the chair down with its back facing Jeck. He plopped down, folded his arms on the base of the chair, and stared. Jeck looked somewhat horrified. Lito had tanned skin, a shaved face, and a short mohawk. Although those traits reflected his character, it was his eyes that startled newcomers. His eyes were bright purple and one of his pupils was permanently dilated; it was quite a jarring characteristic.

"Ya know, Jeck, I've dealt with the Hiezers before, where I came from."

"Oh, yeah?" Jeck antagonized, "Where's that?"

"Bulchevin," Lito said with his eyes wide in his strong accent.

Bulchevin was an exiled continent that split off from the country of Brazil after the Global Quake; this added to Lito's strange character as he didn't speak a work of Portuguese.

"Hah," Jeck yacked, "is that supposed to frighten me? I've visited the exiled continent that equates to half of Brazil. It's no more or less scummy than Senation."

"Maybe on the surface," Lito said, while he pulled Jeck by his hairline to meet his purple eyes. "I've worked in the mines for years at a time, navigating the bright Cryos-lit areas and pitch black rows, with an eye patch on, searching for your precious Ayelan. I must say, Mr. Jeck Stone, I would still be doing that happily if one of your guards hadn't murdered my *familia* off of a hunch."

Jeck tried to remain calm. "Lito, you know this world isn't as stable as it once was. Though the class system is strict, we do not condone murder. What happened to your family is guard brutality, an issue the Hiezers are working to eliminate."

"Too late, *cabron*," Lito swiped a jagged elbow to Jeck's temple.

Jeck was dazed, trying to maintain his focus. "You know, Lito, violence only leads to more violence. Are you going to contribute to an endless cycle? Is that your purpose now?" Jeck said while holding his head.

"Maybe I wouldn't have gone down this path if my mother and brother weren't tased, dragged off to your laboratories, and killed by the guards. Those orders came from high up. No way it was guard brutality. For all I know, it mighta been you who gave the order." Lito pulled Jeck up off his seat by his robe's collar.

"I'm surprised your leader would select such a hothead for a commander," Jeck struggled to say as the grip was slightly choking him.

Lito smiled, "You should see our leader's temper, makes me look like a tame *pequena* bunny."

"If that's so, I shouldn't be worried. Your little group has no hope," Jeck said with malice in his voice.

Lito winked and kicked Jeck's chair back, "Now you can sit on the floor for the next few hours."

Jeck rolled his eyes, "Whatever you say, boss."

Lito took his chair back to his corner of the room, picked up his contraption, and began bobbing his head again.

Briggs inspected his sling as he perused the second floor in search for Blague's room, nearly matching the height of each door he passed. As he approached the last room in the corner, he noticed that the door was left slightly open. Briggs took a moment to notice the massive crowd a floor below him, creating the commotion of a small stadium as they settled. He turned back and awkwardly pushed the door open with his good arm, not being used to leading with his left. He saw Blague sitting Indian style on top of a sleek, black marble desk. His muscular arms were folded and his green eyes pierced right through Briggs, almost as if he were in a trance. Briggs waved his good arm to see if he could snap Blague out of it. Blague shook his head, his pushed-back hair followed on a second delay.

"Hi Briggs," Blague said holding his head with one hand. Briggs saluted by pounding his chest once. "Can you believe this?" Blague pointed to the gold swiveled wall with his knife. "I believe the idea of status is powerful, but it also serves as a slap in the face for those so far below even the thought of it."

"I agree with you, but the Sin followers are settling in just fine, as if they won the lottery. I know your focus is on the Hiezer's despicable regime, but take a look at the good you did toda-"

"We, Briggs," Blague interrupted, "The good we did today." Blague stood up and put one hand on Briggs' good shoulder. "I would be nothing if not for the strong group that we're developing."

"Thanks boss, glad to be a part of the team. My boy is getting anxious. Especially after seeing me wounded. He has dreams of fighting with us." Briggs paused for a few seconds, with worry expressed in his features. "I'm proud, Blague, but fearful of when that day might come."

"Haha," Blague laughed, "he's not even a teenager yet. If we're lucky, we have many years to watch him grow first." Briggs looked down and scratched his head, still worried. Blague punched his good arm, causing Briggs to stumble half a step and look up with confusion. "That thing is a rock. How did a measly little bullet pierce it?"

Briggs laughed, "I feel like a little bitch right now. The doc said I have to sit with the civilians for a month until the wound heals."

"You're a beast. I give it a week before you're on the front lines with me again," Blague said. He looked at his silver watch with a large blue face. "Ok, Briggs, I have ten minutes before I check in with Sabin and Eugene for a rotation update. Do you have the status update regarding Senation's reaction?"

"Yes," Briggs' face turned serious. "Let me start by saying one of our contacts went dark. I don't think he was killed, because he went dark right before we blew the wreckage. It seems too coincidental. My hunch is that we were infiltrated."

"That's troubling," Blague said while thinking about the next course of action. "I'm going to send Lesh to track the person down. Which of the contacts went dark?"

"Nemura," Briggs said.

"That snake," Blague looked down and shook his head. "I swear that evil looking smile of his was almost too obvious." Blague continued looking at the floor, "My feeling is that there's more to his crossover than we know right now. I'll have Lesh get to the bottom of this, even if torture is necessary. Nemura singlehandedly disrupted the integrity of our group. The civilians no longer feel safe. And it will probably take far too long to recover such a delicacy." Blague paced back and forth, spewing all of his thoughts. "Ok, continue with the report."

"The contacts are beginning to rally supporters, civilians and fighters alike. They're not having an easy time though. Senation seems to be divided since the explosion," Briggs responded.

"Of course," Blague said as he hoisted himself back on top of the desk and resumed his seated position. "Senation isn't starved, so the thought that life could get worse is still a viable fear. The Sins as a whole still have something to lose. It's somewhat brilliant planning on the Hiezers' part. It has historically kept uprisings miniscule," Blague said as he recalled the Hiezer's swift silencing of past rebellions. "They generally fizzle out within weeks. Our advantage lies with former professionals and educated citizens that existed at higher social ranks prior to being shipped into exile. Those people know that the world was never fair and that there's a difference between unfair and crippled," he concluded, staring intensely at Briggs.

Briggs nodded without hesitation, "Agreed. So how can we provide safe passage to the incoming followers?"

"Cautiously, in small orderly groups," Blague said as he continued plotting. "We also have to screen any newcomers and keep them temporarily divided from our existing group."

"By all means, my men and I will work to screen as quickly as possible. I expect the contacts to start rolling past the breach within a few days. We have a lot of work to do," Briggs said.

Blague nodded, "Thanks for your report. We'll catch up soon. Please feel free to take this room for you and your son. I'll be transferring one floor up, closer to Jeck."

Briggs saluted once again. Blague hopped off the desk, sheathed his knife, and walked out of the room.

Sabin planted himself on a ledge sitting atop the roof of the mansion that overlooked the Pacific Ocean. He stroked Mars' thick black and grey coat as the wind blew their hair and fur back. Fighters were patrolling the surrounding areas from the roof.

Despite all the filth behind us in Senation, this view is quite unbelievable. Receiving the call from Blague is what I truly needed. Life as a Templos was growing bland. My purpose in this world couldn't be to supply Hiezer guards with specialty food from my hunting expeditions. Sitting like a lame duck for all those years. The monotony of following orders, thinking that it could be worse. What did I let seep into my brain? How could I have grown so soft and narrow-minded? I mean yeah, I manage somehow to always find some fun along the way, but at least I have a purpose now: to fight with an old friend for a just cause. Being in the lower tiers of social class becomes painstakingly rigid over time. Once the fear subsides, that becomes clear. I'm grateful for all Blague did for me in his previous life and all he will do in this one.

Just as Sabin turned to Mars to pet him, Mars' ears became alert. Sabin turned back to look at the ocean. He saw a cargo ship come into sight. That's when it hit him.

If we were to be attacked, it would be by boat through this route.

"Sabin," Blague called out, "where's Eu?"

"He passed out in his room on floor two," Sabin said

as he pet his wolf.

"That's not like him," Blague said while walking up to Sabin.

"He gave me his report ten minutes ago. All is clear on all angles. Although, something just hit me, I just envisioned an attack by boat, through that cargo route," Sabin pointed. "As sad as it makes me to suggest this, maybe we should have Lito trap the shorefront side as well."

Blague stared for a moment, "That's an excellent idea. Let's even take it a step further and set up one scout on the far end of the rocks to get a jump on any suspicious ships. Assign three fighters to rotate shifts."

"Alright, Blague," Sabin said as the wind blew his half cape, "will do."

Blague nodded and walked off. Sabin turned back to soak in the view while petting Mars.

"You're always so pessimistic," a woman said as she smiled and mussed Eugene's dirty blonde hair.

"Jen," Eugene sighed, "can you please take at least one thing seriously? If we're not careful, we're going to be shipped off."

Strands of Jen's long blonde hair fell over her face. Her smile was contagious and whenever she did decide to shoot one off, her eyes became squinted. Eugene loved that about her. Her genuine character was infatuating. Eugene laid back on his comfortable tan colored couch and put his hands behind his head.

Jen leaned over and gave him a kiss. She then got up and

headed towards the door. "See you later, babe," Jen said in an upbeat tone. Before closing the door behind her, she looked back to Eugene, "They have no choice but to recognize that the job I want to do will benefit them much more than the job they want me to do." Eugene stared at her with a look of worry and sighed. She decided to give him a big smile before she stepped out.

Eugene rubbed his brow and looked down. A flash of lightning whizzed by his face and startled him. "What the hell was that?"

He looked up, shocked at what he thought he just saw. In the blink of an eye, a powerful gust of wind slapped him across the face. All of a sudden he was no longer indoors. The faint sound of screaming echoed all around him. Through the muffled noise, he heard Jen screaming as if she was miles behind him. He turned around to see Jen grasping desperately onto his arm.

Her eyes welled up with tears. "I'm sorry, babe," she said, defeated and distraught, "You were right, I should have listened to you."

A Hiezer guard marched over toward them. "Get back on line immediately," the guard said in a militant tone, directing his attention to Jen.

Eugene, horrified, quickly analyzed his surroundings. He felt the tenseness of this situation as he gazed upon a long, jumbled line of people, all of whom displayed a whirl of varying negative emotions. Some were screaming, some crying, some were silent and just stared blankly in front of them. The chaos made the situation difficult for the Hiezer guards as they struggled to maintain order. Eugene felt the anxiety funneling through him as he shifted his gaze to the end of the line, where his wandering eyes focused on three large machines blocking the entrance to a ship. Pipes on the machines had a neon blue liquid flowing through them. He witnessed a guard pull the next person on line, who was lethargic. The guard grabbed her arm and stuffed it under the machine as an extension of steaming hot metal pressed down upon her. Tears ran down her face as her skin sizzled, but she didn't let out a sound. The guard roughly pulled her arm out and tossed her ahead, where she was assigned her new name and then escorted to the ship. Her new, forced identity was now showcased by the glowing blue mark that branded her arm.

Eugene turned back to the guard directing his attention to Jen, his look intensifying. The guard began advancing with a pistol drawn, his patience wearing thin from herding the soon-to-be exiled citizens. Eugene put himself in between the two of them.

"Take me instead," Eugene said as he puffed his chest out to try and stop the guard from advancing.

Jen cried louder, "No, Eugene, you can't!" trembling with fear.

The guard was eye level with Eugene, but he was looking at him through a black mask, revealing no identity. The guard raised his voice, "Stand down, give me..." the guard looked down at his device, "Jennifer Parinto, immediately."

Eugene repeated himself calmly, but sternly, "Take me instead."

The guard raised his pistol and swung it towards Eugene's face. He caught the swing with one hand and swung a fist with the other. The guard toppled over. Two others noticed the altercation and intervened.

"Assault of a guard is a serious crime. You're both going on the line," the guard said in a frustrated tone as he adjusted his mask.

Eugene was breathing heavily, thoughts of what to do next rushed into is head, but he knew he was cornered and done with. He looked up, a splash of searing fire latched onto his face, burning his skin. He swung his head frantically as he felt the temperature rapidly rise. He let out a scream, feeling his eyes melting from his sockets. He shook his head, causing the flame to suddenly cool.

Eugene felt the touch of skin, he opened his eyes and looked to his left. Jen was holding his hand tightly, with a look of fear on her face. The machine was directly in front of Eugene's face now. The guard pulled Jen by her arm. Eugene reached for her but his arms were suddenly shackled. He attempted to scream, but no words came out. The guard tossed Jen to the next guard, her arm glowing with the same stamped tattoo as the others.

"Your assigned name is Asura," the guard read from his device.

Eugene felt nothing as they stamped him.

"Considering your crime happened moments ago, headquarters allowed you to keep your first name so they didn't have to alter the system, which had already been set today. Your last name, however, is now purged. If you so much as introduce yourself with it, you will be punished. Understood?" the guard dictated as he pushed Eugene forward forcefully.

Eugene's furiously twitching arms made his metal shackles ring, as he resisted further with every step. The ship in front of him became blurry. He froze when he realized a snake was crawling up his shoulder and onto his face. His surroundings went dark, except for the hissing snake twisting its body, readying to bite him between the eyes. Its thin fangs were exposed and its pink mouth was visible. Eugene felt the panic fill his chest as his breath shortened.

His vision suddenly began to clear and the snake faded out of existence. He quickly realized he was on the inside of the boat.

Jen was still next to him, holding on for her dear life. The other prisoners were rioting; chaos ensued all around them. A crazed prisoner grabbed for Jen's face with a lustful glare. Eugene turned around and whipped his arm, landing a forceful right hook. Eugene wasn't overly muscular, but he packed a strong punch. The deranged exile flew backward, but quickly recovered and ran back toward Jen, trying to take advantage of the chaos. A huge guard came between them and took them both by the arms and began carrying them off.

"Jen!" Eugene shouted.

Another guard smashed Eugene in the jaw. The guard's device was blinking red, showing Jen's previous and new name. "This Sin is Asura. Part of the reason for this trip to Senation is for you to learn how to obey authority."

Eugene held his jaw and noticed the chain on his shackles was broken, but the clamps were still attached.

"Jen!" he shouted again as she was being dragged further away.

The crazed prisoner overpowered the guard holding Jen and took hold of her. Eugene's anxiety became blinding.

Eugene jolted up from his bed, sweating profusely. He had dried tears on his face and his eyes were stinging. He slid his legs off the bed that he had hoped would provide a peaceful nap.

"Fuck!" he shouted and slammed his fist against the wall of his beautifully decorated room.

A woman settling into the room next door knocked on his door. "Is everything alright in there?" the woman asked.

"I'm fine," Eugene replied, wiping the sweat from his brow. Eugene heard the footsteps of the woman as she walked over to his door.

"May I come in?" she asked in a kind voice.

"Not the best time," Eugene said dismissively.

He walked over to the door and slightly opened it. The woman was taken back by the amount of sweat dripping down his face. His hair was different shades of blonde and brown by the varying degree of sweat in certain areas.

"Sorry to disturb you," Eugene sighed, "a nightmare is all."

The woman had very smooth, tanned skin, a nose ring, and attractively large eyes.

"Alright," the woman said, "hope the dream wasn't too bad." She stuck her hand in between the door crack. "I'm Narene," she said pleasantly.

"Eugene," he said, still slightly embarrassed.

She smiled, "I'll leave you be now, Eugene. Better luck during your next nap."

Eugene smirked.

Briggs gave Kentin a hug, "Just hang out in here for a little bit, ok big guy? The room is pretty cool right?" Kentin nodded and smiled. "Alright, don't go wreckin' the whole place now, ok?" Briggs said as he messed up his hair. Kentin gave a big smile and chuckled. Briggs smiled back and nudged his arm. He shut the door behind him and began exploring the second floor.

I can't believe that fuck, Nemura. He got that little boy's mother killed. Blague is right to set Lesh on him. Time to go find that crazy woman and set her loose.

Briggs held the pristine black and gold railing with his functioning hand and took in the view of the open main floor.

Something doesn't feel right about this whole situation though. Why would Nemura turn on us? He has great reason to hate the Hiezers; he was stripped of his title and banished to Senation years ago. Sure, he's crazy, but he doesn't seem like the type to double-cross for a deal.

Briggs walked up to what he thought was Lesh's room. The lights were off. He pushed the door open slowly and inched his way in. A whizzing sound followed by a thump echoed through the room. Briggs had an idea of what was going on. He reached for the light and as soon as he flicked an ornate light switch, a knife whizzed right above his head and stuck to the wall. Briggs' eyes grew wide as he began breathing heavily. Lesh was hanging upside down with her feet braced onto a ceiling ledge. Lesh smirked and flipped to the floor. She walked over and reached for her knife lodged in the wall, right above Briggs' head.

"Maybe next time I'll forget how tall you are, Briggs," Lesh said in a calm, raspy voice.

She slapped his arm that was now properly bandaged, turned, and walked over to the knives that stuck out of a picture hanging on the wall. Briggs' lips curved inward, as he pretended that the slap didn't hurt.

Earlier, while Lesh was covered in darkness, she traced the Hiezer symbol on the wall with her throwing knives. The symbol resembled two golden waves, which surrounded a black spherical orb. One wave crashed on the top of the orb and the other was inverted and crashed on the bottom. The design was identical to each of Jeck's pauldrons.

"You know why I'm here, I assume?" Briggs asked.

"I have a hunch," Lesh replied, turning to face Briggs, "Blague wants me to flush out the rat?"

Briggs nodded. "It's Nemura," Briggs revealed. Lesh shook her head, "That doesn't make any sense. He's on our side. He's with the Sins. He's murdered too many guards, with a smile I might add, to be against us."

Briggs opened his hands and shrugged his shoulders, "My transponder didn't malfunction. Nemura went dark right before the blast."

Lesh paused and eventually nodded. "Ok, I'm going solo."

Briggs looked disappointed, but not surprised. "Take Sabin, or Eugene. Either of them can cover you."

Lesh shook her head, "No, it's too risky. We have no idea what the Hiezers are planning. Keep all of the talent here. Let me do what I do best," she said calmly, with no hesitation in her voice.

Briggs put his hands up as if he wasn't going to suggest anything further. "Good luck, Lesh. There's a meal being cooked on the main floor, if you want to refuel before you take off."

"How cute, Briggs," Lesh said as she reached for her ration. She took a bite of the bar while staring at him and then ran off.

Blague walked into the room that Jeck and Lito resided in.

"Hah," Blague laughed at the sight of Jeck facing the ceiling, "I see you two are getting along."

Lito lifted his goggles and smiled, looking over at Jeck shackled behind a chair on the floor. Blague walked over to Jeck and stepped on the leg of the chair, raising him slowly upward.

Blague leaned over, his eyes penetrating through him, "Alright, Mr. Stone. Shall we discuss our deliberation?"

Chapter 5

Lesh flipped over the ledge of the second floor onto the main area where food was being served. The wide open space of the black marble floor looked like an abyss in outer space. The civilians moved out of her way as she started toward the front door in a fast trot.

Cherris looked over at Lesh and waved, assuming she was off on her next hunt. Lesh nodded back and glanced down to see Milos at Cherris' side, staring at her blankly. Lesh raised her eyebrow, to see if he would give some kind of response back; he raised both of his eyebrows.

There's still hope for the boy. He's not catatonic, just in shock. It would be a shame if the boy's fate is to become a killer, but even Cherris' love can't erase what happened. I have a feeling that boy will be under my wing soon, unfortunately.

She swiftly continued, noticing the mood shift among the civilians.

Only a few days have passed, and everyone seems to have already forgotten what happened. It's pathetic, really, to be so unprepared. Or do I envy them? To be able to flip a switch and forget it all. To experience joy in such an uncertain time.

She turned to look forward, realizing that she was approaching a twenty foot, massive front door. The golden Hiezer swirls were elegantly decorated all over it. Two Sin fighters were guarding the inside. They scurried to open the door as they saw the assassin approaching.

"Holy shit," one of the fighters said with panic in his voice, "that's Lesh coming this way."

"What in hell are you staring at, open the damn door! Quick!" the other fighter responded.

As the doors opened, Lesh ran past ten fighters in formation guarding the front. She didn't slow down; the Sins pounded their chests in her direction as she passed. She ignored the salute, as she usually does.

"Hey!" a charismatic voice shouted behind her, followed by a friendly bark.

She stopped and turned around, looking annoyed. "What is it, Sabin?" she said as she walked over and knelt down to pet Mars.

Sabin was off to the side, leaning on a wall of the mansion, about thirty feet away from the door. His arms were folded and he had one foot on the wall. His torn cape was flapping in the wind and his golden eyes were gleaming. "Lesh, as much as I want to stick around and search for Ayelan with the scientists, I think I should have your back."

Lesh shook her head, "You'll just give away my position by walking around with the only pet in Senation. Plus, those horrible weapons will probably be the death of me."

Sabin let out a burst of laughter. Lesh smirked back.

"Was worth a try," Sabin said.

"If you say so," Lesh bantered back.

"Be safe, I'll see you in a few days hopefully," Sabin wished sincerely.

"Yep," she responded with rasp in her voice, "Either

then or in hell at some point."

Sabin smirked and Lesh ran off. Sabin became straight-faced as he kept an eye on the direction she headed.

Milos stared at the floor, his shaggy black hair washed over his face as he sat in the corner, dazed. His limbs were spread out, as if he had no life left in him. He kept thinking of his mom. Before joining Blague's movement, she took him almost every day to a black market school, which was taught in a guarded hut. She packed him lunch and hugged him tightly before letting him run along every morning. She knew it wasn't the most formal way of helping her son grow, but it was the best available option in Senation. She knew the teacher from her prior life and trusted her completely. After school, Milos would run out of the hut through the black drapes that masked the activity inside, and jump to hug his mom. She gave off a sigh of relief and a smile every day when she got to see him. The bags under her eyes and her weathered appearance didn't exist for a moment. Milos felt his mother's unconditional love every day. Those memories of her were bright. After his period of thought, he eventually snapped back to the present, leaving him shrouded in darkness. Kentin and another boy ran into Cherris' wagon, where Milos was sitting lethargically.

"Milos!" Kentin shouted, "Let's go explore the back! I borrowed my dad's goggles that Endok made so we can avoid the bombs that were planted." Milos stared at

Kentin, unable to replicate his enthusiasm. Kentin extended his hand, "C'mon! Let's go!"

Milos grabbed on and Kentin pulled him up. "Who's that?" Milos questioned in a cold tone.

"This is Felik, he came with the new group. He was just cleared yesterday!" Kentin said.

Felik extended his hand, "Hi Milos. Nice to meet you."

Milos looked at him dead in the eye, and slapped his hand instead of shaking it. "Hi Felik," Milos said in the same cold tone.

Felik had a shaved head and lanky arms. He was a weird looking kid, but had an innocent demeanor nonetheless. The kids left the wagon. On their way to the back of the mansion, they saw Cherris speaking with a group of adults, discussing safe practices and promising futures. Kentin waved at her.

She smiled and waved back. "Don't go too far kids," she said.

"Ok!" Kentin shouted back.

The kids headed for the back entrance. On the way, they noticed a line of new people, waiting to be accepted into the group. Briggs and his crew were in charge of background checks and psychological evaluations. The kids arrived at the back door, which was also guarded by two fighters.

One knelt down, "Where do you think you guys are going?" he said.

"Just out back, we'll be very careful!"

The guard stroked his beard playfully, contemplating whether or not he was going to let them through. "Only if you stay on the side of the rocks. You have to let Lito and the other people work, *capisce?*"

Kentin and Felik nodded. The guard let them through and told an outdoor guard to keep an eye on them. All three of the boys strolled through the pebbles and sand facing the ocean. Milos stared at the waves as they crashed down not too far ahead of them. In the distance, they saw Lito measuring and pointing to inform his team where to plant the next remote C-4.

"What's going on back here?" Felik asked.

"Those guys are protecting us. We can't let the Hiezers invade our new home!" Kentin responded.

"Didn't you steal it from the Hiezers though?" Felik asked.

Kentin shrugged. Milos thought about that comment.

Did we steal it from them? They're bad, evil, and I want to kill all of the Hiezers. But if we steal from them, does that make us bad too?

Kentin and Felik started running around, collecting rocks in an attempt to skim them over the ocean's surface. Milos trailed behind, contemplating morality.

Briggs headed toward the front door of a warmly lit room as he politely escorted a cleared Sin civilian to the next checkpoint. "Good luck, Malrez, and welcome to our new home," he wished with sincerity. He then motioned to Rodest to let the next newcomer through the line to be evaluated. It was evident in everyone's expression that the day had been long and the wait, grueling. The miserable body language from the incoming group was hard to ignore, but Briggs stood tall, as a commander should, to instill vigor and inspire his team. A less than stable man rushed towards Briggs, as the man was welcomed into the room. The man was wearing a ragged leather jacket and had straggly grey hair that aged his face beyond his years. Briggs hesitantly welcomed him into the room and motioned for the man to have a seat. The man stared down at the black marble desk, seemingly on the verge of tears.

"What's your name, my good man?" Briggs asked, trying to keep the evaluation light.

The man clasped his hands in an attempt to keep them from shaking. "Victor Doran," the man said after a long pause, finally looking up.

Briggs stared back in confusion, "You have a last name. You aren't a Sin?" he questioned.

Victor shook his head.

Briggs got up from his chair, "Then how did you make it this far?"

Briggs started for the front door to find out what was going on. Victor lunged for Briggs' hand and grasped it with both of his. Tears filled his bloodshot eyes. Briggs' first reaction was to tense up, considering this could be an attempt to take out a commander.

"Please, sir, I'm not a threat. I've been searched up and down and pleaded with the earlier guards to let me through," Victor said as tears covered his face. "My wife, my son… they took them both." With a shaky hand, Victor took out a decrepit wallet, letting the tears flow as he shared a frayed family picture with Briggs. "What the hell can I do now, but try and get them back?" Victor pleaded desperately.

Briggs stood tall, looking down at the desperate man. He grew less tense as his mind started to race.

"Hun, the baby's crying again. It's your turn," Briggs said with a smile.

"It feels like it's always my turn," a woman said, smiling back.

"Oh c'mon, Saeda," Briggs said, trying to read a book.

"He's starting to look like you," Saeda said as she rocked Kentin gently.

Briggs took his eyes off the book to smile proudly. He got up and picked them both up effortlessly. Kentin giggled like a typical nine month old would, thinking that he was flying. An incoming sound crept louder and louder from the background, until an explosion shook the ground. The feeling of adrenaline kicked in, boiling Briggs' blood as he watched the fear and terror wash over Saeda's face. Briggs put them down and gently scooped his arm around Saeda to push her along quickly, as another bomb exploded nearby. The flying debris of former huts clapped onto their roof, knocking it off completely. They both looked up as Kentin began to cry. Briggs slammed through their back door, where the shrill screams of the incoming bombs and explosions were no longer muffled.

"Why?" Saeda cried frantically, "We already have so little. Who would..." Another explosion went off, knocking them both off their feet.

Before the fall, Briggs quickly grabbed Kentin and held him securely in his gigantic arm. They were now in the open, as their hut caved inward from the explosions.

Briggs shot up to his feet and extended his free hand for Saeda to grab. "There's no time," Briggs reminded her with a mix of worry and intensity. The sound of stealth jets soaring overhead made the fear of death that much more apparent. Saeda grabbed on and got back on her feet. Briggs sprinted, attempting desperately to get his family to safety. He held Kentin tight as the baby cried uncontrollably and held Saeda's hand as she struggled to keep up in her slippers. Screams echoed in the distance amongst the explosions. Briggs prayed in his head that his family wouldn't contribute to them. They finally broke away from a block of huts and got to open ground, when an explosion hit two huts twenty feet away, blowing their hair back. Briggs ducked and faced the other way to shield Kentin from any fallout. Just as he felt the wind die down, his other arm jerked. His heart fell into his stomach and a huge lump in his throat immediately took his breath when he noticed Saeda was no longer holding his hand. A jagged portion of a hut wall, the size of Briggs, speared Saeda and propelled her fifteen feet away from where they were ducking for cover. Briggs' mind went numb, tears flowed from his eyes as he was forcefully reminded of mortality. He ran to her lifeless bloody body while images of her smile exacerbated the pain. Bodies were spread out from the chaos, some just as broken as the exploded huts. Briggs grabbed onto Saeda's lifeless hand. Her face was still intact, but her eyes were open and lifeless. Briggs sobbed over his beloved partner, wishing with all of his heart that he could have her back.

Briggs snapped back to reality, looking down at Victor, who had fallen to the floor in tears as Briggs rehashed his past.

"I'm a Terra, sir. I did my duty. I carried out my orders. Why would they just take them?" Victor sobbed.

Briggs was holding back tears of his own, very much able to relate. Briggs bent down and lifted him up to his feet, putting Victor's arm around his shoulder. "It's alright, buddy. We'll get this straightened out. And once we do, you can join our cause. We'll help you locate your family and get them back," Briggs reassured.

"Thank you," Victor said, starting to calm down, "God bless you, sir."

Briggs picked up his radio, "Get me detailed records on a Terra named Victor Doran."

"Right away, commander," Rodest replied.

Briggs helped Victor regain his balance and reassuringly patted him on the shoulder. "I've lost family too. We have to stay strong, for all that we have left. It won't do us any good to dwell. And I know, much easier said than done. I've been there, but hopefully we can help you through it," Briggs said.

Victor wiped his nose and nodded, looking up at Briggs with his bloodshot eyes. "You're a good man, Briggs. I hope to pay back your kindness one day," Victor said as he gathered himself and took a seat. Briggs smiled and looked down, happy that he could help. "Ok," Victor said, "I'm ready for the evaluation."

"My intent is to inform the people of Senation of our current situation and continue to let them decide what course of action to take," Blague said calmly to Jeck. "You see, this benefits you too. I'm giving you an opportunity to speak on behalf of the Hiezers."

"Hah," Jeck mocked. "I'm a prisoner in my own place of work. Forgive me if I don't perceive this situation as beneficial. Your little group of savages will claw my eyes out the second you allow them to," Jeck said with malice in his voice.

Blague stared at him for a moment, not reacting to his response. "That mode of thought makes it all too obvious that you barely regard the Sins as people," Blague replied, as he paced around the room.

"Oh, they're people, Blague. Uneducated, lawbreaking, uncivilized people. They deserve every bit of this hellhole," Jeck said while jerking in his shackles.

Blague pulled over the chair Lito was sitting in. "You're so quick to generalize. Your macro level outlook will make this debate a landslide," Blague explained confidently.

"Enough about your nonsensical plan. You seem educated about the situation at hand," Jeck said as he leaned forward, to the point where his shackles pressed against the back of his chair. "You're after the Ayelan for yourself. Playing as noble Robin Hood, but underneath your cloak, you just want to preserve your own life." As Jeck leaned back, the black orbs in his pauldrons reflected the light around him. He looked at Blague suspiciously, but with a smirk. "I've got you figured out," Jeck said.

Blague leaned forward with an unchanged expression, "You're as misguided as your black-cloaked brothers, Jeck. Has it become so cloudy at the top that the only conceived thoughts are of personal gain?" Blague questioned as his stare intensified, watching Jeck nod in a mocking expression.

"Alright, almighty Blague, basking in your ideals. Unlike you, my 'brothers' live in the real world, which if not for them, would be post-apocalyptic. We restored

order on a global scale within six months of the quake."
Jeck said while shifting to a confident demeanor.

Blague sat back, "Does the one great deed
accomplished justify the tyranny that you've built? That's
a little narcissistic, wouldn't you say?" Blague asked.

"Hah," Jeck scoffed, "We've made this world
prosper. Unfortunately, there will always be a lower class,
filled with a false sense of entitlement."

Blague got up and slowly walked behind Jeck's
chair. "Jeck," Blague said as he unlocked his shackles,
"you've grown so weak." Blague began walking toward
the door with a smirk on his face. "I'll release you after
you speak for the Hiezers." He shut the door and locked
it. Jeck remained in his chair to reflect while rubbing his
freed, achy wrists, confused by the last few sentences
Blague spoke.

Lesh ran for what seemed to be hours. A dust storm
enveloped the city, causing her to reduce speed. She
approached the inner city, Clestice, where Nemura was
supposed to keep watch for Hiezer activity. The huts were
multicolored, scrapped together with the most durable
metals available. Each hut was about ten feet away from
the next, each ranging from fifteen to forty feet in height.
The pathways were an unpaved mix of sand and dirt. The
streets were populated, but not overwhelmingly crowded.
Dust storms were generally a great time to loot in
Senation. Everyone wore a hood to protect from the dust
or to blend in while they robbed their neighbors blind.
Clestice was one of the harsher cities, with less guard

patrol than the rest. Lesh paused for a moment, clenching one of her throwing knives in the pocket of her hooded fleece, annoyed that the knife ring on her back was covered. Her brown hair creeped out of her hood and blew in every direction with the wind. Her face remained serious, as she analyzed her position and tried to determine the best place to start her search.

Nemura was stationed in a silver hut east of my location. My best bet is to interrogate anyone that has remained there. But surely anyone involved wouldn't be dumb enough to stick around. Unless, of course, they think us all to be dead. If Nemura is with the Hiezers, then he has definitely heard the status of the situation by now.

Lesh leaped to a crease in the side of one of the taller huts and quickly began to scale it, searching rapidly for the next spot to grab. After about twenty seconds, she grabbed hold of the roof ledge of the hut. She swung around with her back to the wall and with both arms, flipped herself to the top of the roof. She walked to the eastern edge of the hut and crouched down, waiting for a moment of clear sight. When she got it, she paused and let out an uncontrollable laugh.

"Of course all of the huts in sight have been spray-painted silver. Well at least I have my answer. Nemura, you fuck," Lesh said to herself. She began her way back down the hut, when she heard a gunshot coming from the northeast.

That sounded like a high caliber weapon. Anyone with that kind of gun must have connections in this city.

She sprinted off. In the distance, she saw a man with curly hair with a gun pointed at the head of a teenage girl, who had her hands over her head, trembling in fear.

"You little bitch," the man snarled. "Do you have any idea how long it took me to get a decent gold watch into this store? How dare you." The older man's face was shaking in anger.

"I gave it back," the girl said in a petrified tone, "I'm sorry!" she pleaded.

Lesh dashed into the vicinity of the man, shrouding her figure by the surrounding scene, listening to the conversation.

"If I pierced a hole in that thieving brain, no one would ever know," he said as he spit on the girl.

The hooded citizens of Clestice didn't even turn their heads for a second look. The man's pistol hand began to shake, as his anger became exacerbated. He held an old magnum pistol that could pierce three skulls with one shot. Lesh realized it was time to jump in. She dove toward his back at an incredible speed. She knocked the man in the temple and quickly spun to his other side to maneuver his gun to point straight at him, cracking his fingers in the process. He let out a grunt without knowing what hit him. When she realized he was dazed and at gun point, Lesh stood up straight and spun around to face him, gripping his hand with the magnum. She flipped her knife around with her free hand and pointed it to his groin while staring into his eyes.

"I don't think this is where you want to die, old man," Lesh's voice cracked as the words came out. The man looked stunned, releasing his grip on the gun, surrendering to her.

The teenage girl put her hands on the floor and

stared at the mysterious woman who may have just saved her life. "Thank you, miss," she said.

Lesh turned her head, "Stay put for a moment," she said.

The man flinched. Lesh lightly pierced his skin with the knife. He cringed and instantly backed down. Lesh turned her head back to stare the man in the eyes.

"Did you not hear me the first time?" Lesh's voice echoed.

The dust was whirling around them and the wind was howling.

"What's your name?" Lesh asked.

"Morn," he revealed weakly.

"Is this your store, Morn? May we go inside?" Lesh asked rhetorically.

He nodded. Lesh stripped Morn of his gun and shoved him toward the door so that he could open it. All three of them entered. He flipped on the lights. The displays surrounded them with makeshift jewelry, most of which looked like cheap silver.

"On the floor, Morn," Lesh said.

He sat down, muttering slurs under his breath. "Listen lady," Morn said in a southern drawl, "unless you're robbin' me, you best be on your way. This girl over here attempted to thieve my most precious item. She needs to be punished."

Lesh pulled out a knife and stared at it, but didn't respond. Morn had curly grey and black hair, a strong nose, and a sunken in, chiseled face, with a black goatee. He wore a tanned trench coat without a hood. Lesh removed her hood. He stopped talking for a moment, a bit startled. Lesh's slim, fierce face, coupled with strangely attractive dark circles under her eyes, made her a unique sight.

"I'm not going to take any of this material from you," she riddled.

"What do you want then, sweetheart?" Morn asked.

She smirked and walked over to him quickly, placing the point of her knife under his chin. "Tell me what you know about Nemura," she said in a chilling tone.

The teenage girl reacted with a shift of her weight and a slight twitch. Lesh quickly turned her head.

"Am I interrogating the wrong person?" Lesh asked herself out loud.

The girl shook her head fearfully. The silence was eerie. Information was obviously being withheld.

"I'm not known for my patience. I'll flip one of these silver coins," she said as she stood up and plucked one from a display. "Depending on the landing, one of you is about to lose a finger, after I pull out the nail of that finger," Lesh threatened.

The girl hesitated, "You must be with the Sin movement. Everyone in this town knows that Nemura is with them, too," she said. Lesh looked over, unconvinced, as she flipped the coin. As soon as it landed in her hand, she closed her fist.

"Now, now hold on a second, sweetheart," Morn said in a nervous tone. "Nemura went AWOL from Clestice and had a new group of goons cover his tracks."

"Oh?" Lesh challenged. She slowly opened her fist.

Morn started moving toward Lesh, to beg. "I'm

being true to ya! My sources tell me he skipped town or went underground. No one's heard or seen that snake since that explosion a week ago."

I don't sense that this hothead is lying. Nonetheless, I have to find out if he knows more.

Lesh took a few steps back over to Morn, knelt over, and grabbed his hand. "It landed on tails, so you're up first," she said. Lesh didn't remove eye contact with him as she slowly aligned the knife where his chosen fingernail rested.

"Lady, I told ya everything I know. Information about him ain't worth any pain!" Morn pleaded.

Just then, the lights flickered and four hooded figures rushed past the main glass window of the store. Lesh looked down and noticed a blinking red dot coming from the teenage girl's jacket.

"You little bitch," Lesh said.

The girl got up and ran toward the back of the store, taking cover. Lesh swung off her cloak, exposing her knife ring. The main glass shattered as two hooded figures jumped through it. Another kicked open the front door. Lesh jumped and perched on top of one of the displays. She flung the knife in her hand in the direction of the first attacker she laid eyes on. The person quickly shut the door, letting it catch the blade. Lesh unsheathed two more knives from the lower portion of her ring and flung them toward the two covered figures charging from the glass, while propelling herself backward onto another display. One of the knives pierced an attacker in the abdomen causing him to drop to the floor, screaming in agony. The other knife struck another attacker in the throat, who was now bleeding out face down on the floor. The door swung back open with two more attackers charging at her. Another one slowly entered from the broken window. Morn crawled frantically behind a corner display. The teenage girl charged Lesh and tried to grapple her from behind. Lesh spun and jumped at the last second, with one foot trailing the other in midair. She kicked the girl twice with one spin. Blood from her mouth splashed the ceiling and a tooth fell to the floor. Lesh spun back toward the two assailants right in front of her, who were swinging blunt metal poles toward her face. She unsheathed a knife from the top of her ring. She ducked one swing and slashed open one attacker's gut and spun a third time to cut the other's neck. As soon as the knife pierced his neck, someone grabbed her arm. The last thing she saw was the figure of a woman, right before a pole was used to jab her in the temple.

Chapter 6

Eugene looked more solemn than usual, as he led a group of six scientists to search for the hidden Ayelan chemical. They analyzed every inch of the underground research facility that rested directly below the main floor. Sabin frequently checked in with Eugene to follow up on the progress of the searches while they were in session. Although they were assigned to work collaboratively to recover the chemical, Eugene didn't mind that Sabin's presence was spotty.

I can't believe how long it's been since I lost Jen. And the news, the news that she died that day on the boat to Senation. Why am I rehashing all of this now? These goddamn dreams are recurring way too often. Eugene held his head. *I failed her when she needed me most.*

One of the scientists beckoned the group over. In the furthest corner of the room, he stared intently at an object. "This has to be it," Endok shouted. When Eugene walked over to see, the other scientists cleared a pathway for him. "Eugene," Endok said as he leaned in to inspect his findings, "look at the points in the wall glimmering with light. If you pass by from different angles, you'll notice the shades of orange turn to gold."

Eugene raised his eyebrow. "That sounds like the chemical's unique characteristic, but I have a feeling breaking through the wall isn't the answer. How would the Hiezers access the chemical for testing?" Eugene questioned.

The other scientists started thinking out loud. Endok remained quiet for a moment, standing there with thick glasses and a lab coat that was much too short. An idea immediately came to mind and he pointed to the mid-section of the facility.

"It's over there. There has to be a code that unlocks the Ayelan. It's the only part of the facility that has a database mainframe," Endok explained.

Eugene looked convinced, "Let's get Briggs and his team involved to crack the code and extract the chemical."

Endok looked over to Eugene, "And what do you plan on doing with it if we can extract it?" Endok asked curiously as he pushed his glasses up to his face.

"What's your concern, Endok? Do you think we're going to chase immortality like the rest of this wretched world?" Eugene questioned, sounding impatient.

Endok looked down, "No, I spoke with Blague many times and I believe in his vision. He's a just man," Endok explained.

Eugene sighed, "Then what's the problem?"

Endok regained his posture, "You must understand, Commander, from the perspective of a scientist like myself, the discovery of Ayelan and Cryos is brand new. The possibilities are endless. The Hiezers haven't even begun to see its potential." Endok caught the attention of the other scientists that were gathered around.

Eugene raised his hand. "Enough, Endok," he commanded, "Let's get our priorities straight. We have to maintain custody of this mansion. The first step in doing so is to extract the chemical and let Blague hide it. At that point, we will no longer have to bluff. The Hiezers won't invade if we threaten to destroy the chemical."

Endok pondered, "I understand, I'm just curious if we will eventually conduct our own tests, in a controlled environment of course."

Eugene lowered his tone, "My assumption, if all remains settled for our group, is yes."

This conversation sparked excitement among the scientists, and so they began rattling off different theories to each other. Eugene dismissed himself and called Briggs on his radio.

Jeck strolled behind Blague as they walked toward the northern pathway on the first floor. Blague didn't even glance over his shoulder to check on the uncuffed prisoner that he had taken.

"Are you ever going to decloak, Jeck? That outfit must be getting rather disgusting at this point," Blague mocked.

"Hah," Jeck yacked, "Well according to you, I'll be walking safely out of my old fortress unscathed in a few hours. Isn't that so, Blague?"

"Depending on your behavior, potentially," Blague said.

The gold, ornate swirls decorating the walls danced as they passed the rooms. Both of the opposing personalities approached the presentation ledge with confidence. Blague's vision of creating a community, in which information flowed transparently, was about to be underway.

This is an essential step for our group's growth. I'm already perceiving team-oriented divisions within the population. They're collectively forming a functioning community without even noticing it. Confidence is growing as a result of our victory. I want to make the growth rapid, by instilling choice and free will. Implementing change with as little bloodshed as possible may seem like a laughable thought, but I will still strive toward it.

"Alright everyone," Blague boomed, with an echo to follow, "gather up and inform anyone working to cease for a few hours. Jeck and I will present our positions in thirty minutes, without holding anything back from you." Blague looked at his watch and turned back to Jeck.

"Your Cryos mark is different," Jeck said, curiously.

Blague looked up, "It differentiates me, doesn't it?"

Jeck looked confused. "All of the marks are designed to be uniform. It's a stamp. Yours has slight imperfections and a unique shape," Jeck continued.

"Let that tunnel-vision mind of yours try and muster why that may be," Blague riddled back.

Jeck scoffed, "You're nothing but a jester masking the same ambitions as the Hiezers."

Blague turned away, realizing the conversation would go nowhere.

"You ever get those moments, Eugene, when your past hits you like a ton of bricks?" Briggs asked.

Eugene sighed, "Yeah, now more than ever."

"You think it's because we found a moment that we're out of harm's way and our bodies now have the time to catch up with all the shit we've been through?" Briggs continued to question.

Eugene shrugged, "That's probably it."

"Man, it's like pulling teeth talking to you today," Briggs said as he leaned his folded arms onto the mainframe computer.

Eugene smirked, "You know, I was hanging out here just fine before you started yapping." They both shared a laugh.

"Fine then, no point to stop now that I already annoyed you," Briggs said with a smirk. "I remember when I was a boy, my parents and I were Yuprains. My father had just gotten this big construction job. I was only thirteen, but I was already bigger than him. Not to mention, he had a busted leg."

"Let me guess," Eugene interrupted, "Good guy Briggs to the rescue?"

"That's not the point!" Briggs said jokingly. "So I volunteered to join and help out, to pull my weight for once. We showed up on site five minutes early and joined the crowd in two single file lines. My father turned to me, 'Keep your mouth shut, Joel, it's for your own good' he said." Eugene folded his arms, showing some interest in the story. "Here I am, thinking I'm doing a good thing and helping out, but as soon as I got there, I realized, fear was the only thing that mattered on the job. Good deeds didn't count for anything and the workers beside me were conditioned for years to let fear run them. I looked up at my father, who never let a hint of insecurity show at home; I saw him crumble at the sight of his bosses. I looked ahead to see a girl that looked younger than me with crystal blue eyes. She was escorted by a tall dark haired man with black, mirrored aviator glasses and a long trench coat." Briggs broke eye contact because two scientists began to loudly argue their theories near the Ayelan. He looked back to Eugene, "And I thought to myself, my dad's afraid of a little girl?"

"Hah," Eugene let out a laugh, "It's impossible for a kid to understand what real power could do to somebody. If you abide by it long enough, without putting up a fight, it can transform you. To your dad, that little girl probably looked as tall as you are now."

"Yeah, she was calling the shots, tasing people who weren't working hard enough. My blood was boiling. I would ask myself, 'How could these grown men allow this to go on?' Once I got over the initial shock and the day went by, I saw my dad's knee buckle as he fell to the ground with a slab of concrete on his back. I rushed over and grabbed the concrete and threw it to the ground and kneeled to help my father up. As soon as I looked up, the girl and large man were right in front of us. She had an emotionless expression and was revving her live taser. I tensed up. My father grabbed onto my arm tightly and looked at me with intensity, 'Don't do it,' he said. I unclenched my fist and kneeled back down with my father. We both took the shock therapy," Briggs finished.

Eugene shook his head, "Yuprains were almost treated as shitty as the Sins."

"Well, it's only one class level of difference, so I guess it's all relative," Briggs said, shifting his position on the flat cylindrical computer. "Anyway, that's the day I realized that this world isn't right, and I had to do something about it," Briggs said.

"Here you are now, one level lower, and still fighting," Eugene said jokingly.

Briggs waved his hand dismissively, "C'mon, Eugene. Don't buy into their hierarchy. I'm ten levels higher mentally, with a great leader and a sad mope of a friend," Briggs said, punching Eugene's shoulder.

Eugene lost his balance and muttered, "Fucking asshole."

Eugene sat on the floor with his legs spread out in a corner of the research facility. Briggs and two of his technicians analyzed the database, with Endok a few steps back, pondering solutions. The other scientists were scattered, basking in the glory of their new found facility. Eugene inspected his gun as his mind wondered.

As a Remdon, our employment was so clear. I remember the call coming through the transmitter which rested next to the kitchen wall. Jen always resented that moment. It was a little reminder that you are under the control of a higher power.

"Eugene and Jennifer", an unidentifiable voice projected, followed by the image of a guard mask that appeared on the small screen of the transmitter. "Present your IDs," the guard said.

They both held up their barcoded cards with their name and class symbol stamped on it.

The guard would proceed once the cards were scanned, "Report for your job assignments."

I'll never forget the feeling of being so trapped. Acceptable jobs for Remdons were so limited. Jen was to gather crops within a large group. I was military support with a long range rifle. The fear of being demoted a social class was at the front of our minds whenever we were performing our duty. I'll never forget the day Jen hit her breaking point. All of those articles she read about how to report on events. She wanted so badly to become a part of that. Unfortunately that job was reserved for Dactuars, the class immediately below the Hiezers. Anyone with a brain knew that the mass projection of events was heavily filtered and controlled by the Hiezers. It drove her mad. If I stopped her she would still be here, but I have to repress these thoughts, again. These dreams have to die out soon.

The door directly at the top of the steps of the facility swung open. "Twenty minutes until the rally," one of the fighters shouted, "Work is to be temporarily ceased."

Eugene looked up. "Alright, we'll be up in five," he shouted back.

Time to start focusing on the issues at hand. I have to help make this group maintain integrity and breakout of this hell hole that we call Senation.

Eugene quickly stood up, "Briggs," he yelled, "let's give it a rest and stand by Blague."

Briggs nodded and twirled his finger in the air to round everyone up and head upstairs.

Kentin and Felik loved going out back. The soldiers that kept watch grew a liking to the curious boys. Kentin knew Milos was suffering and always dragged him along, even if he was unpleasant. Lito spent the last few days organizing the booby traps at the back entrance. Anytime a ship came into vision, the patrol on watch would signal for everyone to hide. The kids hid behind the rocks; Kentin always being the most excited to play spy. Lito took it a little more seriously. "*Puto!*" he shouted whenever he got the signal. At that point, he and his team would promptly trot to the back entrance door and go inside. Periodically, Lito would come over to where the boys were playing to hang out with them. He would lift his goggles up and play along with their imaginative scenarios that changed on a daily basis.

When everyone was out back, a solider called out, "Blague's speaking in fifteen minutes. Cease work temporarily."

Felik was staring at one of the bomb-squad workers planting C-4. "Who do you think controls the bombs?" Felik asked Kentin and Milos.

"Either Lito, my dad, or Blague," Kentin guessed.

Felik nodded, "That's a scary job."

"Yeah," Milos agreed, "especially if you mess it up."

Kentin turned to run for the door and the other boys followed.

Blague watched as the civilians and fighters gathered on the main floor. He noticed lots of new faces; the faces of Sins that came to join the movement. Blague had a lot of faith in Briggs and his ability to maintain order in a cautious manner. The first floor ledge where Blague and Jeck stood, jutted out about eight feet over the main floor, allowing them enough room to move around in the spotlight. The golden swirls of the first floor began on the wall behind the speakers; it looked as though Blague and Jeck had golden wings of abstract design. Blague stood there wearing a jet black shirt with sleeves that stopped right below his shoulders. His Cryos mark was purposely exposed. His pants and shoes were a mix black and blue, all form fitting active combat wear. His exposed arms looked extra defined in this lighting and his veins pulsated. His Desert Eagle was strapped to his right hip and his blade was strapped to his left. His posture remained that of a leader's and his confidence never swayed. Jeck remained in his Hiezer cloak and refused to remove his orbed pauldrons, which complimented the design on the walls behind him. Jeck looked like a young fifty years of age. He was polished and arrogant, as you would expect a high status egotistical individual to look. His face was chiseled, but full. His discomfort was masked by his attitude. His hands dressed in black and gold gloves remained clasped behind his back, assuming an authoritative stance as he readied himself to speak. Blague's commanders began lining up on the main floor, directly below the ledge. The fighters were scattered to keep order and patrol the exposed areas. Blague looked down from the ledge and noticed that Lesh and Sabin were missing.

Sabin looked at the transponder where a blinking light remained stationary for an entire day. His half cloak and hood flew in every direction from the intense dust storm. Mars trotted behind him with his head down, trying to cover it from the dust.

Either she found that little pebble I tossed on her back and disposed of it, or she's captured, or worse. I'm glad I planted that tracking device on her. She's way too valuable to lose.

Sabin and Mars trekked through Clestice as concealed as they could. The sight of Mars would definitely raise some eyebrows. The dust storm was beneficial in the sense that the people trekking outdoors had little interest in anything, but getting to their huts safely. Sabin proceeded east, where he noticed each hut was painted a metallic silver. Mars barked and sprinted to the jewelry shop, where he smelled Lesh's scent from her spilt blood. Sabin jogged after him. "What is it boy?" he said as he approached the bloody scene, "Oh my, this isn't good." Sabin pulled the knife out of the door and inspected it. "This is definitely Lesh's," he looked around at the mess of bodies.

Guards will be all over this scene as soon as the dust storm dies down.

He patted Mars on the side, ran to gather Lesh's knives, and then ran outside back into the storm. He looked at the knives inside his coat.

This is unnerving, I hope she's still breathing, we can't be without her.

As he approached the blinking red dot on his transponder, he slid on his metal gloves, which had open creases at the joints of his fingers. The palm of each glove had the end of thick wiring securely clasped to it. He pulled out a double-sided curved black blade that had the other end of the wiry rope clasped to it. He and Mars contemplated how to best break into the hut where Lesh's tracking device remained still.

Chapter 7

Lesh spit blood out of her mouth onto the ground. A man took his mask off and gave a sinister grin to Lesh. He had a long, silver goatee and wild, silver hair. His face was thin and sharp and his body was of average build. He pulled down his leather protective covering to reveal a fresh wound on his neck.

"Look at this, you little bitch," the man said, laughing. "You almost got me! And you didn't even know it was me!"

Lesh's eyes regained focus, but remained hazy from the countless jabs to the temple in an attempt to keep her unconscious. "Of course I knew it was you, Nemura. Why do you think I went for the neck?" Lesh quipped in a cracking voice.

"Going against big, bad Blague's orders? Surely he wants me alive," Nemura said with a mocking grin.

"I have reign to use my own judgement," Lesh shot back. "You're a Hiezer now, what's there to talk about?" she questioned.

Nemura's grin transformed from genuine to sarcastic. He slowly lifted her face by the chin with his blunt metal stave. "You think you've got it all figured out don't you?" Nemura asked, looking at her curiously in the eye. He looked over at the scarred woman next to him and then passed a look to the men behind him.

Lesh followed with her eyes and noticed the teenage girl standing up straight with them, sporting a bandage wrapped tightly around her face. Her eyes shifted to a hunched-over Morn, kept in a corner under the careful watch of a guard. Nemura gave a nod. His crew began to unmask; all of them wore grey combat clothing with a strange, red symbol on the left of their chests.

That isn't a Hiezer mark, for sure. It's not a mark of any of the other social classes either. Is this another uprising?

"You look like you're starting to have an epiphany, Lesh," Nemura said mockingly.

The woman next to Nemura stared blankly at him. She had four deep scars on her face; two of which started from her right eye and extended all the way down to her chin, and the other two mirrored the same marks on her left side. She had medium length blonde hair. Her eyes had no focus whatsoever. It was as if a corpse was standing in the room. The men behind Nemura were of all different shapes and sizes. The common denominator was the symbol they wore. Lesh's Cryos mark began to shine.

"Oh?" Nemura noticed, "There's life in you yet, Lesh. I expected as much from you. You put up a hell of a fight for someone who was ambushed," Nemura said as he tilted his head back, while holding eye contact. "Everyone, do not reveal your Sin names to this one here," he said loudly as he pointed to his chained up prisoner. "It's bad enough she knows mine, heh," he laughed.

Lesh's eyes communicated fire, but her expression remained unchanged. She looked up to inspect the chains that kept her raised off the ground, then looked down quickly to notice her feet chained together.

"Look all you want, you aren't leaving this place. I haven't yet decided whether to kill you or hold you as collateral for the resources I can exploit from your group," Nemura said as he leaned his face in to meet Lesh's. "But I imagine you'd be a hard prisoner to keep," he said as he showed his teeth.

Lesh remained undaunted. "You let civilians die for no reason, Nemura," she said coldly, "Even the weak deserve a chance."

Nemura's grin faded for a moment, "Unfortunately, it was time to make my move. We now know we're destined for greatness," he replied.

"You sound more psychotic than usual. Did someone hypnotize that peanut residing in your head?" Lesh asked with a smirk.

Nemura laughed in a high pitch and slapped more blood out of her. "You're making my decisions too easy," he said as his face changed to a more serious expression. "I've seen something that you can only dream of," Nemura said in an excited whisper. "A land mass that sprouted from the quake and was only discovered eight months ago," he continued as he raised the volume of his voice. "Auront, it's called. Since I just decided you're a dead woman, I have no problem at all sharing our future. This land mass was discovered by a Dactuar, Jason Brink, who was an explorer of our post-quake world. In a trip to analyze the shift in the Antarctic continents, he passed over a landmass that had no indication of ice or any other life for that matter. He later took both me and my comrades here," he gestured around the room. "The terrain was hardened dirt that resembled concrete. That wasn't the strangest part though," Nemura lowered his voice, "There were geysers shooting an ominous dark red smoke."

Lesh's brow moved, *what the fuck is this guy talking about? What planet is he living on?*

Nemura looked up, entranced. The scarred woman focused on Nemura for a moment and then promptly lost focus again, although it was obvious she was listening.

"I wasn't yet worthy to land on the island, but Jason did. Since then, he's reached a higher state of consciousness. He only landed for three hours and had already become a more powerful thinker than Blague or any of the Hiezers. He's enlightened." Nemura looked at Lesh, "Sounds nuts right?" Lesh stared blankly at him. "It's something you would have to witness to believe, unfortunately. We are now convinced that a higher power has caused the Global Quake and is communicating to us through Auront. Now I'm not much of a godly man, but some stream of greater power, some force has the ability to elevate us," he said.

Lesh let the mumbling settle for a moment.

"So, you've traveled across the world in hopes to receive a hallucinogen that seemingly has permanent effects?" Lesh asked and paused for a moment. "So, you're a junkie that hasn't even had the drug yet? And that's why you let people die?" her voice cracked.

"I never took you as such a caring woman, Lesh, I'm stunned," Nemura flashed his ear to ear grin again. He looked at his pocket watch, "I'm in no rush. We have at least two hours before our transport arrives." He pulled over a stool and sat to the side of Lesh, so he can address her and his group. Morn was shaking his head in confusion and disbelief. "Let's change the subject," Nemura decided. "How about a history lesson on our fine prisoner here? The master assassin, the mysterious killer, the, the, prisoner of a junkie," Nemura burst out laughing. His crew let out some snide chuckles to support their superior, all except the scarred woman, who remained somewhat catatonic. "Lesh here," Nemura gestured to her with his hand, "wasn't always such a crazed killer or so the legend goes."

Lesh slowly shook her head, "Don't bring it up, Nemura. I understand that you have great sources of information, which is why we welcomed you in the first place, but this isn't necessary, so don't do it," her voice faded as she spoke the words.

"Aww, a soft spot? Could it be?" Nemura questioned as he put one leg up on a peg of the stool, becoming excited that he was able to extract some emotion. "So as I was saying, Lesh wasn't always so unique. It was a normal day in the ranks of the Terras. Her older brother was a bit of a rebel, carrying out his duties haphazardly. One Hiezer guard in particular took note of him and eventually grew to despise his ability to skate on the edge of being de-ranked."

Morn's attention was grabbed; watching Lesh in action astonished him and he was very curious to hear this story. Lesh tried to analyze her surroundings instead of reliving her demons. She noted the spread out dim lights, few and far between, hanging from the high ceiling. Around the edges of the hut were mesh metal ledges with staircases stretching to the top.

Nemura backhanded Lesh. "Pay attention!" he shouted. Lesh shot a dirty look at him.

You're going to regret this.

"Her brother operated in this fashion for years, until one day, the guard taking note decided to put a stop to it. He followed her brother to where he checked in for his job as an architect. The guard watched as her brother immediately bailed on his duties, to explore the world as he saw fit. The guard followed him for a few hours and when he was far enough away from all the activity, he seized him," Nemura said as he turned to observe his audience, who was captivated. "The guard covered his mouth from behind and slammed him in the back with the blunt end of his gun," Nemura animated the motion to more vividly describe the story. "'Bring them out,' the guard radioed to his unit. Both he and Lesh's brother were in a mountainous region in Vermont. In a deserted area, elevated rocks rested on both sides of them. A black transport vehicle pulled up behind them. Out came a young sixteen year old Lesh, if you can imagine it," Nemura laughed, "Followed by her mother and father, all of which had ties around their mouths and their arms held together by their respective captors. The guard holding her brother knocked him down and took off his mask." Nemura paused for a second, "What were your names at the time? My memory's a little hazy."

Lesh clenched her jaw.

"Heh," Nemura huffed, "Well anyway, the guard's expression was nothing less of satisfaction. 'Alright,' the guard said, pointing an assault rifle at the brother's head, 'let's test your will.' The guard pulled out a pistol and handed it over to the brother and stepped behind him, pointing his rifle directly at the back of his head. Lesh was terrified, if I heard correctly," Nemura motioned to Lesh for rhetorical confirmation. "'Heh,' the guard said, 'now you have a choice,'" Nemura snapped his fingers, "Chase! That was his name!" Nemura shouted. "'Now you have a choice, Chase, kill yourself with the pistol I just handed to you or murder your family in cold blood and you get away scott free,' the guard said with an intensity."

Lesh's eyes became bloodshot and her Cryos tattoo began to glow brighter.

Nemura smirked when he saw some emotion in Lesh's face. "The guard said, 'If you so much as flinch, you're done.' The guard stiffened his position and put his finger on the trigger. Groans came from Lesh and her parents. Chase stood still for thirty seconds, which I'm sure felt like an eternity. 'Time's up, Chase,' the guard poked the gun at the back of his head. Chase, with a shaky hand pointed the gun at his own head. The guard took pleasure in the visual. But, a few seconds later, Chase turned his shaky hand slowly, pointing the gun toward his father, who showed no fear. The guard's satisfaction turned to disbelief. Chase, the witty rebel, had absolutely no honor. The guard behind the father quickly moved out of the way, and Chase fired. Lesh couldn't believe it," Nemura said, laughing, "She must have thought he took a noble shot at the guard holding his father, so he could break free and make a heroic escape. Nope!" Nemura slapped Lesh's face lightly. "Chase shot his father right under his nose, in the top lip. The most awkward spot to shoot someone. It pierced the back of his throat and eventually rendered him motionless, and he bled out on the floor. The groans that came from Lesh and her mother and the expression! That must have been a sight," Nemura mocked.

Lesh shook in her chains. *If I snap his neck now I'll never get out alive. I have to endure this until the moment is right.*

"Next, Chase pointed the gun to his mother. The guards were all shocked at this decision. Tears ran down the spineless rebel's face. Lesh squirmed then similar to how she's squirming now," Nemura said, cracking himself up, yet again. "He fired!" Nemura pulled the trigger of an imaginary gun to Lesh's face, "He fired, and this time, he really fucked up. He shot his mother in the stomach, so she bled out slowly. Chase, not being able to see straight from the tears, fear, and shame, quickly shifted the gun to his little sister. Now this is where the coward made a big mistake! He couldn't have known of course. But Lesh here, was extracted by the Hiezers at the age of ten and was trained as ranged special forces for six years. The higher ups got wind of her incredible agility and plucked her from her family for most of every day. Only her parents and higher ranking guards knew. It was classified information. But thank god for that, right? Otherwise you wouldn't have made it this far! Chase took his shot and you shifted, with that unnatural speed of yours."

Lesh's mind wandered as she faded in and out of Nemura's story, recognizing that his version was all too accurate.

It made me sick when Chase looked at me with his cowardly face. I'll never forget that moment.

At the time, Lesh was able to analyze the traumatizing blood spatter all around her. Her training and her adrenaline didn't allow her brain to disbelieve the horror or shut it out. She had to embrace it.

Nothing but instinct and intuition took over my body. That and the despised thought of my cowardly brother.

"Chase shot the guard in the lower abdomen, which would have got Lesh right between the eyes if she hadn't dodged it. Lesh being the instinctive assassin that we all know her to be, unsheathed a knife strapped to the wounded guard's leg and flung it at her brother's face. His eyes rolled to the back of his head and blood from his pierced forehead poured out." Nemura paused, winded, "Now tell me that's not drama?"

Nemura's audience had mixed reactions; the teenage girl had tears in her eyes, Morn looked solemn, Nemura's crew looked impressed.

"I know," Nemura said, nodding his head, "I lived in awe and in fear of this woman since I learned this story, until now of course."

I'll never forget holding my crying and screaming mother before the pain stopped.

Lesh twitched in her captivity, ready to make her move.

Nemura looked over at Lesh, satisfied with himself. "If that wasn't bad enough, old partner, your group is done for. My boy right here," Nemura pointed to one of his larger crew members, "extracted intel that the Hiezers were moving in on your precious new home. They're going to waste anyone in their way." Lesh held back any reaction. "They're storming by boat any day now," Nemura warned. "They're going to thin the Sin population and regain territory, two birds with one stone," he explained slowly.

"You bled with us Nemura. Why would your tone be so mocking?"

Lesh questioned, trying to hold back her fury.

I have to warn the others, even if I die trying.

"Because," Nemura shouted, "had I stayed with you and your petty territory battle, I'd be dead in the mansion with you! I represent life! Life that happens to be mocking death!"

Lesh heard a sound on the second level and glanced up when Nemura and the lifeless woman weren't looking. The others didn't notice because the dust storm caused a similar racket every minute.

That bastard! How did he track me? Mars is going to have a new owner once I'm done with him.

Sabin entered and drew his double sided, stringed blades quietly. He motioned to Lesh to be silent, then winked at her.

Pain in my ass.

"Nemura," Lesh said, changing her tone, "you talk too much, old partner."

Sabin watched Lesh grab on to the chains with her shackled hands and backflip, gaining height and kicking Nemura in the face in the process. She began shifting her body weight and repeatedly flipping to climb further up the chains that held her captive. Nemura's crew drew their weapons.

Time to dance.

Sabin flung one of his blades and ducked down. He tugged on the wire of his blade, which was leveraged over the ledge of the second floor. The blade slightly changed direction, catching the large man in the chest. Sabin jumped down to the main floor as the blade impaled the man. He flung the second blade toward the back of the room with intense force, while whipping the wire of the first blade that stood in the impaled man. The blade retracted like a boomerang, clashing with Sabin's metal glove as he caught it. His instinctive abilities allowed him to multi-task the two blades gracefully. He didn't possess the footwork that Lesh did, but his talent was evident in maneuvering his unique weapons. Sabin's second toss impaled another of Nemura's men. Morn looked shocked, as he followed the blade swing around the man's neck twice before sticking him. He then ducked frantically and began looking for his confiscated magnum. One of the wiry ropes wrapped around Sabin's arm. He spun around twice, gathering enough momentum on one of his blades to fling it back toward him. He aimed the incoming blade at the scarred woman, who was charging him with her gun drawn and began firing, temporarily focusing her eyes on Sabin. At the last second, she ducked the blade that would have decapitated her. Lesh, who carefully observed the massacre unfold, released her grip on her chains and pushed toward the scarred woman. With her chained feet, Lesh drop kicked the woman in the back with the force of her fall, slamming her into the ground. Lesh swung through the air, still harnessed by her chains.

Nemura, trying to find a clear shot, finally got it once the scarred woman was out of the way. Sabin whistled and ducked. Mars burst through the door and charged Nemura as he fired. One of Nemura's followers jumped in the way with a blade drawn, trying to stab the wolf. Mars lunged forward after a wild swing by the follower. Mars latched onto the back of his arm. Blood immediately started to spew all over his fangs. Nemura looked back and ducked. He refocused his aim to Sabin, who was clearly the greatest current threat. The scarred woman, who Sabin realized would be quite beautiful if not for the abnormal persona, got up and regained her posture. She also aimed at Sabin. The few crew members left standing started to rally alongside Nemura. One tried to help the man being decimated by Mars. Sabin, now in possession of both of his blades, threw one high, causing everyone to duck in fear. The scarred woman shot again, barely grazing his cloaked arm. Sabin jerked the wiry rope in his desired direction while jumping for cover. The blade slashed right through the chain that held Lesh up. The instant she dropped to the floor, she flipped horizontally, catching one of Nemura's men in the face with the chain on her feet. Nemura shifted his aim to Lesh, but she maneuvered around him and took cover, with bullets trailing behind her every move. Sabin exposed himself once he caught the blade. He rolled up the wiry ropes around his arm so they had shorter range and swung them in a circular motion, one trailing the other. He shifted his swing to his left side and swiftly changed to his right, alternating from side to side. The scarred woman charged with her stave, but had to jump out of the way when Sabin's blades picked up speed as he moved toward her.

Nemura realized this could end badly. "Back out!" Nemura shouted to the remaining four of his crew and the teenage girl.

They started making their way to the back door of the hut. One of the members had a clear shot at Mars and didn't want to leave without inflicting some kind of punishment on the invaders. Mars bared his teeth at the man. Lesh and Sabin were too far on opposite sides to intervene. A shot went off. Lesh's ears went deaf for a moment as she was making her way to save the wolf, but someone beat her to it. Morn fired his magnum that pierced the head of the man holding Mars at gunpoint. Sabin stopped his swinging blades while his eyes focused on what had just happened. He stood in shock for a moment.

Mars!

Sabin dashed around a cargo crate to get a clear view. When he acknowledged what had happened, he exhaled with a sigh of relief. Sabin dropped his metal gloves, with the attached blades hitting the floor. He then drew a long barrel pistol from his back.

"I generally use this for long range, but I might make an exception if you don't drop your gun right now," Sabin said.

The door slammed as Nemura and the remaining members of his crew escaped into the dust storm. Morn dropped his gun and put his hands up. Lesh stood up straight, still shackled.

"I saved your pup, hotshot," Morn said, shifting his eyes to Sabin without moving his body. "You owe me a thank you if anything now, not any death threats."

Sabin looked at him curiously, "I wonder what your story is."

"It's true," Lesh said, "he saved Mars."

"Listen to 'er," Morn pleaded.

Sabin whipped his gun back into its holster. "Want to chase them, Lesh?" Sabin asked.

"No," she responded, as she spit out some more blood. "We have more important things to tend to. We have to inform Blague immediately that the Hiezers are storming by boat," Lesh said.

"My transponder is jammed," Sabin explained, "No communications are getting through."

"They're jammin' the signal. It's obvious," Morn said in his drawl. "Let me help ya. My store is a wreck now and that's the only thing that was holdin' me back before," Morn explained.

Sabin and Lesh looked at each other. Mars barked, walked over to Morn and sat by his feet.

"I guess it's already been decided," Sabin said with a smile.

Lesh noticed one of her knives held captive in Sabin's belt as he cut her chains. "This will be the last time this happens, thank you, and don't say a word back to me if you know what's good for you," Lesh said.

Sabin put his hands up with a big smirk and closed lips, as she put her arms around his back to reclaim her artillery.

"We're lucky to be alive right now," Morn said, "I thought we were done for."

Lesh let out a laugh. "You have no idea how far away that reality was."

"Aw c'mon, no credit whatsoever for that?" Sabin asked.

"Some," Lesh said with a smirk, "but enough of that. Let's get to Blague now."

Sabin nodded, "We're approximately thirty two miles from the breach point, so let's get moving."

"Morn, you can join us for now," Lesh said in an irritated tone.

Chapter 8

Jeck stood tall on the center stage with his hands clasped behind his back. The crowd wasn't sending pleasant vibes in his direction. "Ladies and gentlemen of Senation, over forty years ago this world was in peril, separated by the devastating Global Quake. The disarray was mitigated and eventually reversed thanks to a community that knew how to act. Today, you know this community as the Hiezers," Jeck paused to gauge his audience. "It's easy to lay blame on the leaders sitting at the top. But ask yourself this; is there not relative order in your lives? Yes, some of a Sin's misfortune might not be totally justified, but have you not noticed the attempt to properly maintain jobs and food supply?" Jeck motioned around the audience with his hands, "I don't see anyone starving here. Sure, that may be due to hard farming work, but where do you think the initial seeds came from? That's right; we supplied them from the top."

The crowd scoffed, each person rehashing their own traumatic experiences with Hiezer guards.

"I know that we are hated, but if nothing else, I would appreciate an understanding that we strive for the betterment of the people on a grand scale."

Someone screamed back, "Bullshit! You're referring to the upper classes. Sins are dirt to you!"

Jeck put his hand up for the man to settle down. "We do not regard the Sins as dirt, but you must understand that the exiled continents are named as such for a reason. Some of the punishment is a lesser allocation of resources and more guards to keep order."

"Those guards murdered my family!" another audience member shouted.

"Again, people of Senation, guard brutality is not sanctioned. These instances are rogue acts. We are working rigorously to curtail and eventually eliminate these atrocities." Blague stood behind Jeck in the corner, forming his rebuttal. "We have an entire world to watch over and so the Hiezer's responsibility is never ending," Jeck explained. "One thing we can strive to improve is hearing the exiles' concerns and frustrations. In time, we can make Senation, Bulchevin, Hekata, Faltier's Crest, and the rest of the exiled continents a more livable existence," he projected.

Expectedly, the audience was not receptive to Jeck's speech, but they weren't throwing rocks at him either. A civilian doctor loudly told his own story, "I've been stripped from my former life due to a strict, unreasonable rule, which has rendered me, and my family torn and beaten. All of the promises in this world can't erase that."

"I'm deeply sorry for your hardship, but the strict rules have been carefully articulated and implemented to maintain appropriate order among the classes. It gives the people a purpose by creating a ladder to climb and a hope to one day enjoy the freedom that each higher class gets to take advantage of," Jeck explained.

"That's ridiculous," Chella yelled. "That doesn't

apply to your audience," she said with anger, "There's no way to break out of exile!"

"That is incorrect," Jeck responded. "We have implemented two rules to break through to higher classes. The first is to present viable information to capture career Sin criminals, and the second is to submit the discovery of the Ayelan chemical to Hiezer authorities." Jeck heard the people mumbling to each other after that last sentence. "I see that I'm stirring some uncertainties. Let it be confirmed that the submission of the Ayelan chemical will result in an automatic promotion of three social classes for the individual and that person's immediate family. Let it also be confirmed that maintaining your position as an uprising against the Hiezers will result in a catastrophic end for you and your loved ones. We have crushed hundreds of uprisings since we've initially maintained order. Is it really worth following this man?" Jeck questioned while pointing to Blague, who stood quietly without a reaction. "Citizens of Senation, come to your senses and help us maintain order and prosper on a global scale. We value all life, but we also understand that our systems were built to sustain the necessary structure. Don't throw your lives away for a futile cause. Thank you for hearing the other side." Jeck ended as he gave the Hiezer salute to his audience; his index and middle finger rested on his eyebrow and his ring finger below his eye.

The salute frames the eye, which symbolizes the vision of the Hiezers. The crowd's reaction was mixed. Some people were angry and some were curious. Jeck walked to the back as Blague moved forward.

"Not bad," Blague said with a grin.

"Fellow Sins," Blague boomed as he stood at the very tip of the ledge. His hands were open, embracing the crowd. "You've followed me through hell and back this past year. We've suffered, we've laughed, we've lost, but most importantly, we've grown. And as we grow, we share a collective idea that serves as the glue holding this group together. We all feel slighted, crippled by the authoritative power standing tall above us. We all strive for the betterment of our people, our families. Up until this great victory, we have been stunted and discarded by the world. What's worse, even if we have the drive to pursue greatness, we are further beaten down by the guards surrounding us. We are nothing but rats in a cage to the Hiezers. It's evident in Mr. Stone's words," Blague gestured to Jeck. "How does a Sin rat get out of the cage?" he asked rhetorically. "By finding the cheese and giving it up? And by giving up another rat? If this doesn't sound like imprisonment and oppression, then I don't know what does. The younger generation that was born into this amazing crowd before me, has suffered greater than anyone who has had the opportunity to live a higher quality of life. Since birth, they have been trapped in a forcefully sheltered life, thanks to rules set forth by the egotistical community with the grand scheme of maintaining order." Blague paced from side to side on the platform. "I will not get overly political at this point in time. I want you all to know that I'm very far from being an anarchist. What I want is a fair shot for all of us.

Everyone who has had the privilege to read a history book knows that there was once a time when societies weren't crippled. They may have had an unfair start, but hope was always existent. I stand before all of you today, giving everything I have to bring that hope back for the Sins, whether we deserve it or not."

The crowd was listening intently and most of the audience nodded their head as he spoke. Blague turned to Jeck. "I know that this debate is incredibly unfair, considering I've bled with this group, but nonetheless," Blague turned back to the crowd, "I want this to be the first step in an effort to create transparency, by providing this group with all sides of the story before making decisions. The Hiezers are even darker than what we've all seen from the guards. They've been known to perform human experimentation with the Ayelan and Cryos chemicals. Their research orientation, mixed with the power that they've assumed, has gotten them drunk and rendered them blind on their quest for human life preservation. For that reason and many others, carry on with me in our new home and fight with me to gain back our freedom!"

The crowd cheered for him. He pounded his chest once. His commanders pounded back, followed by the crowd behind them.

Blague looked over at Jeck, "You're free to go, Jeck, as promised. I'll have you escorted out."

At that moment, a piece of marble to the far west end of the main floor slid to the side, exposing a hole in the wall. The sound echoed and the few that heard the movement amongst the cheers turned their heads to look.

Everyone else contagiously followed suit. The fighters and commanders drew their weapons and so did Blague. Blague jumped off of the ledge to the main floor.

"Hold your fire!" Blague shouted, as he made his way to the marble.

A security camera slid out from the hole, at the same time a projector screen slowly lowered from the first floor to the main floor. As Blague and his commanders made way to the screen, the image of a man dressed in a Hiezer robe appeared. His pauldrons were of a sharper shape than Jeck's. The man had shoulder length black hair and wore a discrete golden crown, with a small black orb in the center.

"That must be a highlord," Briggs whispered to Eugene.

Eugene nodded without taking his eyes off of the image in front of them. The man had a slightly extended, thin nose, large hazel eyes, and proportionately high cheekbones. He was an attractive, somewhat feminine looking, well-groomed man.

He slowly clapped, "Impressive speech, Blague, or whatever you call yourself these days." Blague stood in front of the screen with an icy expression. "Such a bold takeover, holding one of my men hostage and sabotaging my fortress," the man said as he tilted his head to inspect the crowd. "There was critical research being performed here. What gives you the right to hinder my operations, Blague?"

Blague stepped forward slowly. Briggs motioned for him to stay back, but Blague waved him away.

"Mulderan, don't you think you've caused enough pain in

this lifetime?" Blague asked.

Mulderan stared at Blague, straight faced and unblinking. "I don't see it that way, Blague. I have always made decisions keeping in mind the greater good of the people. All of my past decisions that may have caused pain were not made lightly. I have a heavy heart, but I'm glad that my prophecy became self-fulfilling in the end. The people are now reaping the benefits that resulted from the risks I have taken." Mulderan waved his hand, "But those are my burdens to bear."

"You've always been incomprehensively twisted. We're prepared to give everything to tear down the current class structure," Blague fired back.

Mulderan squinted for a moment, "Maybe I'm missing something, but from my perspective, it doesn't seem that the structure is yours to alter. You're outnumbered and out-gunned, as usual. You will fall and your movement will perish. These aren't just words, I've backed them up many times before," Mulderan said smugly.

"This time is different. In all of those other movements you crushed, you weren't fighting me." Blague flipped his gun and shot the camera down. "Briggs, disable the projector and screen," Blague said.

The crowd watched Mulderan rise from his throne-like seat. He didn't show any emotion. His face remained of stone as he slowly walked over to disable the camera on his end.

"Start defense preparations and then meet in my room in two hours for a meeting," Blague said, as he turned to his commanders. "I suspect we will be under attack shortly."

Many of the Hiezer research and development laboratories focused on military improvements, including aircraft modifications. One of the improvements was installed on Mulderan's black, stealthy jet that flew past Old New York, which was now half submerged due to the quake. This new technological improvement, called turbine flutters, enables any aircraft to land similarly to helicopters, by having powerful thrusters guide the landing of the jet. Mulderan was in deep thought, with his chin resting on one of his fists, waiting to arrive at the Hiezer research fortress in Old Massachusetts. As the strategic highlord, Mulderan was constantly traveling, making sure the resources allocated to each division were producing the desired results.

I have to be sure this uprising doesn't gain traction. Underestimating him would be a foolish mistake. Battle plans have been set into motion. I'm going to have to prioritize the crippling of this group of Sins. They have already managed to make this movement a political nightmare. We've never been stormed, let alone lost a fortress. Once I receive word that the Ayelan has been extracted, I will have the Senation fortress carpet bombed and we will build a new structure. We are far passed the point of being diplomatic with the Sins. They must be kept at bay so society can continue to flourish.

"Sir," a stewardess called, "we will be landing in forty minutes. Can I get you anything?"

Mulderan waved her away, annoyed that his thoughts were interrupted. The flight was smooth; the flight technology built into the jet was advanced and the cabin pressure synchronization made it feel as though you were sitting on a cloud.

Humanity is not likely to survive another catastrophe in its current state. I must continue pushing the limits through experimentation. It's my responsibility to prepare our species for harsh conditions. We must maintain civil society or all is lost. My sorrows will be outweighed by the greatness I achieve for the greater good.

The jet slowly came to a stop in mid-air. The thrusters repositioned to slowly lower the jet to the landing location. Four guards appeared with drawn rifles to escort their highlord off the plane. Mulderan wasn't totally defenseless; he sported his preferred black stave with golden Hiezer designs swirling on both ends. To match, he carried a similarly designed rifle. Both weapons were neatly strapped to his back, covered by his cloak. The guards stood at attention as Mulderan rose from his seat.

"Let's move quickly. My allotted attention to each matter today is severely limited."

The guards nodded and led the way. Mulderan's hair whipped behind him, as he approached the windy climate in Old Massachusetts. He took a moment to inspect his surroundings, but then retreated back to the thoughts that were racing through his head. He felt the burden of strategizing the survival for the entire world. Mulderan approached the two Hiezers awaiting him in front of the research facility.

"Have you located a new donor?" he asked one of them, staring without a blink, making the Hiezer squirm.

"We believe we have," the other Hiezer said, as he raised the device to show the person's name and 3D picture.

Mulderan's eyes shot to the Hiezer that was speaking. "She will do," Mulderan said in a cool tone, "Where is she located?"

"Faltier's Crest," the Hiezer responded. "The exiled continent near the Old U.K.? This clearly shows how randomly dispersed the DNA requirements are," Mulderan pondered out loud. "Alright, and how many milliliters of Ayelan do we have in the Old U.S.?" he asked.

"Ninety total," a guard responded.

That's less than I had hoped.

Mulderan nodded. "Seize the girl, transport her to the facility in Faltier's Crest, and begin the process of creating the shot. For both of your information, the highlords have decided the next recipient," Mulderan said.

The two Hiezers looked at each other. The bolder one asked, "What's the candidate's area of expertise?"

Mulderan paused for a moment, "A weaponist, seasoned war strategist, and excellent council, my wife." Mulderan proceeded past the steps, while the two Hiezers began whispering to each other as they fell in line behind the guards. They continued trekking until they approached the entrance to the facility.

"Who was that guy on the big screen?" Kentin asked Milos and Felik.

Felik shrugged his shoulders, "I don't know, but he looks cool. I like his crown."

"Do you think he's going to try to take the mansion back?" Kentin asked.

Milos nodded his head with his arms folded, looking down. "That guy means business. You can tell," Milos said.

"How can you be so sure?" Felik asked.

"I don't know, I just have a feeling," Milos responded.

"Let's go downstairs and help my dad get ready in case that guy attacks us!" Kentin shouted with energy.

"Ok!" Felik yelled back excitedly.

Milos motioned for Kentin to lead the way, unenthusiastically. The fighter guarding the door smiled at the boys and opened the door as they charged for the stairs.

"Slow down boys. No need to crack your heads open on the stairs," the fighter warned.

The laboratory looked like an enormous robot to them. Gears, life sized enclosed vials, and buttons surrounded the entire facility. They visited every other day, with Kentin molding a new imaginative adventure for the other two boys to partake in. Briggs, a few of his men, and Endok huddled around the computer station in the center attempting to crack the algorithm to release the Ayelan container. Now that danger was predicted to be imminent, the pressure to crack the code was that much greater. Kentin and the boys ran to Briggs. Milos grinned after realizing that Kentin looked like a baby version of his dad. He was husky with a tiny stomach and his face was full. Their mannerisms were identical, making it impossible for Milos to overlook the resemblance.

"Any way we can help, dad?" Kentin asked, standing tall.

Briggs looked at him, worried, but proud. He attempted to hide the overwhelming stress he felt and smiled, "Yes boys! Go play by that shiny corner over there," he pointed and then knelt down to their level. "If anything moves, even slightly, you three will report that to me, ok?" Briggs asked, sharing his son's excitement.

"Roger!" Kentin replied.

The three ran off, ecstatic to contribute. Milos sat Indian style on the floor and pulled out the knife he had in the back pocket of his pants. He inspected it and reminisced of the time he had to use it. His mom's face kept popping into his head. First with the loving face that he remembered growing up, but then it shifted into a face of screams and blood, straight out of a nightmare. Tears ran quietly down his face. Kentin and Felik patted him on the back in an attempt to console him.

Blague sat at the head of a round table in his room on the fourth floor. He had his elbows on the table and both of his hands pushing his hair back, lost in thought, waiting for his commanders to join him. A vivid picture entered his mind.

"You're to be a part of something greater than yourself, Elaina", a shrouded figure lectured. Blague felt a tremendous amount of pain from the memory. *"Appreciate that you will*

help your partner and you will help me save this world," the figure continued. *"Stop this, don't go through with it! You're losing your mind!" Elaina screamed, shaking in her chains.*

Blague slammed his fist on the table. "That wasn't one of my memories. That's the second time this year that this happened," Blague said to himself. "I'm sure it's not something I've concocted in my head either. Something about that felt very real."

Just then, Eugene, Briggs, Lito, and the other commanders walked in.

"Any word from Sabin or Lesh?" Blague asked.

"Not as of yet," Eugene replied. "I have a feeling Sabin went searching for Lesh. Something doesn't feel right," Eugene continued with a worried look.

Briggs nudged Eugene, "Those two are fierce fighters. I'm sure they're just fine."

Eugene sighed, "You live in a bubble."

Blague listened while pondering what could have happened.

Drino, the battle-ready recruitment commander chimed in, "Blague, when do you suspect this attack will happen? My cadets are well trained and will be at your beck and call," he explained in a militaristic fashion.

"I predict within twenty four hours. Mulderan wouldn't have shown his face if he thought we had a shot to survive. He thinks that a rebel group doesn't have the capacity to prepare quickly. Although, he may not underestimate us considering we're accomplishing groundbreaking feats. I would expect a small army from him to extract what they came for," Blague responded to Drino, staring intensely. The side conversations stopped and the commanders listened intently. "Before we speak logistics and positioning, there's some history you should know about our enemy, now that you've all met him. I knew Mulderan in another life. I've witnessed his evolution first hand. He has grown ruthless and colder to emotion than I could have ever imagined. He believes in one thing, the greatest good in terms of continuing our survival as a species. He believes that him and his group are the best suited to rise to the task. He views us and any other rebellion as a nuisance that must be silenced," Blague explained to his commanders.

"*Hermano*, how do you know the highest lord of the Hiezers?" Lito questioned, looking at him with a puzzled expression.

"I knew him before he was a Hiezer, Lito, when we were younger," Blague answered vaguely. He then put up his hand for Lito to hold off. "There's more. Understand that our enemy believes in good, but also keep this in mind: he sacrifices human lives as "donors" to the recipients of the Ayelan shot. He extracts the DNA from the spinal cord of the victim through a process that renders the person lifeless when completed. This is the type of man you're dealing with. Commanders, know that he will not stop to think about the lives of children or show any mercy. Guard them well so we can overcome this threat," Blague concluded.

"How could the leaders at the top condone such a thing?" Briggs asked.

"Because the benefits of the Ayelan shot are tremendous. If administered correctly, it can preserve a human life by about three lifetimes," Blague responded.

"Makes sense that they were bumping the Bulchevin miners a few classes up from Sin if they found the Ayelan," Lito said.

"That's unnatural," Drino said. Eugene jumped in, "Who's to decide if one life is worth the preservation of another's?" "How the hell does that even work?" Briggs questioned.

Blague pointed to Drino and Eugene, "I sit before you in part because I couldn't agree with you more." Then he pointed at Briggs, "The shot is a mix of Ayelan, Cryos, and human DNA. The unfathomable amount of resources thrown at scientific research produced incredible results after the quake. The scientists discovered that the mix of those two chemicals with a rare DNA strand can result in the preservation of human cells, as well as enhanced cell regeneration. Endok and his group are keen to these facts. Feel free to pick their brains when we overcome this threat." The commanders looked at each other and began conversing. "Ok, Eu, lead on logistics," Blague ordered.

Eugene nodded, "I will be coordinating snipers on the roof and through the windows on each floor, facing both the front and back of the mansion, as these are potential threat points.

"Drino, are any of the new sniper cadets ready to be thrown into battle?" Blague asked.

"Two," Drino said in a raised, stern voice, while holding up two fingers. "I'll provide you with their details after this meeting."

Blague folded his arms on the table and looked down, listening intently to the plans.

"Ok, my location assignment for snipers will vary

depending on visible threats," Eugene said as he shifted his gaze, "Lito, what is the remote explosive status?"

Lito looked at Eugene and fired two fake finger guns at him and smiled. "We're all set *amigo*. *Mira aqui*," Lito pulled out a device which showed a map of where the explosives were planted. Lito's long arm stretched over the table to share the map.

Eugene nodded, "Make sure all of the fighters are aware of the situation and to avoid blast radius."

Blague lifted his head and stared at Lito for a moment. "Further to that, Lito, if this mansion is stormed, make certain that our fighters remain invisible until explosives have been detonated. We're operating under the assumption that the Hiezers do not know which coordinates contain explosives. Any positioning of our fighters outside of the mansion will give away safe coordinates," Blague said.

Lito nodded, "Roger that, boss."

Eugene nodded in agreement. "Briggs," Eugene said as he looked over his left shoulder, "how are we on communications?"

"We've been jammed since Mulderan appeared on that screen, which further indicates to me that we're in imminent danger," Briggs replied.

"Fuck," Eugene said, shaking his head. Drino and the other commanders expressed similar concern. "Ok, what about the extraction of Ayelan?" Eugene questioned, switching topics.

"We've cracked most of the encryption and have approached the final algorithm. My best people are on it. I expect Rodest will be able to crack it shortly," Briggs said confidently.

"Alright, please keep us informed on the progress," Eugene said. "Lastly, has the screening process been strict and successful?"

"Yes, all of the adults have been given rigorous testing both psychologically and socially. We are confident in our process," Briggs said to Eugene.

Eugene took some comfort in that. "Volaina, can we send a scout to find the whereabouts of Lesh and Sabin?" Eugene asked.

"No," she said in a Russian accent, "All of our scouts and spies are deployed. Communications are jammed so Briggs and I think it's too dangerous to send any of our reserves."

Eugene was not happy with that. Although he disliked Sabin, he recognized his and Lesh's value. "Alright," he said after a pause, "please do what you can to scout them out personally, within close vicinity."

Volaina nodded.

"Drino," Eugene pointed, "please organize the fighter positioning and arming. Forward your map to my device when completed."

Drino pounded his chest, "Roger that," he said eagerly.

"Volaina, since your reserves can't be deployed, please have them organize the medics," Eugene said. "Briggs," he continued, "please have your men keep the scientists safe while dealing with the Ayelan."

"I will, Eugene," Briggs said, punching his arm, "I'll see to it personally."

Eugene looked around the table, "Alright, we're all

set. Let's save our home." Everyone pounded their chest.

"We will come out on top," Blague said confidently, "Let's do so by minimizing the damage."

Everyone nodded and proceeded to work.

Chapter 9

On the main floor of the mansion, Cherris stood at the center of a circle of mothers and children. She preferred to stay near her wagon, which was large, comfortable, and contained everything she needed to help out the orphans and less fortunate families within the group. Fear was beginning to spread since Mulderan made his appearance, leaving the people feeling unsettled and wary.

"We're all going to have to pitch in so that Blague and his team can successfully protect us," Cherris said.

"What can we do but hide at this point?" one of the mothers said, holding her little boy tightly in her arms.

"There's plenty for us to do. Help the medics prepare for battle, keep food and supplies flowing for the fighters, and keep the morale support high. That's what we can do," Cherris said with high hopes. "I'm going to need help pushing my wagon to the southwest corner of the mansion. I'll house anyone who needs my assistance," Cherris continued.

"Which rooms are set up for medical assistance during battle?" another woman asked.

Cherris pointed and the circle of people followed with their eyes. "Room 1-N, 2-N, 3-N, and 4-N," Cherris responded. "The rooms are directly above each other. We expect, if battle is to erupt, that the main floor and fourth floor medical rooms will be most occupied, considering we have most fighters stationed on the roof and the main entrances. We all have to pray for our group and our families," Cherris concluded.

"I want my daughter to grow up here," a mother confessed, "This shelter and this group is everything I could hope for as she grows up."

The other mothers agreed with her. "I want to help anyway I can," another mother asserted.

Cherris smiled. *Please let us keep this home. These people deserve a break.*

Everyone was winding down from a long day of intense preparations. Briggs allowed Kentin to have a sleepover with Milos and Felik in Cherris' wagon, which was now in one of the safest locations in the mansion, tucked away in a corner. It was about midnight and Kentin was snoring loudly, annoying Milos, who would have been unable to sleep regardless. After about an hour of twisting and turning in his sleeping bag, Milos got up to see if anyone was up at the other end of the cart. There was a group of kids sleeping, but one sleeping bag was empty. It was hard to make out who was who with only the faint shine of Cryos marks as the only source of light.

Is that Felik's sleeping bag? What could he be doing at this time at night? Maybe he wants to continue helping the medics prepare. Maybe I should go give him a hand. I don't think I'll be getting much sleep anyway.

Milos flipped over his green sleeping bag and got up

quietly. Cherris generally maintained a light sleep outside of the wagon to listen for any potential threats. The wagon had a large cloth ceiling that was held up by multiple durable support beams. It was strangely cozy, mostly because of Cherris' motherly hospitality. Milos slowly tiptoed toward the back exit of the wagon. He jumped off to the floor and peeked around the side. Cherris was sound asleep with her back against a wall of the wagon. She looked exhausted. Milos scratched his head and pulled out a small device for light. Most of the rooms had no lights on and the other wagons scattered around the main floor were all dark. About twenty feet away, Milos saw a small glimmer of light and heard a very faint sound coming from a small open space within the structure of the mansion. He tiptoed over to see if it was someone who could use his help. As he got closer, he heard what he thought was Felik's voice. Milos was confused. As he inched toward the crevice, he slowed down. He was now sure it was Felik's voice, but he was speaking very strangely in a very low tone, almost a whisper.

"Coordinates 17.5 through 14.2, safety zone. Coordinates 67.3 through 71.1, safe passageway through front entrance. Ayelan concentrated in laboratory basement, unmoved," Felik's voice slightly echoed outside of the nook.

What is he saying? Why is he talking about the Ayelan that Kentin's dad was talking about? Milos was finally close enough to sneak a peek at Felik. He stuck his head out just enough to catch a glimpse. *I can't believe it. Felik was giving the same weird sign as that Jeck guy did when he finished his speech. That's the same sign the guards did before one of them killed my mom.*

Milos began breathing heavily, his thoughts started to race.

Felik is bad, he has to be bad.

He peeked again. The device Felik was speaking into displayed a 3D image of a person with the same attire as Jeck.

"You've done well and you will be rewarded accordingly," the 3D image responded to Felik. "Now retreat back to base. The mansion is no longer safe."

Milos felt his heart beating through his chest. All of the energy he'd been lacking for weeks rushed through his body at that moment.

I have to warn the others. No, I have to stop him now. I acted too slow before, that's how I let my mom die. I'll never let that happen again.

Milos drew his knife and glanced into the nook once more as Felik put his device away into his pocket. Milos saw the opportunity and stormed in while Felik was turned to the side. Time slowed down for a moment, while Milos could hear nothing but the sound of his own pulsating heart. His instincts quickly took control over his body. He lunged forward and stabbed Felik in the stomach. Blood gushed as Felik dropped his device and keeled forward, staring Milos in the eyes with a look of disbelief. Milos' face was filled with rage. Felik quickly overcame the shock and desperately punched Milos in the jaw; the force of the punch was not that of a child's. Milos fell to the side but held on to the knife, dislodging it from Felik's stomach. Felik screamed in pain as the force of the punch caused the wound to open further. Blood trailed in the direction Milos was thrown. Felik tried to stop the blood flow by covering it with his hand. He gasped for air as blood dripped through his fingers. Felik screamed again and charged Milos. Milos, rehashing all of his initial suspicions of Felik, regained his posture, knowing that he had to stop him. He dodged Felik's clumsy charge, causing Felik to slam his shoulder into the wall that Milos was leaning on. Although Milos was frightened and couldn't believe the situation that was unfolding, he knew he had to finish what he started. He stared at Felik, who was dazed from the blood loss, struggling to regain his position. A flash of his mother being shot in the head blocked out his vision. Milos pulled Felik's bald head back and opened his throat with his knife.

Cherris woke up from the screams and rushed over to the scene, only to see the massacre all over the walls. Milos dropped the knife and slid to the floor with wide eyes and no trace of emotion.

Felik was bad, he wanted to kill more of us like the guards did the day of the bomb. Felik was bad. I had to stop him. I had to kill him.

Eugene sat in a marble chair in his room, and rubbed his temples, while taking a breather from the long day of planning. Narene had just finished a night shift in the medical room. She sat on a chair next to him, smiling; her nose ring shimmered in the light.

She put her hand on his, "You did great today Eugene," she said genuinely. "I saw you coaching and arranging your snipers. You're doing everything you can to protect us. I appreciate that," she finished.

Eugene looked over and sighed, his shoulders were hunched. His confidence was low regarding the Hiezer threat. "Thank me when this is over and we're both still here," he said.

"No," she said calmly, "I think I'll continue thanking you now. Do you know what I did today?" she asked. Eugene shook his head. "I tended to a child, in a real medical room. Not some rusted hut. It was a real, legitimate medical room. I haven't been able to do that since I was a Terra eight years ago. I thank you for letting me act as a nurse again and letting me help someone. The fighters made that possible. You made that possible," she said, leaning in. Eugene looked at her, not saying a word. She leaned in further and kissed his cheek, staring into his eyes.

Just then, his device rang. He looked down to see Cherris' name pop up. He gave Narene an apologetic look and picked up.

Blague's voice echoed through, "Get down to the main floor near Cherris' wagon, southwest side."

Eugene kissed Narene quickly on the lips, "Sorry, sounds like something's wrong."

She nodded, bit her lip, and folded her arms. "See you later?" she asked.

Eugene smiled on his way out of the door, "Hopefully," he said.

Eugene rushed down the stairs toward the corner of the mansion that had some light coming from it. The pitch black marble floor added to darkness surrounding him.

As he rushed toward the dimly lit corner, he noticed a silhouette of Blague, Cherris, and Briggs standing near a wall. As he approached, he pushed Briggs' big arm out of the way so he could have a look.

"What's going o-... shit," Eugene said. Blague nodded. "He's just a kid," Eugene said, shocked, "Who would do something like that?"

Cherris looked at Eugene and frowned, pointing to Milos who was sitting, holding his knees with a towel over his legs.

"He won't say a word," Briggs said.

"Isn't that the boy who lost his mother?" Eugene whispered to Blague.

Blague nodded, holding his hand to his chin, thinking and staring at the young corpse on the floor. Blague and Eugene walked over to Milos, who stared at the floor. Briggs radioed for someone to come clean up the mess before making his way over.

Blague bent down and put a hand on his knee, "What could he have done to deserve this, Milos?" Blague asked calmly.

After about a minute, Milos realized Blague wasn't moving until he got an answer. Milos looked up and tensed his brow, angrily. "I had to, he was bad," Milos admitted.

Blague's eye twitched, "Bad? How was he bad?" he said aloud to himself. Blague saw that a transponder laid next to Felik's body; he quickly stood up.

Eugene looked at him, puzzled. "What is it, Blague?" Eugene asked.

"I just came to a very harsh realization. I don't think

Milos was to blame in this situation," Blague said.

"Um," Eugene responded, while pointing to the blood bath they were both now walking toward.

"Briggs," Blague said in a commanding tone, "take off this boy's shirt and flip him on his stomach, quickly."

Briggs hustled and Eugene walked over beside him, confused. Blague stopped walking at Felik's feet and stared at his back for thirty seconds. Briggs and Eugene looked up at Blague, not quite sure what he was trying to accomplish. Cherris stood next to Blague, still horrified from what had happened.

"Do you see the discoloration?" Blague asked all three of them.

They inspected the skin along the spine and began to nod.

"What color do you see, Eugene?"

"Orange," he said.

Briggs made a face like Eugene was crazy.

Blague's eyes moved to Briggs.

"Gold," Briggs said.

The mark was small, but apparent.

"This boy, what was his name?" Blague asked.

"Felik," Cherris said.

"Felik," Blague continued, "was not a kid. He was probably around forty," Blague said, still thinking.

Cherris looked up at him, "Have you gone mad, Blague?"

Blague ignored the comment, noticing the puzzled look on everyone's face. He knew he would have to explain. "Felik was injected with the Ayelan shot when he was young. He was brought up as a Hiezer and trained as a spy." Blague extended his hand toward the body. "This is a product of weaponizing human preservation. The Hiezers stunted his growth physically and trained him mentally for many years."

Briggs, having never seen the effects of the infamous Ayelan shot, was in disbelief. "You can tell all of that from discoloration on his back?" Briggs asked.

"I know that mark," Blague confirmed, "and judging by how small it has become, chances are he's quite old." Blague looked over at Milos huddled up in the corner. "I'm even more perplexed by how an actual boy managed to outsmart and overpower an adult," he said.

Eugene pointed to the blood leaking onto the floor from Felik's stomach, "It looks like Milos may have gotten the jump on him. There are two wounds." Blague continued staring.

"So the Ayelan shot would have made him live like this for another forty years?" Briggs asked.

Blague shook his head, "More like another hundred and forty years. The shot increases the regeneration rate and reduces the death rate of human cells throughout the body."

Although Eugene was taken aback by the matter at hand, he knew he had to focus on the imminent threat that they faced. "We have to interrogate Milos, immediately," Eugene abruptly said.

Cherris looked upset, "Please don't, Eugene. He obviously can't handle anything right now."

Eugene looked up at Cherris, "We have no choice. What if he heard a conversation that could prevent us all from getting killed?"

Blague turned to Cherris, "I'm sorry, but he's right." He put a hand on her shoulder, "We'll need you there for his support."

Cherris' eyes were glassy, fearing for the boy's wellbeing. She closed her eyes and nodded, "We need to help him."

Blague stood silent, not knowing what else to say. Eugene stared at Felik's corpse.

This Hiezer experimentation is straight out of a horror movie. He's not deformed, but something just doesn't seem right. I got goosebumps when Blague said he was an adult. What kind of fucked up world are we living in?

Eugene stood up and gave Blague a look, motioning to get moving.

Briggs looked around for a moment. Then he excitedly said, "Guys, local radios have been operational, but outside signals have been jammed since Mulderan appeared on screen. Could Felik have caused that?"

Briggs looked to a corner in the nook that they stood in and Eugene shined a light in that direction. The blood stained transponder was sitting there. Briggs ran over to the device and pulled out some small tools to dismantle it. "Eugene," Briggs said while tinkering, "try to radio Sabin."

Eugene pulled out his communication device and shifted to Sabin's channel, "Does anyone copy?" They all waited a moment, then Eugene shook his head. "Nothing," he said solemnly. They all made their way toward Milos.

"Eugene, is that you? You son of a bitch!" a voice came out of Eugene's device.

Blague started to laugh and Eugene rolled his eyes, but smirked. All of them were relieved to hear Sabin's voice.

"Sabin," Eugene said, "where the hell are you?"

"Been busy, buddy, I have Lesh and some cowboy next to me jogging our way back to the mansion. The dust storm in Clestise slowed us down for a day or so. We're a little fatigued, but ok!" Sabin screamed through the wind hitting the radio.

Everyone looked even more relieved to hear that Lesh was alright too.

"Do you ever shut up?" Eugene asked, jokingly, "We will send Volaina to escort you back."

"Oh!" Sabin said, "That's ok, we found her too!"
"Ok," Eugene replied, "then get your asses back here."

"Oh, boy! Someone gets cranky past his bed time!" Sabin responded.

Briggs chuckled.

"Alright," Eugene said, "I'll see you not too soon." He turned off his radio, sighed, and continued to walk toward Milos.

Milos heard the faint sound of laughter as he stared at his blood soaked hands and the blood stained cloth that covered him. He was unarmed, cornered, and in shock. A faint ringing filled his ears and his heart continued to beat at what felt like three hundred beats per minute. The sweat dripped down his face from his straggly black hair.

Felik was my friend. Why did I hurt him? Why did I kill him? He was my friend.

Briggs knelt down, "How are you holding up?" he asked, being careful not to treat him like a little kid, considering he just murdered someone.

Milos' ears continued to ring. His small Cryos tattoo was shining through his shirt. He looked straight past Briggs and the others standing before him.

Cherris knelt down on the opposite side. "Milos," she extended a loving hand, cupping his face, "everything is going to be alright," she said with tears in her eyes.

Blague stared at Milos while everyone attempted to snap Milos out of his daze by offering kindness and support. Blague realized he was numb to compassion now. "Get up," Blague said in a calm tone, with no room for question.

Briggs and Cherris looked back at him. Eugene's eyes opened a little wider and looked at Blague with his arms folded. Milos' ears stopped ringing for a moment and his attention focused on Blague.

"Good," Blague said, "you're back." He flung Milos' bloody knife to the wall next to him. "I believe that belongs to you," Blague said as he then walked up to Milos and extended his hand. "Get up, Milos, we need you," he said, penetrating through Milos' fog.

By now, most of the civilians residing in wagons throughout the mansion had heard some rumbling in the southwest corner of the main floor. Flashlights were scattered throughout. Some ventured near the incident, but a few fighters called in by Blague and Cherris were sent to reassure people that everything was under control.

"Did you hear any transmissions with Felik and the Hiezers?" Eugene asked. "Is that why you attacked him?" Eugene continued probing.

Milos stared blankly for a moment, then hesitantly nodded his head.

"What did he say?" Eugene asked, getting impatient.

"It didn't make much sense," Milos said in a low, mellow voice. "He just kept saying a bunch of numbers, then the Hiezer he was speaking to said that Felik did good. I knew he was bad for sure when he gave this sign," Milos said while he demonstrated the Hiezer symbol.

Blague looked at Briggs, whose eyes lit up. They both said "Coordinates" at the same time.

Cherris got up and turned around, covering her arms with a raggedy shawl, "They must be close. We're all in great danger, aren't we?" she said.

Everyone looked at Blague.

"We've been prepping for this. Everyone will know what to do," Blague reassured.

"Can we please address the murder and reinforce that it will not be condoned?" Cherris asked.

Briggs looked to Milos. "What you did may have saved some lives and for that I'm thankful. But, there was another way. You could have gotten someone else and trapped him," Briggs said in a sincere tone. "I know you've been through hell, but don't create unnecessary chaos because of it," he continued.

Milos looked down. *I killed him because he deserved to die.*

Milos stiffened, "Commander, if I didn't act, he may have gotten away and caused more pain for others,"

Milos said.

"You could have died!" Cherris jumped in.

"But I didn't," Milos answered back, his expression changing to anger. "What if it was Kentin who was next on Felik's list? Would you still be upset with me?" Milos asked.

Briggs stood up in shock from the boy's response.

At that moment, a fighter yelled from the top floor, "We're under attack! Through the back entrance!"

Eugene's jaw tensed.

"Eugene," Blague said, his strategic plans rushing through his head, "rally up the commanders and start moving. Briggs, get Endok and extract the Ayelan now, then hide it! Cherris, get Milos and the kids to safety. It's time to show the Hiezers that the Sins will not fold."

Chapter 10

Lito leaned over the ledge of the roof, glued to a set of binoculars. He watched the ship unload Hiezer militants as it sat, anchored not too far offshore. "*Puta, mierda,*" Lito said as he slammed his hand on the ledge of the roof. Snipers were stationed to the left and right of him. "Hold 'jur fire boys!" Lito exclaimed.

The Hiezers started to pour onto the shore via small boats as the sun was beginning to rise. Most of the Sins had already been working around the clock. A mix of exhaustion and adrenaline began to stir amongst the fighters.

Eugene ran up the marble steps leading to the roof. He flipped his rifle from the strap on his back. "Everyone is in position, but we have new intel that our safe coordinates may have been leaked to the Hiezers," Eugene said.

Lito turned to Eugene slowly, in disbelief. "How?" Lito asked, "We were so careful every step of the way. How, Eugene? Another mole?" Eugene nodded his head. "Briggs screened everyone," Lito replied.

"He screened everyone except for the kids," Eugene said, giving Lito a quick glance.

"You've got to be shitting me," Lito said, slamming the roof ledge again.

"I'll explain later. The enemy was one step ahead of us, thinking far outside the box." Eugene took aim with the snipers stationed beside him. "There's only one threat at the back entrance?" Eugene asked.

"So far, *mijo*," Lito responded, focusing his attention back to the ship. Lito felt his heart drop into his stomach, his eyes involuntarily grew wide. "You were right, they're lining up against the rocks, where the boys were playing while we set up the explosives."

The guards began forming a single line and advancing toward the mansion. Lito looked at Eugene and started laughing.

"Have you lost your mind?" Eugene asked while sighing.

"No no no no, none of that, amigo," Lito said, still laughing. "The mole didn't catch what we did during the night shift last week it seems. Hahaha," Lito continued his maniacal laughter. "Mira," Lito pointed to the rocks, "Look with your scope between the rocks."

Eugene looked for a moment and then smiled with him.

"'Ju ready to cause some chaos?" Lito asked, looking psychotic with a huge smile and one of his pupils dwarfing the other.

"You stuffed C-4 in the rocks just in case," Eugene said.

Lito couldn't contain himself; it was a last minute idea. The soldiers relied on Felik's instructions, confidently advancing since no bombs had yet been detonated.

"Hold 'jur fire," Lito said to everyone, "and duck,

they probably have snipers getting into position too. As soon as the shore is swarming with them, we will begin detonating and cause them to break ranks."

Blague radioed Lito, "I just checked the front breach point pathway. There seems to be no threat from that side. I'm now at the back entrance on the main floor with the fighters and snipers. Are you almost ready, Lito?" Blague asked.

"*Si*," Lito responded, with his detonator in hand. The device had multiple buttons to set off the remote explosives in certain areas. "Here we go," Lito said to himself. He peeked out to see a swarm of Hiezer soldiers quickly advancing in multiple rows, hugging the rocks. "Now, Eugene!" Lito hit a detonator at the same time Eugene swung his rifle over the roof ledge, taking aim.

His sniper subordinates followed his lead. Explosions burst out of the seemingly safe rock pathway, jolting the entire line of soldiers. Some were thrown into the air as others quickly spread out to avoid the explosions.

"Aim for the ship!" Lito screamed amongst the cries of agony caused by the bombs.

Eugene shifted slightly. He took a deep breath, keeping his red line black rifle steady. He fired, piercing the eye of a sniper who had his sight on one of his infantry. Eugene quickly ducked as he spotted two other Hiezer snipers within the boat. Lito peeked out to assess the damage with his binoculars. Eugene signaled for the other snipers to get down, but it was too late. One of them flew backward from the impact of a bullet that sliced through the side of his head.

"Fuck!" Eugene screamed, "Get down!"

He beckoned another sniper to crawl over to him. A large horn went off, coming from the ship. The Hiezer soldiers were scattered throughout the beach as the battle ensued, running in fear of potential land mines throughout the area.

Lito Hissed. "Not yet, not yet," he said quickly to himself. "The ranks should be storming any second." Lito pulled out his device and radioed Blague, "Can you hold them?" he screamed. A blanket of sound comprised of gunfire and panic covered the battlefield.

"The fighters are holding them. They're piling up outside," Blague responded.

Lito heard intense gunfire before the radio cut out.

"Fire two shots quickly at the ship from the furthest corner," Eugene told the sniper as he pointed, "Go!"

The sniper hustled over, fearful of the chaos developing below him. Eugene watched carefully as the sniper got in position. Lito lit a stick of dynamite and carefully tossed it toward the soldiers, who were trying to take cover behind the rocks. The explosion set off a blaze of fire, blood, and rock that spewed in all directions. The sniper cadet flung his rifle over the ledge and fired two shots toward the ship and ducked back down. Eugene saw his opportunity, as he flung his rifle over the ledge, positioned right beside Lito. He took aim, catching a Hiezer sniper repositioning himself to aim at the corner ledge. Eugene fired, barely leaving his scope there long enough to see the bullet penetrate the soldier's eye, propelling him backward. Eugene quickly shifted his rifle, focusing on the second sniper who was aiming toward the same corner through a window of the ship. Eugene fired; the soldier's rifle tumbled out of the window as he used both hands to grab the wound on his neck. Eugene ducked down and took a breath. He looked over to the sniper who fired the decoy shots and gave him a nod. He was a skinny man in his mid-twenties with blonde, long hair on the top of his head, and shaved sides. He looked terrified even though this wasn't his first battle. The horn sounded again. The whole side panel of the ship facing the shore lifted upward as the ship began to tilt. Endless amounts of soldiers dove into the water to reach the shore.

Lesh, Sabin, Morn, Mars, and Volaina were scouting the breach point from the front entrance. The four of them were using this time to recuperate after their missions. They quickly ate the meals that Volaina brought to them. Lesh was the only one who seemed unaffected by her recent ordeal.

"If there aren't any threats in the front entrance, then shift rotation. We're about to be overwhelmed," Blague calmly said to Sabin via radio.

Sabin began equipping one of his metal gloves, keeping his pistol hand free to aid in long-range combat. Volaina quickly whipped her jet black motorcycle around and sped to the front entrance to help. The others sprinted behind her, fatigued, but no less dedicated.

As they entered the mansion, a fighter barricaded the enormous front door in an attempt to buy some extra time in the event they were to be stormed from the breach point. The main floor was decorated with carts, wagons, and supplies, all resting on the black marble floor and huddled near the front entrance. This set up was meant to keep the civilians safe from the battle erupting on shore. Morn was shocked to see so many Sins working together as a community. People were helping each other and providing comfort in such a chaotic time. He watched nurses and doctors wheel injured fighters to the dedicated medical rooms, as orders were shouted to maintain effective battle positions. It was quite a sight for any Sin who was not a part of Blague's original group. There was something unique about this community; they had a sense of hope. Sabin directed Mars to his room and headed toward the roof to catch up with Lito and Eugene. Lesh ran toward Briggs. He was sprinting with a vial in hand, while Endok struggled to keep up behind him.

"Stay with the civilians, Morn, and help protect them," Lesh said.

"Alright," Morn responded in his southern drawl, still trying to process all of the chaos around him.

"Lesh!" Briggs stopped for a second to put his free arm around her. "You've looked better!" he said with a smile.

Lesh smirked back, her lips still encrusted with blood from the beating Nemura had given her. "Is that the chemical?" Lesh asked.

"We finally extracted it. Now we just have to hide it," Briggs replied as he picked up the pace.

At that moment, an explosion rattled the mansion. They both looked up for a moment, when they noticed the sound of helicopters flying closely above them.

"Shit," Briggs said to Lesh and Endok, "the roof is being compromised."

Briggs ran to the hole that Mulderan's hidden camera sprouted from and placed the vial there. Lesh ran behind Briggs with a limp.

"Ready to join Blague?" Briggs asked Lesh.

She nodded.

Sabin approached the staircase leading to the roof, when suddenly a group of snipers and fighters rushed in. "What the hell is going on?" Sabin stopped one of them forcefully to ask.

"The Hiezers just landed on the roof! They boxed in our fighters sniping shore side," the Sin responded.

"Then why the fuck are you running inside?" Sabin raised his voice.

"Because Commander Lito just threw a bomb at the helico-"

An explosion rattled the staircase and a massive flame engulfed the corridor. Sabin released the fighter and ran toward the nearest window on the fourth floor. He opened the window and pulled himself out from the ledge. He had his string blade between his teeth and his half cloak was flapping in the wind behind him. He heard explosions close above and saw a portion of a burning helicopter directly above him.

I have to help the fighters get off that roof.

He took the blade out of his mouth and threw it with force toward the roof. The blade caught onto the ledge. Once he tugged it to test if it would hold, he began pulling himself upward. As he approached the top, wrapping the wiry rope around his arms as he leveraged himself, he heard screams and gunfire directly above him. When he reached the roof, Sabin grabbed onto the ledge with one hand and worked to dislodge his double-sided blade with the other. His attention was momentarily directed to a soldier who was thrown by the impact of a sniper's bullet; the solider spun off the ledge of the roof with blood squirting out of his shoulder. Sabin turned his attention back to the blade as a scream echoed below him. Sabin put the blade back between his teeth and with both hands, gracefully boosted himself over the ledge. Time slowed as a chaotic canvas filled with blood and destruction was painted in front of him. He saw Lito hiding behind a large piece of helicopter scrap, with only his mohawk peeking through. He then saw Eugene and his black rifle stationed between two corpses. Only a few other Sin fighters remained on the roof. Most of the Hiezers were either dead or critically wounded from Lito's dynamite, but ten or so still remained. Sabin's moment of assessing the situation was over. He had an advantage, since all of the soldiers were facing the remaining Sins. Sabin threw his string blade under the body of an intact helicopter. The blade pierced the leg of a soldier who was shooting toward Eugene. The soldier let out a scream and dropped his gun. Sabin yanked the wire, sending the guard face first onto the floor. With his other hand, Sabin drew his long barrelled pistol and aimed it toward a soldier who was heading for the mini-gun equipped on one of the helicopters.

If he begins firing that, it's all over.

Sabin struggled to keep his arm steady with the guard writhing in pain, kicking his impaled leg and shaking the wire. Sabin paused for a second to aim as the soldier on the helicopter was about to fire. Sabin fired at the Hiezer, causing the soldier's hand to almost burst. Blood splattered all over the mini-gun. Sabin fired again, this time hitting him in the stomach. The soldier fell off the step that hoisted the mini-gun. Sabin knew that bought him a few seconds. With great force, Sabin swung his hand back, painfully whipping his blade out of the soldier's leg. The bloody blade retrieved back into Sabin's metal glove. Noticing that some of the guards had spotted him, Sabin took cover behind a piece of the burning helicopter. Fighters were slowly starting to come back out of the staircase, which led to the roof. They fired shots toward the Hiezers which further diverted their attention. Eugene aimed with the little vision he had between the two corpses and fired at a Hiezer, who was running to aid an injured soldier. The bullet pierced his chest and slammed him into the side of the helicopter. Two soldiers on the opposite side of the roof noticed Eugene's exposed sniper barrel and began firing. The corpses danced as the bullets from the automatic rifles penetrated them. Eugene groaned, feeling the sting from a bullet, radiating all the way down his arm. After hearing Eugene's anguish, Lito became enraged; he plucked the pin from a grenade and bowled it over to the two soldiers. It rolled under one of the two, tearing his body apart from the shins up. The other soldier dove out of the way just in time.

"Sins, out!" Lito roared.

The fighters pooled back up the stairs. Sabin

revealed himself and flung his blade downward, aimed at the guard that survived the grenade blast. He pierced him right in the neck and quickly retracted the string blade back to his hand. The incoming Sin fighters finished off the last few soldiers. Lito rushed over to Eugene and kicked the corpses off of him. It didn't look good, as blood covered Eugene from head to toe. He lied still in his sniper position. Sabin rushed over as well. They both stood there in shock, not knowing what to say about the bloodbath in front of them. Sabin and Lito exchanged looks, stunned. At that moment, Eugene's gun went off, scaring the shit out of the both of them.

"You didn't kill the one near the mini-gun," Eugene said, turning his head to look up at Sabin.

Lito and Sabin smiled at the nice surprise. Sabin gave Eugene a joyful kick.

"Argh, you piece of shit, that's where the bullet grazed my arm!" Eugene screamed at Sabin.

Sabin backed up, "Whoops," he said, still smiling.

Lito took hold of Eugene's other arm and hoisted him up. "We thought you were done," Lito said, relieved, "All that blood from the *muerta*, we thought it was from you."

Eugene shook his head, "Not dead yet."

The fighters radioed in for water supply and extinguishers to put out the fires blazing on the roof.

Lito looked over the ledge. "The light armored guards are charging fast. It's almost time to blow the entire beach."

Blague, Briggs, and a few Sin fighters pulled the large back door until it finally slammed shut. Blague looked at his watch and pulled out his radio. "Ten seconds, Lito," Blague said.

"Copy," a strong Latino accent replied back to him.

Blague and Briggs looked through the peepholes of the massive doors. "Get back, everyone!" Blague yelled.

"Into positions!" Drino shouted at his Sin ranks.

Blague eyed the light armored guards charging at full speed, spread throughout the shore, trying to out run any potential detonation.

Briggs looked at Blague, "They almost seem suicidal."

"I suppose they believe in their cause with the same intensity that we believe in ours," Blague responded, not removing his eye from the peephole.

All was quiet for a moment, except for the sound of footsteps sprinting through sand and gravel. Briggs' eyes widened as he heard the boom of an explosion. He saw sand and rock propel into the sky far off into the background. The explosions cascaded closer and closer to the mansion, until the entire building shook. Blague took his eye away from the peephole and braced the door shut, using all his strength. Briggs ducked as soon as the visibility outdoors was nothing but sand and smoke. He braced the adjoining door. Both doors jolted open a few times, as if a tornado were trying to break in. The explosion was far enough away not to harm the two men.

"Briggs," Blague said putting a hand on his

shoulder, "I want you and Lesh to guard the civilians. They're going to need you. The Hiezers aren't done yet."

Briggs nodded with a painful look, considering he wanted to be on the front lines with Blague.

"Drino!" Blague yelled, "Sins! Move out now!" Blague pulled open the door and ran out first, using the smoke as cover.

The first group of light armored guards is done. We have thirty seconds at best before the next set start arriving.

Blague attempted to visualize the surrounding environment, since there was no visibility from the effects of the explosion. Blague envisioned the large ocean and rock pathway on the right and the large mountain-like rocks on the far left.

Blague looked at Drino, who was now right behind him, "Shield fighters out first, followed by assault rifle support. Give them hell," Blague commanded.

Drino pounded his chest and began yelling his orders.

Blague ran toward the rock pathway on the right. Once he reached it, he boosted himself up the few layers of rock and jumped over to the other side. As soon as he hit the ground, he quickly sprinted toward the Hiezer ship. He heard a mass of soldiers running in the other direction on the opposite side of the rocks.

I have to stop this attack from the source and I don't have much time.

His veins were bulging out of his head, as he nearly doubled his usual speed. Flashes of terrifying images from his past rotated into his vision, altering his judgement and increasing his rage. He pulled the pin of a grenade and threw it far over the rocks, attempting to cause chaos amongst the Hiezer ranks. He pulled the pin of another, and another, all the way down his path toward the ocean. Before jumping in, he noticed a black jet slowing down toward the roof of the mansion. He dove into the water, swimming furiously toward the ship, trying to avoid the pathway of the outgoing soldiers.

If they catch sight of me, I'll have no chance of taking out their commander. Their masks probably have built in goggles, so I'll have to take the long route.

When Blague finally reached the ship, he pulled himself up from the side of the ship that was tilting into the ocean. Blague's combat wear was drenched, leaving a trail behind his every step. He unsheathed his black carbon steel blade, realizing that there were no guards on the back side of the ship; all focus was on the progress of the invasion. Blague searched the back of the ship for an entrance. He stealthily climbed up to another level where he was able to carefully open one of the metal doors. He snuck into a dark black room; the only faint light was emanating from his Cryos mark. He heard orders being dictated nearby. Blague slowly crept down to the first floor of the ship, which was artfully crafted with high quality metals. The vessel appeared to be brand new, and so the floor didn't creek as Blague waded through different areas of the ship, helping to keep him incognito. Blague counted eight guards surrounding the commanding officer, who was plastered to his binoculars, shifting quickly through different parts of the battlefield, yelling orders into his radio. A few snipers on the floor above were getting into position. One of the soldiers had black camo paint framing both of his eyes and was armed with a machine gun. Blague snuck up behind him, covered his mouth, and jerked his body behind a pillar. The soldier's swinging machine gun made a clamor, but the outside gunfire and swaying of the ocean masked the noise. Blague stuck his knife through the guard's temple, staring at him in the eyes as he did it. He looked up, to make sure no one heard. He looked down and noticed he was still dripping and leaving water marks everywhere he turned.

"Jet 05 landed successfully, snipers. Cover fire for arrival," the commanding guard shouted.

Blague realized there was no more time. He took out a flashbang, sheathed his blade, and drew his deep blue Desert Eagle. He took the open shot he had at the commander and let the flashbang fly. The last thing Blague saw before he took cover behind the pillar was the bullet piercing the back of the guard's neck and the binoculars flying into the air. The flashbang went off, as Blague sprinted up the stairs and began firing at the snipers in position. He hit the sniper positioned closest to him, once in the shoulder and once in the side, causing him to bleed out on the floor. The other guards on the floor below were yelling about the intruder who was onboard their vessel. The two remaining snipers repositioned, aiming at Blague's location. He took cover behind a corner pillar as high caliber bullets crashed into it. Blague took out his last grenade and threw it around the corner to the walkway where the snipers were located. Blague jumped off the second floor ledge as soon as he heard the snipers scrambling to dodge the incoming explosion. As the guards were regaining their sight, they also felt the agony of bullets piercing through their bodies. Blague landed on his feet in plain sight on the first floor, just a few feet away from the commander he shot dead. Blague's brow was tense, as he quickly aimed and fired at the multiple recovering guards. He quickly shifted, pulling the trigger before any one of them could lift their weapon to return fire.

I can't let the Sins down. We have to end this fight.

As the last guard on the first floor fell, a sniper bullet grazed Blague's calf.

"Shit," he grunted as he stumbled out of the way to reload his gun.

A familiar voice came through the Hiezer commander's radio. "I'm descending to the roof of our fortress. Be prepared to cover. My pass-through will be swift," a voice said.

Mulderan is here?

Blague jumped up and shot three times in the sniper's direction. He missed his shots, but succeeded in making the sniper reposition. Blague stood up, steadied his aim, and fired again. The bullet broke the sniper's scope and penetrated his skull. Blague, wasting no time, limped over to the binoculars on the floor. He saw Drino and the Sin ranks holding the back door against the Hiezer militants. He shifted his vision to the roof. He felt his heartrate increase, as he watched Hiezer guards marching down an opened platform of a jet, surrounding Mulderan with large bullet proof glass shields and assault rifles. The guards murdered all of the Sin fighters who remained on the roof.

He came personally to reclaim his territory. The outcome of this battle will now be pivotal for the survival of this group.

Chapter 11

Cherris looked up to the fourth floor from her wagon. Terror ran through her body as she saw Hiezer guards storming the building. There were two groups of guards; one was aggressively headed toward the main floor, and the other marched slowly with long, clear shields headed toward a room on the fourth floor.

"Briggs, Lito," Cherris pleaded, "protect the civilians, they're inside the mansion!"

"I'm coming!" Briggs responded in a panic.

"Sending soldiers to assist you, Cherris," Lito said as background explosions muffled his voice.

It was too late. Cherris beckoned the parents around her to hide in the wagon with the kids while the other civilians were either hiding or working in the medical rooms. She mustered up the courage to stand tall against the guards that were approaching. Most of the Sin fighters were called in to help defend the back door. Cherris held her head high. Her hands were shaking under the cloth she was holding. She moved her silver and blonde hair out of her face. She counted seven guards and another sprinting toward the hidden Ayelan, with a device in hand. The Hiezer guards stopped in front of her.

If they get the chemical that Briggs hid, it's all over for us.

Cherris slowly picked up the radio, figuring this would get her killed. "They know where the Ayelan is, stop them, now!" Cherris yelled with terror in her voice.

The guards aimed their rifles at her. She closed her eyes and tilted her head up, dropping her radio and accepting her fate.

Don't give up Blague. Give the Sins a better life.

She felt wind blow against her face, followed by a bang; it wasn't a gun shot. Cherris opened her eyes, confused by what just happened. She saw the back of a man, rising from his fall. He had a grey scarf wrapped tightly around his face and grey hair spilling out of a cloth that he wore over his head. The rest of his body was draped in ripped cloth wrapped around his torso and most of his arms, leaving just his forearms exposed. He wore ripped grey pants and old combat boots. After Cherris' glimpse of the man, gunfire erupted. The mysterious man that fell from the sky slammed down a huge riot shield, deflecting all of the bullets aimed at Cherris. He pulled out an ancient rifle and turned to her. She was stunned to see that the man's eyes were smoky grey with no pupils. His forearms had shimmering Cryos blue veins.

"Get to safety," the man said through a voice changer, raising his eyebrows.

Both fearful and confused, Cherris gave a quick nod, accepting her second chance however short lived it may be. She watched sparks fly in all directions off of the giant hunk of metal. The man rested his rifle over the top of the shield. He peeked through the vision hole in the middle and began firing back. Screams came from the wagons located on the main floor, as parents feared for the fate of their children. Sin fighters rushed in, refusing to open fire against the guards who were standing near the civilian wagons. Instead, they sprinted in an attempt to get a better position.

Briggs and two of his men opened the large metal basement door and immediately opened fire on the guards. Briggs strafed, hip-firing two sub machine guns at the group of Hiezers. The guards became frantic, trying to dodge the incoming bullets from various directions. They violently fell within seconds of the fighters unloading their guns onto them. Once the threat was over, Cherris peeked out of her wagon, only to see the strange man standing ten feet in front of her. He stood up from the cover of his shield and then shoved a lever down on the large hunk of metal; it quickly consolidated into a smaller piece of metal, about the size of his arm. The man looked older and was of average build, but contained enormous strength. Effortlessly, he began walking toward a corner of the mansion, carrying the chunk of metal that was no lighter than it was in its expanded form.

Briggs ran over to Cherris, giving her an odd look and motioning to the strange man. "Who the hell is that?" Briggs said to Cherris.

"I don't know, but he undoubtedly saved my life and the lives of the people in my wagon," Cherris replied.

Briggs shifted his eyes to the man walking away, and then looked back at Cherris with a raised eyebrow.

She shook her head, rethinking and remembering the hectic scene that just unfolded, "There was one more!" she said with renewed panic, "He was going after the Ayelan! Find him, Briggs!"

Lesh and Volaina remained on the fourth floor, tracking the marching guards to see where they were headed.

Volaina tapped Lesh on the shoulder, "They're going to Jeck's holding room."

Lesh turned back, "Blague didn't release him yet?"

"No," Volaina replied in her thick accent, "Blague had him detained since the Mulderan broadcast." Lesh looked at her with slight confusion. "I'll explain later," Volaina said.

The guards turned and entered Jeck's room.

"Cover me," Lesh said.

She began sprinting before Volaina could answer. Volaina drew her silenced assault rifle and aimed it at the guard standing watch outside of Jeck's room. The guard turned his gun to Lesh as she rounded the corner. Volaina fired, hitting the guard's leg. Lesh pulled a knife from her ring and threw it, hitting the guard in the shoulder, forcing him to drop his gun. Volaina finished with a shot to the head. The guard's face slammed into the wall from the impact. Volaina followed Lesh as she continued sprinting, ignoring the pain in her leg. Lesh reached for her knife that was lodged in the guard and dove into Jeck's room, slamming down the light switch before anyone could turn around. The brief image that she mentally noted before killing the lights was that of a tall Hiezer untying Jeck's blindfold and a force of shielded guards protecting them. Volaina, realizing Lesh's plan, shot out the hallway light to make sure the room was pitch black.

"Hold your fire!" someone shouted within the room.

Lesh quickly dashed in a zigzag pattern very low to the ground. She maneuvered around a shielded Hiezer and stuck a knife into his chin, drawing the attention of the other guards. She then back-flipped to the opposite side of the room, removing herself from the attention of the alerted guards. Lesh took hold of the guard closest to her, pulled his head back, and slit his throat. She hastily dragged the guy out of the room as the guards closely encircled their leader. Using her keen eyes that were already adjusted to the darkness, Lesh tossed the Hiezer corpse to Volaina's feet in the hallway.

"You're up," Lesh said in her raspy voice.

Volaina scrambled to put on the padded vest and jacket, took the guard's shoes and mask and snuck into the room, slowly backing into position. She then hustled over to the light switch in her new concealing armor. As soon as the light flickered, Volaina could see Mulderan with his stave drawn, ready for hand-to-hand combat. Once Mulderan saw that the there was no longer a threat in the room, he twirled the stave back into the holster on his back.

"They got one of us," Jeck said pointing to the guard bleeding out on the floor.

"No more mistakes, Hiezers," Mulderan said in a firm, cold voice. "Extract the Ayelan and depart immediately. I'm already behind schedule," he said, arrogantly. "Give the locator to Jeck," Mulderan said to one of the guards.

Volaina picked up the bullet proof glass shield that

was lying on the floor and returned to position. The small army began marching down to the main floor, protected with shields from all angles.

Kentin followed the Hiezer guard that reclaimed the Ayelan capsule from inside the secret wall. The guard had thrown off his mask and black uniform in the hopes that he would stay hidden long enough to reunite with Mulderan. He wanted to be the hero that won the battle of the Senation fortress. Kentin made sure to stay clear of the guard's sight. He was boiling up inside, trying to get the attention of a fighter to help stop the intruder. Everyone around him was either sprinting to reload, shouting into a radio, or being carried to a medical room to be treated. The guard began to pick up speed, noticing Mulderan and his group exiting the room on the fourth floor. That's when Kentin jumped in front of a Sin fighter and pointed.

"He's a guard and he has the chemical, stop him," Kentin said quietly enough so that the guard wouldn't hear him.

The Sin fighter and Kentin trailed the man, as the fighter contemplated if the kid was right. The guard turned slightly, feeling eyes on him. He immediately realized that the two of them were following him. The guard swung around and opened fire. The two of them dove to the floor with no cover in sight. Bullets buzzed past them. The guard grew frantic, knowing that he was horribly outnumbered within the fortress. The Sin fighter shot back, aiming for the legs to avoid shattering the invaluable vial. One bullet connected. People peeked their heads out of their hiding places, terrified that the battle was pushed onto the main floor. The guard cackled and fell to the floor, catching himself with his good knee. The guard and fighter aimed at each other and fired again. The Sin fighter was hit in the chest, but before the effects took place, a successful retaliation shot hit the guard in the stomach.

After a few seconds, both were lying on the floor, struggling to take their last breaths. Kentin was terrified, his body was trembling as he watched the two men bleed out. However, he knew how important that vial was to his father, so he picked himself up, screamed for help, and ran toward the dying guard. Kentin stared at the man, who was coughing, causing the blood to seep faster from his stomach. Kentin reached for the vial and began to pry it from the guard's fingers. The guard's strength was waning and Kentin was pulling with all of his might. The vial didn't appear to be cracked; the thick liquid shimmered its multicolored composition through the hard glass container. Finally, Kentin took hold of the vial and ran toward Cherris' wagon, hoping to find his dad.

Drino lifted his head from ducking yet another explosion. Sand and soot covered his face. The men and women around him continued to defend the entrance with ferocity. The Hiezer guards were in disarray, since their commanding orders had gone dark about an hour ago. Drino realized that Blague's rogue operation was successful, which gave the front lines the ability to hold off the massive amount of incoming troops. Drino had a defined jaw and a permanent five o'clock shadow. He was as muscular as Blague, but had a stiffer demeanor. Everything about Drino screamed intensity, which is one of the reasons he was put in charge of formations. Drino's hair was bright blonde and parted strictly to the left side. He preferred being on the front lines, equipped with a heavy machine gun. The deep scars on the sides of his face were evidence of that.

"Sins! Squad B, rise!" Drino yelled. His voice faded out at the end of his call because of the endless screaming around him.

Squad B heard and promptly rose from cover, unleashing a storm of bullets and grenades from launchers. A group of charging guards fell, some of which tried to retaliate, but the wave of bullets was too intense. After about ten seconds of straight fire, most of the Sins found themselves having to reload. Drino and his squad were spread out directly behind the door, ready to defend it with their lives. A line of Hiezer guards with solid blue bandannas tied around their arms were slightly hunched and sprinting forward. They jumped over their dead brethren in hopes to avenge them.

"Squad X!" Drino said, looking to his other side, "Fire!" Drino's staggered voice was chilling.

A squad of Sins began firing from the rocks on the east side. Drino and his squad fired as well. This group of guards was more adept to the Sin's strategy; they spread out to confuse the fire coming from Squad X and they kept up the pace, sprinting toward Drino's squad. Drino swung his heavy mini-gun into position. He pulled the trigger and the chamber began to spin. Within a second, a barrage of bullets propelled from his gun, mowing down four Hiezer guards within his line of sight. What seemed to be the leader of the blue bandanna guards hopped over a barricade that Drino had been using for cover. He whacked Drino across the face with his assault rifle and kicked him backward. Drino shook his head and split out blood. Before the guard could reposition his gun to aim, Drino lunged forward and jabbed him in the ribs with brass knuckles. The guard stumbled forward, but tried to swing his gun again to disable him. Drino dodged and purposely dropped his mini-gun, causing it to land on the guard's leg. The guard fell to his knee. Drino didn't give him a moment to gather himself. Instead, Drino knocked off the guard's helmet and proceeded to beat his face to a bloody pulp. One of his fists caused serious damage, opening the side of his face with each pound from the brass knuckles. Other guards were breaking through to Drino's barricade. Although his squad did their best to fend them off, the fighters were forced to cease fire to avoid hitting their own. One Sin fighter attempted to restrain the breach by lighting a flame thrower. She advanced slowly as the guards pulled back. Drino looked up to find himself with a group of guards in his line of sight. He grabbed his mini-gun and opened fire. With intensity and determination, he was ready to end this battle.

Briggs was in position with fighters and civilians, ready to defend the main floor as Mulderan, Jeck, and the guards descended down the steps. Jeck stared down at a device as he proceeded onward. Mulderan's eyes faced forward, analyzing the situation. As soon as one of the shielded guards reached the main floor, a Sin fighter opened fire, resulting in a chain reaction. The Hiezer guards braced on to their shields as they shook violently while the incoming bullets ricocheted off the bulletproof glass. Mulderan motioned to his team to speed it up. Jeck lifted his head and pointed toward the east end of the mansion.

Briggs poked his head out from behind the wagon. The sight of his imperiled son caused a tingling sensation throughout his entire body as a brief state of shock left his eyes wide and mouth open. A jolt of energy charged through him, every cell in his body forced him to run.

Kentin sprinted while sobbing, protecting the Ayelan filled vial with both of his hands.

Lesh looked over the ledge of the fourth floor, to watch the escalating situation. She drew the knives from her back. Although she had an aerial view of the battle, she was too far away to get a clear shot. She swung her arm to release the throwing knife with all of her force, throwing a Hail Mary out of desperation. She repeated the motion several times. This bought Briggs some time to reach Kentin.

Between the gunfire and projectiles raining from above, the guards were struggling to maintain composure. Mulderan drew his stave after watching one of his guards get punctured in the shoulder by a flying knife. Mulderan whirled the black and golden stave above his head, swinging it in all directions. He deflected three of Lesh's knives with precision.

"Dad!" Kentin yelled as he recognized the mountain running toward him.

Volaina realized that she wouldn't be able to successfully exit the mansion disguised as a guard, since the situation was getting out of control. She dropped her bullet proof shield and drew two silenced pistols, firing at the guards surrounding her from within the circle of shields. After a few of the shielded guards dropped to the floor, she swung toward Mulderan, whose eyes pierced right through her, with his stave already in motion. The impact of the staff whipping across Volaina's face knocked her helmet off and sent her slightly airborne before hitting the ground. Mulderan's protective circle was diminishing.

"Recover the Ayelan, now," Mulderan said, pointing toward the boy.

The guards prepared to fire. Kentin lost sight of the Hiezers as Briggs' body covered his entire view. Briggs quickly bent down to scoop Kentin up and move him to safety.

He hugged Kentin tight, "It's ok, bud, I've got you." Kentin shut his eyes, relieved, holding on to the vial as tight as he could. Time stood still for that moment, as Kentin felt a vibration; he opened his eyes as Briggs fell to his knees. The pupils of Briggs' wide eyes constricted. He remained straight faced, trying not to show pain. Kentin's relief quickly morphed into anguish. Briggs took four more hits.

"Dad!" Kentin cried. One of the bullets that pierced his back exited through his chest.

Blood dripped down his huge body, oozing from all of the open orifices. Kentin was horrified, but Briggs maintained composure and looked into his son's eyes.

"I'm sorry Kentin, but I need you to be strong. This group is your family now."

Tears fell from Kentin's eyes, "Why are you saying this, dad? You can't die."

Briggs looked pained and his eyes began to glaze over. "I love you, son. I'll always be with you."

Briggs hugged Kentin tight as he held back tears to try and be strong for his son. His vision was beginning to darken.

How can I leave my boy alone in this world?

Chapter 12

Three days after the devastating attack on the mansion, Sabin and Blague leaned over the ledge of the roof, both with heavy hearts.

"The toll is dire," Blague said to Sabin, as he gazed into the distance.

It was a sunny warm day. The faint stench of blood still whirled around the beach, acting as a constant reminder of the hell the Sin community had just endured. Sabin looked down while petting Mars.

"Briggs was a good man," Sabin said, looking slowly up at him.

"He was, and so were the sixty other fighters who perished. The despair among the community from losing their loved ones is heart wrenching," Blague responded. Sabin put his head back down. "Briggs' funeral will be held today at six. Grab Eugene and Kentin. All three of you will help me do the honor of burying him on the far side of the rock path," Blague said.

Sabin looked a little surprised, "Isn't that a bit much for the kid?"

Blague paused for a minute, "Perhaps, but this world has grown cruel and although it's a hard task for Kentin, it will help him to realize that he's not alone. He has us."

Blague's radio rang, causing Mars to bark frantically.

"Blague, it's Cherris," she said through radio.

"Go ahead," Blague said.

"Now that the dust is beginning to settle and the people are starting to calm down, I want you to come down to the main floor. There's something I've been meaning to show you," Cherris said.

Blague looked at Sabin and Sabin shrugged. "Alright," Blague said, "I'll be right down."

"How's Lesh doing?" Sabin asked.

Blague smirked at Sabin, "Careful, Sabin. Every time you mention her, your eyes nearly turn heart shaped." He tried to hold back a laugh as the words came out.

Sabin looked at him with confusion, "What the hell are you talking about?" Sabin asked, as he began to laugh with Blague.

Shit! He's on to me. Is it that obvious that I have a little crush?

"The feelings you have for her are written all over your face," Blague said as he turned his back to begin walking down to the main floor. "I'm in your head now, old friend. Sometimes you make it too easy," he said while pointing to his head.

"Hah, you're a real bastard sometimes," Sabin responded while laughing.

"We all have to have our fun somehow. You want to join me in seeing what Cherris found?" Blague replied.

"Sure," Sabin answered, tapping Mars on the side to come along.

As they continued down the stairs, Sabin noticed that the medical rooms were still operating intensely. Many of the wounded soldiers were in critical condition and needed constant attention. The main floor was full of grievances and love, spread throughout the rooms and wagons; some families were devastated and some rejoiced in the victory, but overall it was obvious that the Sins were kind and supportive of each other.

"It looks like the amount of supporters has tripled since we got here," Sabin commented.

"It nearly has. Thankfully we have over two hundred fighters strong. We had nearly three hundred before the battle. We would all be dead right now if Briggs didn't protect his son. The Ayelan would have been dissolved or taken and this home would have been bombed moments later," Blague said, looking down as he proceeded toward the main floor.

"So I heard," Sabin replied. "I was helping wrap up the battle out back with Drino at that moment. That dude looks like he was born to yell and kill on the battlefield," Sabin said half-jokingly. "Can't trust a man with hair combed so perfectly," he continued, making himself laugh.

They both approached Cherris. Blague gave her a hug, followed by Sabin.

"How're you holding up?" Sabin asked.

"I'm fine, dear. It's the broken families that are suffering. But anyway, I wanted you to meet this odd person who saved my life. He's been sitting in the corner behind my wagon for almost three days now. The kids are scared to even go near him."

As Blague and Sabin followed Cherris alongside the wagon, they saw a man sitting in a corner Indian style, with scarves wrapped tightly around his face and cloths draped around his body. His smoky grey pupil-less eyes darted back and forth in rapid motion. Sabin walked by, leaned over, and waved a hand in front of his face. The man didn't respond.

Sabin stood up straight and shrugged, "I think he's sleeping."

Cherris walked over and put a gentle hand on the man's shoulder. His brow slowly tensed. A few grunts projected through his voice changer, distortedly. He blinked and his eye movement ceased. He stood up and exchanged looks with Sabin and Cherris.

"What's your name?" Cherris asked.

The man dusted off the cloth draped over his shoulder and looked up at her, staring into her eyes. "I have no name," the man said, his response echoing through his voice changer.

Sabin poked the metal constricted riot shield resting on his arm. The man jerked his hand away and looked at him, annoyed.

"Mind yourself," the man said.

Mars barked at the man. He looked at Mars and bent down, offering his hand. As he extended it, Blague, Cherris, and Sabin looked at the veins jutting from the man's arm, radiating Cryos blue. Mars sniffed his hand and licked him. The scarves covering his face moved upward, feigning a smile.

"I haven't seen a tame beast in what feels like a century," the man said.

Blague took two steps forward, to get a closer look at this unique individual. "What will you have us call you?" Blague asked.

The man rose, looking eye to eye with Blague, as his eyes widened. "Your cause has led me here, though I will not reveal why." Blague raised an eyebrow. "So, I understand that I'm not offering you much in terms of trust," the man took a step closer to Blague, "but I hope that my saving one of your key people awards me the privilege of having peace with you." The man extended an arm to shake Blague's hand. "You can call me Niro, I suppose."

Blague extended his hand to meet Niro's. "My name is Blague and I thank you for protecting Cherris. She's invaluable to me."

Cherris put her head down.

"Can you see out of those things?" Sabin asked.

Cherris smacked Sabin, "Don't be rude."

Niro chuckled, which echoed in different tones. "Yes...?" Niro motioned toward Sabin.

"You can call me Sabin."

"Yes, Sabin. I can see perfectly fine," Niro said.

"Why in hell are your pupils white then?" Sabin continued to probe.

Niro shifted and took a step back with his heavy combat boots to have a better view of all three of them. "You ask a lot of questions," he said to Sabin.

"You're a curious person," Sabin responded.

Niro looked down at his arms, "I've been exposed to the horrors of this world. That's the cause of my discoloration; pay it no mind."

Blague analyzed the man. Something about him was very strange. His unique features were only a part of it, and he couldn't quite put a finger on the rest.

"Where did you come from?" Sabin asked.

"That's a loaded question," Niro responded. He turned around and walked back to his corner. He leaned on the wall, folded his arms, and after a moment, his eyes began to rapidly dart back and forth again.

"Whelp," Sabin said, throwing his hands up in the air, "I guess we lost him."

Blague was unusually silent. Sabin waved his hands in Niro's face, and again, there was no response.

Briggs looked strong on the outside, but deep down I always knew he was soft. If he was stronger, more concentrated on survival, his kid wouldn't have been frantically running in the midst of gunfire. Fuck you, Briggs.

Lesh hung upside down while holding herself up with her busted leg, trying to fight through the pain. She flipped back down and grunted.

"You really think that's helpin ya?" Morn said, leaning on a wall, still wearing his tanned trench coat with his revolver strapped to his belt.

Lesh shot him a look of death. "In my line of work, you have to fight through pain," Lesh said, "Are you really in a position to judge?" She looked at Morn then looked at Milos, who was sitting down with his hands chained behind his back on the adjacent wall. "I've been left with two of the most unstable Sins in this establishment," Lesh said as she flipped back upside down, catching the ceiling ledge with her foot.

"Heh," Morn said, "look who's talking, sweetheart." As the last syllable left his mouth, a knife whizzed past his greasy hair. Morn froze.

"You know, I'm still considering forms of torture for you," she said.

Morn stood there in shock, while Lesh flashed him an upside down smirk. Milos fidgeted, causing the sound of his chains to rattle through the marble room.

"Why's that boy in chains there?" Morn asked.

"He volunteered to be restrained," Lesh said.

"I killed my friend," Milos muttered, "I don't deserve to be free."

"Ya must have had good reason, boy, if you have a conscious like that," Morn replied.

"He did," Lesh said, flipping back down to the ground. "He murdered a traitor and probably helped preserve our home," she continued while walking over to Milos.

"Sounds like the normal life of a Sin, boy," Morn said, "You'd best get used to it."

"He will," Lesh said, leaning down until she was eye to eye with Milos, "You're going to learn to control your demons." Lesh pulled him up by his shirt, "But it's not going to be easy."

Milos looked up at her, his shaggy black hair draped past his eyes. "You can't fix me, Lesh," Milos said.

"Heh," Morn scoffed.

"You're right," Lesh's voice cracked, "You have to fix yourself." Lesh let go of Milos' shirt, letting the back of his head slam against the wall. He cringed, but didn't mutter a word.

"I don't know how long you been cooped up in here, Milos," Morn said, "but I reckon that since your friend's pop died a few days ago, he could probably use some support."

Milos looked up, "Kentin's dad?" Milos asked.

Lesh stood there quietly. Morn nodded.

Milos put his head down and asked himself quietly, "Briggs died?"

This kid isn't going anywhere. He can't even help himself. I'm not going to mother this boy, but I can toughen him up.

"Morn, go get to know some of your new family," Lesh said.

Morn scoffed, "As you wish, sweetheart."

As Morn shut the door behind him, Lesh kicked Milos in the side.

"Get up," she said.

Milos slowly rose, using his legs to push his back up against the wall. Lesh kicked his leg out, causing him to fall back down.

"Too slow," she said in a cruel tone, "Stop moping."

Milos got up a little bit faster, his face cringing from the pain. Lesh, showing no emotion, kicked him back down. Milos looked up at her. Her hair was shimmering, her eyes had dark circles under them, but her skin was smooth around all of the cuts and bruises. She was a fierce, unique commander that would not put up with any bullshit; Milos was learning that quickly.

"Do you think I'm going to have pity on you, because you're making faces?" Lesh asked, almost laughing through her words. "What good would that do for either of us?" Lesh kicked him down again. "What are you thinking, Milos? What's the first thought that comes into your head?"

Milos got up a little bit faster. "That I killed my friend," Milos said.

Lesh smacked Milos in the face, making him fall on his side. "Despair?" Lesh said, disappointed, "What is dwelling in a skewed thought about your past going to do for you right now, in this situation?"

Milos didn't respond. He tried to process what she was saying. He stood up straight, hoping that this is what she wanted from him.

He's not giving up. Maybe this kid can make it.

Lesh grabbed him by the hair and jerked him forward. She took a knife out of the bottom side of her ring and sliced Milos' shackles right down the middle.

"Defend yourself, Milos. Do you still have life in you?" she asked.

Milos nodded timidly. Lesh faked a punch to his face and he flinched. She then swept his legs from under him.

"Milos," Lesh said as she rose from her kick, "I asked you if you still have life in you."

Milos got up again, this time a little bit faster. He put his fists up; the severed shackles rattled as he moved his arms. Lesh threw a punch, holding back force. Milos used both of his arms to block the incoming punch. Lesh's hair swung with her, as she curtailed her strength and her speed, but put enough force into her strikes to cause some pain. Milos found himself face down on the floor again.

"Dwelling again, Milos? That's all you're communicating to me with your body," Lesh said, dropping her fists to her side.

Milos jumped up again, his face looking more determined this time. He put his fists up and charged

Lesh. She side stepped his punch and tripped him.

"Get up you fool," Lesh said, taunting him, "How are you going to save your friends if you're on the floor?"

An image of his mother being shot flashed through his mind. Milos jumped up, this time with rage. The small Cryos mark on his arm began to shine. He charged Lesh while swinging frantically, just to be tripped down and kicked again.

"Don't you see?" Lesh asked. "It doesn't matter if you're dwelling in sadness or boiling with rage. You have no control over either. Your body is reacting to your emotions. You'll never land a blow in this state. Get up and show me that you're not a ball of useless energy."

Although Milos was conflicted, he kept getting up. His rage didn't allow him to feel any pain, but it also made him predictable. He continuously charged Lesh, slamming onto the floor after every attempt.

"You're going to make the same mistakes every time, until you maintain some control," Lesh said.

He began to tire after an hour of endless bruising. It was only at the point of exhaustion when he started to realize that Lesh was right. He was beginning to think clearly again, but he lost all of his furious energy. Milos breathed heavily, as sweat dripped down his face, but he kept his fists up and his head focused.

Eugene laid still as Narene redressed his wounds on one of the medical tables. The doctors and nurses were running on very little sleep, but were finally able to address the needs of the less critical patients. The more critical cases were either stabilized or failed at this point. Narene's tired eyes still had a glimmer of light in them. She artfully performed her job, never letting her smile escape her face.

"I'm so happy you're safe," Narene exclaimed to Eugene.

"It was a close call up there. I lost good men," Eugene said as the scene replayed in his head. He sighed when he thought of Briggs, who was probably the closest with Eugene.

"I know you're suffering, but you're not alone," Narene said smiling. Her nose ring glimmered in the makeshift hospital's fluorescent white light, shining in Eugene's face.

I feel guilty being with Narene, but she is great. Maybe it's time I let myself feel again.

Eugene reached for her hand. She stopped what she was doing and held it for a moment. Flashes of Jen's beautiful smile and squinted eyes rushed through his head, conflicting with the image in front of him. Narene leaned in and gave Eugene a passionate kiss. One of the doctors walked past the room with bloody gloves held away from his scrubs. He looked over and smiled through his mask, then coughed loudly so that Narene would hear. Narene pulled back and smiled bashfully at the doctor. She looked back to Eugene, who awkwardly smiled back at her.

"I'm going to get some rest now if that's alright, Narene," he requested politely.

"Sure," Narene said while she finished dressing his wounds. "Hopefully my shift will wind down sometime tonight. I'll see you later?" she asked.

Eugene smiled and nodded at her. She smiled back and walked out of the room to tend to her next patient.

I'm getting sick of this war, even though it seems to be tipping in our favor. The Sins are still looked at as discarded fodder and most of us outside of these walls believe that. I don't know though, I have to give Blague some credit. He's making some powerful strides. I guess patience is only my strong point on the battlefield.

Eugene looked at the Cryos mark on his arm. The line where the bullet grazed him didn't affect his mark.

This mark is a constant reminder of that nightmare. Eugene put his arms behind his head. *Who am I kidding? I just lost two junior snipers that I've been training for months and one of my closest friends. This hell continues on.*

"Eu," Blague said through the radio, "one hour until burial. Bring the boy."

Eugene sighed as he picked up his radio, "Copy."

Blague looked up at the sun that was beginning to set. He stood with one foot on the base of his shovel. Briggs' body was covered with a large white cloth, rippling in the wind.

I didn't anticipate Mulderan paying us a visit so soon. His spying on my debate with Jeck must have escalated the threat in his mind. He witnessed with his own eyes the momentum this group has gained.

Blague looked down at his shovel as his hair fluttered in the wind. A flash of light in his head gave him the goosebumps. Moments later, he was enveloped in thought.

His wife was being escorted by a shadowed figure. Her head was down, stunned that the man in front of her was dead set on going through with the process.

"Mulderan Grenich," she said slowly, "may you live forever with these horrors that you've caused."

Mulderan turned around, the shadow of him faded; his face was now clear in Blague's mind. He lifted Elaina's chin with his gloved fingers. Mulderan stared into her eyes, with his defined and emotionless face. "Your DNA is of the rarest on this planet. You're going to directly contribute to the survival of our race, whether you can comprehend your value or not."

She looked back at him. Her features were beautiful, but her eyes reflected despair. "It's funny what power can do to a person. You were always on the brink of madness, but now you've hopped over the edge," Elaina said. "Why don't you sacrifice yourself for your grand cause?"

Mulderan let out a laugh, "I gladly will when the time is right. But for now, I have to ensure that our survival is guaranteed."

"You've never sounded so lost," Elaina said.

Mulderan turned back around and signaled for her escorts to continue. "I won't forget you, Elaina, and neither will your partner."

Blague's eyes opened wide, feeling like he was slapped in the face. "These visions are odd," Blague said to himself. "It's as if I'm piecing together the events leading up to her extraction. Events that I wasn't even there to witness."

Blague shook his head then looked up to see Eugene, Kentin, Sabin, and Mars making their way over the rocks. Kentin's head was up high as he conversed with the others. Blague put his hand up to say hello.

Everyone reacts differently to traumatic situations; this kid is a clear reflection of that.

As Kentin arrived, Blague knelt down and put his heavy hand on Kentin's shoulder. "I'm sorry, Kentin. I would have taken those bullets for your father if I could have."

Kentin teared up, looking at the cloth spread over the huge man. "I want to be strong and I want him to be proud of me, no matter where he is right now," Kentin said.

Blague nodded and stood up. He handed Kentin a small shovel, "We will help you achieve that goal."

Sabin pet Mars and then tapped the wolf to go stand by Kentin's side. Kentin grabbed the shovel, then turned to pet the wolf who cried, feeling the boy's sorrow. They all began to dig.

"When I finally made it to the main floor, I saw the fighters pushing the Hiezer's up the stairs to the roof, unloading a storm of bullets at their shields," Sabin said while digging. "I watched Mulderan walk away, as if nothing was happening around him. That man changed since I last remember him. He shows no fear," Sabin finished.

Eugene looked up, "I watched him deploy onto the roof as Lito carried me down the stairs. He saw how few of us were left and just pointed to the squad trailing him to clean up the mess. He has a very odd and ruthless demeanor, so I would have to agree. I didn't know you knew him too?" Eugene added.

Blague looked up, staring at the two of them in a

daze, his thoughts racing. "The man you saw is a finished product," Blague began. "He was in the making for a very long time. His father, Orin Grenich, was the creator of the Hiezer initiative after the Global Quake. He was a strategic mind who came from an old way of thought. He wanted to help people and make the world a better place. So he created the Hiezers from a broad sea of contacts. He was the CEO of a large company at the time, which enabled him to extend his reach on an international scale to stop the chaos that the world was rapidly succumbing to," Blague said, recalling the chain of events.

Kentin listened intently, as did Eugene. Sabin continued digging, well aware of the Hiezer history.

"When I was on sniper patrol in my past life, I used to hear of the Grenich name, but I was so far removed from upper leadership that it meant nothing at that time," Eugene said.

"Yes, Orin was not a man known to boast or broadcast," Blague responded, "Mulderan naturally inherited his position as a highlord."

Eugene nodded, breaking from the digging to listen.

Sabin slammed his shovel into the sand and gravel, "There was always something off with him, Blague. Everyone knew it deep down."

Blague stared at Sabin, "That's true because he never responded to emotional events and he always took a calculative approach, starting with the big picture, the "greatest good." That thought process made it almost impossible to relate with him on a personal level," Blague continued.

"How well did you know him?" Eugene questioned.

Blague waved that question away. "I only knew forms of him," Blague answered vaguely. "The worst of which was created the day he scrutinized a decision made by his father. The decision to stop the research of Ayelan, once Orin got wind of a psychotic scientist making significant progress through human experimentation. Mulderan believed cutting off that momentum would significantly hinder the needed progress for the Hiezers. After the decision, he worked closely and secretively with the scientists to complete the Ayelan injection. Once Mulderan was comfortable with his accomplishment, he called a surprise meeting with the highlords to display his achievement and prove that his father's leadership was counterproductive. Ultimately, he wanted to prove that his father was unfit to lead. The highlords, mostly in shock, realized the capabilities of the unique man presenting in front of them. Mulderan took control of the Hiezers and condemned his father to death," Blague finished.

Eugene looked at Blague with confusion, "How did he assume such power so easily?" Eugene asked.

"From what I heard, it wasn't done overnight. It was a six day meeting consisting of scientific human displays and Mulderan's persistence. His father was disgusted with him. Orin's skills in rhetoric were hindered by the audacity of his son. The result of that meeting was the birth of a monster. The current state of this world is a result of his perseverance," Blague said.

Eugene had trouble digesting the information.

"We have to stay sharp," Blague said to everyone, "We pushed Mulderan back for now, but I'm sure he's planning our demise."

"We won't let that happen, Blague. Don't talk the bastard up too much," Sabin said smirking, "Besides, it's much more fun to root for the underdog."

Blague gave a half smirk, "You're right, Sabin. I shouldn't underestimate our movement. We're fighting for something far greater than domination and preservation. We're fighting for hope, which is something Mulderan has no concept of."

Eugene sighed. "Well don't be too optimistic either," he said as he motioned toward Briggs' body with a nod.

Blague turned to look at Eugene with his green piercing eyes, "Briggs definitely would want us to be optimistic, Eugene. Why don't you help us keep his spirit alive?"

Eugene looked down and continued digging, as did the rest of them. After fifteen more minutes of labor, they carefully lowered Briggs' body into the pit. Kentin helped cover him. His eyes were filled with tears.

"I'll miss you, dad," he said in a scratchy, exhausted voice. He pounded his chest, "I'm going to be strong for you."

Eugene knelt down and put an arm around Kentin. "Don't ever forget him, Kentin. I know I won't. He loves you with all of his being, wherever he is," Eugene finished.

Kentin nodded and wiped his eyes. Blague looked down at the grave. They all proceeded to say goodbye in their own way. Blague then slammed a wooden stick down and carved a "B" in it.

"We'll make this a stone grave one day soon, once

we're more established," Blague said.

Kentin didn't fully understand, but he said "Thank you" anyway.

"*Gran jefe*," Blague's radio sounded.

"Yes, Lito, what is it?" Blague responded.

"I think you should come see this. Meet me at the breach point," Lito said.

"All commanders, meet with Lito," Blague broadcasted.

Blague and his crew walked to the breach point, where people were being held back by the fighters. Once Blague had a clear visual, he slowed down his walk.

As anticipated, the word has spread.

"There must be a thousand Sins," Drino said.

Blague turned to his commanders, "We need builders and a new head screener. This is now a Sin fortress. Protect it with your lives."

Chapter 13

"Four months have passed since the battle," Drino shouted, his voice echoing amongst eighty cadets.

The training room was the size of a school auditorium. A golden Hiezer symbol flowed to the center point of the ceiling. Stone floors and walls surrounded them. Drino paced up and down the rows, inspecting his new cadets with a grim expression. His Cryos mark was shimmering, as his sleeveless shirt served as a good source of intimidation, exposing his white muscular arms. Drino had two squad mates assisting him, disciplining the new fighters.

"It could be any moment," Drino yelled as he inspected the cadets. "Any moment when we're stormed again. Or worse yet." He spun to look a cadet in the eye, "A mole could already be in our home, trying to murder your family. And you stand here, useless to our cause. Waiting for someone to protect you," he said waving his hand with disgust. He spit on the floor, "Is that the contribution that you want to make?"

"No sir!" the room echoed.

Drino walked over to a cadet, "What's your name, soldier?"

"Chella," she shouted.

"Do you want to protect your family, Chella?"

"I lost my family, sir!" Chella replied.

Drino paused for a moment. "Then what do you fight for?"

"A better life!" she screamed.

Drino stood up straight. His scars creased as a smirk crept up his face. He nodded at Chella and continued marching slowly down the rows. "You, what's your name?" Drino yelled.

"Oscin, sir!" he screamed.

"Oscin, do you want to learn how to protect our home?"

Oscin looked at Drino with a sarcastic grin on his face. "I know how to fight, sir," Oscin replied.

As soon as the word 'sir' slipped from Oscin's lips, the back of Drino's hand connected with his face. As the cadet's face jerked toward the floor, he spit out a little bit of blood. Drino yanked him by the collar, lifting his feet off the ground, pulling him toward his face. Drino's strong features and strictly combed blonde hair distinguished him from the rest of the people in the room.

"Don't get smart with me again, boy," he said in a harsh whisper.

Oscin nodded, even though he was angry and embarrassed. Oscin was sloppily unshaven; he had black messy hair and looked like he just rolled out of bed. He was also one skipped meal away from being stick thin. He was not an ideal candidate for a fighter position.

"And you reek of alcohol. Shape up or get out," Drino said as he released him from his grip. "Cadets!" Drino yelled as he walked toward the front of the training room, "I'm through with speaking to useless Sins. So let's change that fact right now. Get into formations and prepare for training!"

It was a beautiful day in Senation. Sabin slammed the dice onto the table, watching them tumble with an ear to ear smile across his face. Lesh stood, leaning against the wall behind Sabin, watching the breach point for any trouble. The dice landed two sixes. Sabin hit the table and laughed. He pointed at Lito and laughed again, then he turned to Mars to pet the top of his head with excitement. Lito scratched his mohawk, upset from losing, but couldn't help but join in on Sabin's infectious laughter. Lesh looked over at the two commanders and the surrounding fighters and rolled her eyes.

Sabin looked back at Lesh, "Ah c'mon, have a little fun!" he joked.

Lesh smirked at him, "You're an idiot."

Sabin waved his hand at her, and then he extended his half cloaked arm to Lito, "Pay up, buddy."

Lito blew him a sarcastic air kiss and flipped two coins over to him. Sabin sat back, with his freshly trimmed black and white beard and his golden eyes that were full of life. Just then, Mars barked. Sabin hit the table with his knee as he rose quickly from his seat. Lesh tensed up and reached for the binoculars on the table. She saw the fighters guarding the breach point holding their hands forward, not allowing three people to pass.

"Looks like we've got some trouble," Sabin said.

Lesh picked up the radio, "Blague, you should make your way to the front entrance. We may have intruders."

"On my way," a calm tone responded.

Sabin and Mars charged toward the breach point, running on the strip of pavement that was recently renovated. As they approached the point, Sabin noticed the fighters guarding the entrance in a defensive position.

"Let us in! We seek words with your leader," a deep, fake sounding voice called out.

Mars bore his teeth and began barking. Sabin slowed his pace to observe the three hooded figures standing at the entrance. They wore combat ready clothing under cloaks that had sleeves extending past their arms and large hoods that shadowed their faces.

"Remove your hoods," Sabin raised his voice.

The figure in the middle stepped forward. "No, Templos," the man said in a distinct, arrogant tone, "but we will surrender our weapons if you will allow us words with your leader, Blague."

Sabin was taken aback by the knowledge that this shrouded man possessed.

My arm is covered. How could he possibly know I'm not a Sin?

Sabin motioned to the guards, "Search them."

The fighters patted down each of the three cloaked intruders. One was a woman, the other two were men. As the woman's cloak rippled from the frisk, Sabin noticed a symbol on the side of it. It was red with two horizontal lines, one longer than the other, and another vertical line that slashed down the middle. All ends of the symbol looked as though it was made with a paintbrush. The thought registered immediately.

That's the symbol that Nemura and his crew wore. Lesh

mentioned that he was babbling about some enlightened being.

The guards threw the cloaked intruders' guns to the ground behind them.

"Are you satisfied now?" the main intruder asked with his arms spread to either side. "Let us speak with Blague," he asked again, gaging Sabin's reaction.

Sabin was no longer impressed. "Did Nemura feed you a tad of information, smart ass?" Sabin asked with a smile.

The hooded figured let out a laugh. "Well, I guess your small game hunting days are over, huh?" the man asked rhetorically.

Sabin kept his cool, "You're a little behind on your intel, hooded freak."

A hand gripped Sabin's shoulder, "What do we have here?" Blague asked.

Sabin turned around to see both Blague and Lesh.

Lesh tensed up as soon as she noticed the symbol on each cloak. "Let them in," Lesh said with her voice cracking. "Better yet, give them their weapons back so at least it's a fair fight," she finished.

The hooded woman cracked her knuckles.

"Blague," the main figure said, "is this any way to greet guests?"

Blague analyzed the three of them and then leaned his head over to Lesh, who whispered something in his ear.

The main figure put his hand up in a strange gesture, "I understand that we aren't exactly allies, but we aren't enemies either."

Blague didn't react to that statement. "Let them in,"

Blague said, gazing at the guards.

The wind was lightly rippling the robes of the hooded guests as they walked down the pathway toward the mansion. The leader slowly lifted his head and looked up toward the roof, his face shadowed by the large hood.

"Snipers," the man said loud enough for everyone around to hear.

Blague stopped and turned around. "Protection," Blague responded, staring at the man as if he could see his face.

The sun reflected off of Eugene's scope as he repositioned. The man raised his hands, as if he were presenting something huge behind him.

"Are you on drugs?" Sabin asked, scratching his head.

"I see great potential here. Harmony can be had between all variations of people, but not before the chaos has calmed," the man riddled in a confident and strange voice.

"Are you questioning whether we are part of the chaos or part of your harmony?" Blague asked.

"That's one way to view it," the man said as he continued forward.

Blague lifted his chin, trying to decipher the odd man's intentions.

"This world could improve, Blague," the man said as he lifted his hood and pushed it back.

Blague looked at Sabin and Lesh, trying to gauge their reactions, neither of which showed any sign of recognition. He turned his attention back to the man, whose skin was tinted a deep red hue. The tips of his medium length hair were colored in the same tone and his eyes were a brownish red as well. His demeanor was odd and there was no hint of angst in him.

"My name is Jason Brink," the man said, "although, I do not perceive myself as I once was."

Sabin looked over at Blague in deep confusion. Blague didn't exchange the look. He was careful to focus his attention on Jason. He took whatever Jason said seriously for the time being, especially considering a person wouldn't leave himself unarmed in Senation without a plan.

"Well, Jason, you already know my name and my motives," Blague said, "so please, reveal why you're here."

"In time, but first I must explain my current state," Jason said, tilting his head toward the sky.

"Definitely drugs," Sabin said again.

Jason ignored the comment and looked back toward Blague. The two people behind him remained hooded and unmoved.

"I'm privileged, you see, for I've discovered something so monumental, so transcendent, that it has altered my entire perception. I no longer perceive thoughts in a linear fashion. My entire understanding of time has been lifted to a new level. I am enlightened, by some greater force than you and me," Jason said.

"How did you reach this enlightenment? How long have you been this way?" Blague asked, purposely playing his game.

"All of my thoughts are current, so I couldn't tell you the answer, as I no longer understand the dimension you live in," Jason responded.

He looked at the back of his hand, then tilted his head and spun his hand around, inspecting it. Lesh stood tense, staring at the hooded male figure.

"What I can tell you, Blague, is how I became this way. You see, I was an explorer as a Dactuar, how long ago or how far ahead I couldn't tell you, but one thing is certain, a discovery has been made. The smoky continent of Auront, is the strangest gift of our world. And I would only reveal such a discovery to an ally," Jason said as he paced slowly.

Lesh cleared her throat, "You're talking about the iceless island near the Antarctic continents."

Jason's head jolted to Lesh, locking his reddish eyes with hers, "You appear to have stumbled upon very delicate information." His intense stare quickly dissipated as he returned back to his enlightened demeanor.

Lesh smiled mockingly at Jason, "I guess you can't see everything."

"I see enough, Lesh," Jason said cryptically, "I can estimate the amount of people residing in your fortress just by the vibrations it produces."

Sabin rolled his eyes, "What bullshit," he said while putting his hands behind his head, stretching.

Jason jolted his head to Sabin and stared intensely again, "One thousand three hundred and forty eight persons."

Sabin raised his eyebrows. "Huh, that's pretty good. Sounds about right," he said, still keeping light about the situation.

Blague remained confident and calm regardless of

the bizarre things the man standing in front of him was saying. "Tell me, Jason," Blague said, taking a step forward, "You're analyzing whether or not we can participate in your harmony." His Cryos mark began to shine, "But what do you expect in return?"

Jason stared at Blague for a moment and said, "You know, I'm not as selfish as you may think." He turned and gestured to the two hooded figures behind him. "One of these two will be the next to be enlightened; I will share the greatness that has been bestowed upon me."

Blague took another step forward, "You seem to not understand the situation. Why would we accept your enlightenment as law?"

Jason boldly stepped forward, his arms awkwardly extended parallel behind his back, "Because, by no choice of my own, I have become a god," he said as he locked eyes face to face with Blague.

"Just say the word, Blague," Eugene's voice echoed through his radio.

They stood halfway between the mansion and the breach point, completely exposed on all angles.

"Your welcome here has just run out," Blague said, drawing his Desert Eagle.

"Surely you wouldn't shoot an unarmed man," Jason said, not at all worried.

"A man? No. A god? Perhaps," Blague said raising his gun to Jason's temple.

"I already know I get out of this situation alive. Why do you think I surrendered my weapons?" Jason asked.

"I've already constructed your story from the facts you've given me," Blague said. "I know you aren't lying.

You're actually convinced of your delusions. You're merely piecing together reality from what we're saying and doing it at this very moment. You're more confused than enlightened, my harmonious ally. But unfortunately, we have to descend into chaos." Blague pointed his gun to the male figure, "Pull back your hood, Nemura."

"Lesh smelled you from a mile away," Sabin said.

Jason slowly nodded at the hooded figure, who pushed back his hood exposing a huge smile on his face.

"Long time no see, Blague. Wish I could say the same for you two," Nemura said, motioning to Sabin and Lesh.

"This was your big reveal?" Lesh asked.

Nemura laughed, "You're going to say hi to your brother for me soon." Nemura's silver hair lopped to one side as he bent forward to continue his laughing fit.

"This is the type of harmony you're seeking, Jason?" Blague asked. "This man betrayed us and caused innocent people to lose their lives. He's indirectly responsible for creating an orphan out of a child. He also held one of my commanders captive."

"I chase something far more valuable than intentions or integrity. I'm interested in the ability to create connections. And I'm sure that you very well know that Nemura has made many. He has an ability to gain knowledge through connections with people, which is why he has been nominated for greatness," Jason said, lifting his hands as he spoke. "Connectivity is evolution and my enlightened state will allow connection to transpire through thought. All in due time," Jason raised his index finger up toward Blague and whispered, "I know your fate."

"You're dismissed," Blague waved him away with his gun.

"Of course, but not before I turn your world upside down." Jason jerked his head back, as the tips of his burgundy hair flew back. He nonchalantly motioned to the female figure to remove her hood.

"What do you want?" Sabin blurted out.

Jason looked at Sabin, "I want more followers. I believe Auront can create a collective mind that can transcend us to a greater god."

"Holy shit," Sabin said, "I can't take this nonsense anymore. I'd rather be on house cleaning duty than listen to another word from this freak."

Jason ignored him and motioned again to the female figure. She slowly pushed her hood back before he began to walk away.

Eugene steadied his crosshair on Jason's forehead, from the roof of the mansion. The man's arrogant stance made Eugene want to pull the trigger that much more. All eyes turned to the woman. Lesh tensed up even more, as she saw yet another familiar face; the unfocused woman had just revealed herself. Goosebumps immediately covered Eugene's body, as tears uncontrollably ran down his cheeks when he saw the woman's scarred face. He could've sworn he was seeing a ghost. As his vision became blurry, he tried to convince himself that he must be mistaken. Eugene wiped his eyes with a shaky hand to try and clear his vision. He focused his scope on the woman, this time knowing he wasn't mistaken.

"It's Jen," Eugene said out loud to himself. He remained in position, still in shock from the woman standing in front of him. Eugene repositioned his scope to Jason, who smirked at Blague and turned around, making his way back toward the breach point. Eugene frantically stood up and threw his gun to rest on his back. He then sprinted to the stairs. He began to sweat profusely, in an unhealthy panic.

I gave up on her. I selfishly pronounced her dead, when she needed me most.

Eugene jumped down another flight of stairs, pushing people out of his way.

It must be some sort of sign. All of the dreams, all of the memories rushing back to me.

Narene looked over the balcony of her room when she heard all of the commotion. She got a glimpse of Eugene running frantically to exit the mansion. Gasping, she rushed over to the closest person she could find, trying to find out what was going on. Eugene opened the front door of the mansion.

Please be alright. Hold on Jen, I'm coming.

Blague looked back at Eugene, perplexed, as Eugene ran toward him in a panic. Sabin looked surprised and confused. He began to walk toward Eugene with his hands up, motioning for him to stop. Blague quickly realized what was happening and holstered his gun.

"Jason," Blague called, "she stays with us."

Jason turned around and shook his head. "Chaos has already ensued," he shouted back, "Embrace it."

Nemura looked confused as to why Blague had said that.

"Whoa, whoa, whoa, whoa," Sabin said, bracing for impact.

Eugene saw right through Sabin and almost knocked him over. The only way Lesh was going to stop him was to put a knife through his throat, so she stepped aside. Blague dashed to his right, stuck his arm out and grabbed Eugene. Eugene's momentum caused Blague's planted feet to slide back slightly. Dust was kicked up all around them. Eugene was unintelligible at the moment.

"Eugene, snap out of it. You know something's not right," Blague said.

Eugene wrestled frantically, as Jen walked further into the distance. Eugene unintentionally elbowed Blague in the jaw causing him to release his grip. Blague shook his head in reaction to the strike and looked up at Eugene, who was stumbling to reconnect with his past. Jason, Nemura, and Jen were handed their weapons and proceeded to make a sharp turn east. As Eugene began to catch up, the soldiers guarding the breach point tensed up in confusion, watching one of their commanders rush forward with no composure. Eugene screamed Jen's name, but no words came out of his mouth. The only thing he could hear was his heart beating through his chest. All of the years he spent with Jen replayed in his mind, including the last moment he saw her, when she was taken away in a boat and grasped for his hand. There she was with shorter hair and a few scars, but the same person he knew and loved.

"Jen!" Eugene finally yelled.

Nemura turned first, remembering Eugene's voice from his time with the Sins. The other two turned slowly, the screams were falling upon deaf ears. Eugene caught up with them and dropped to his knees in desperation. He looked down, then back up to the female hooded figure. Nemura drew a gun and pointed it at Eugene. Eugene's eyes widened. Seeing her face up close made it all the more real, but something was wrong. Her eyes were lifeless and unfocused.

Nemura laughed, "Why are you acting like a lunatic? That's so unlike your usual moodiness," he said, aiming the gun at Eugene's head.

Jason stepped forward, "Nemura, these two had a strong connection once. It has been felt. The fate of this meeting was determined as soon as we stepped foot on their soil."

"Jen, don't you remember me? What the fuck is going on?" Eugene yelled.

Nemura walked closer to him with a big smile on his face. "Asura, you mean? This is classic," he said as he laughed, "Was she your old sweetheart?"

Jen remained straight faced and unmoved.

"She's broken," Nemura said, getting in Eugene's face. "She doesn't feel anything. She's cold and loyal and lethal."

Eugene just kept staring at Jen in disbelief. Her scars looked like permanent tears streaming down her face, but her expression was stone cold.

"Do you know how I found her?" Nemura asked as his eyes glimmered, excited to inflict pain. "She was being raped mercilessly in a hut by Sin boat harborers."

Eugene shifted his bloodshot eyes to Nemura. He jerked his body and whacked Nemura in the face with the butt of his rifle and slapped the gun out of his hand. Nemura stumbled to the floor, holding his face, still laughing.

"Those scars on her face were still fresh, but her life was already taken from her. Five huge men were having way too much fun," Nemura recalled, not holding back any details. "By the look of Asura, it looked like they'd been at it for days. Hah, you should be thanking me, old buddy. I saved whatever was left of her!"

Eugene reached for his rifle, but Jason quickly appeared right in front of him, face to face. Jason put one hand over his face and yanked the gun from him with the other, the strap slapping Eugene in the face as the rifle was pulled from him.

"She's just a ball of rage who doesn't speak, but she believes in us and our enlightenment. Otherwise, she wouldn't follow us," Nemura continued.

Blague, Sabin, Lesh, and a few guards had their weapons drawn as they walked up to Jason. Jason motioned to Jen, who then picked up Eugene, flipped him onto the ground, and held a gun to his temple. Jason put his hands up, motioning to the approaching Sins to stop moving.

"There's no need for additional chaos. Your commander is mine. Concede," Jason commanded.

Nemura walked over to Eugene, "She looked kinda sexy naked and torn up."

Eugene jerked in anger, but Jen tightened her grip around his neck and pressed the gun harder into his temple.

"They were passing her around like a rag doll. I never liked you, even when we were on the same side. I don't know why Blague picked you as his right hand man, but that makes this all the more fun," Nemura said smiling.

"Back up," Jason said with no room for question, "We are departing."

"I could impale the bitch from here," Lesh said to Blague.

"Hold off, it's too risky. We're going to have to play this one out, unfortunately," Blague said.

Eugene, Jason, and his followers boarded a jet that had just landed.

"Are you with them, Jason?" Blague called out, recognizing the Hiezer-style jet.

"In no stretch of time," Jason called back, "We are the Aura, and now Eugene is a part of it."

Chapter 14

Blague walked into the mansion and continued toward Cherris' wagon on the main floor, not acknowledging anyone in between. Sabin and Lesh followed closely behind, all three of them trying to figure out how to best handle the situation. Sabin whipped out his tracking device. Lesh leaned over to see a small dot blink on and off the screen, traveling south at a very fast pace.

"That was a good throw," Lesh admitted to Sabin. "They didn't even notice what happened.

They're clueless about being tracked, kind of like how you were," he said as he looked over at her and smirked.

Lesh huffed and shot a death look back at him.

Cherris stared at Blague as he calmly walked over to her. "I know that look," Cherris said.

Blague stared into Cherris' eyes for a moment, not responding to her words. After a short pause, he began, "We have a new threat and they took Eugene. I'll explain shortly, but first, do you know of any pilots among our group?"

Cherris looked down to think for a moment, strands of her silver and blonde hair washed over her face as she thought. "No one comes to mind, but there's a good shot that Drino has one among his cadets."

Blague turned his head to Sabin and gave a nod to him. Sabin walked off to radio Drino.

Blague turned back to Cherris, "Have you heard anyone speak about a continent called Auront?"

Cherris shook her head.

Lesh walked forward and said, "Apparently it's an island very close to the Antarctic continents that has no ice and omits red smoke from the ground. Nemura babbled on about it when he held me for dead."

Cherris shook her head, "I've never heard of anything like that."

"Apparently that continent caused a man to permanently exist in an altered state. His name is Jason Brink, and he calls his group the Aura. We don't think he has any affiliation with the Hiezers, but we're not exactly sure. And we don't know how many followers he has," Blague said.

The sound of boots walking slowly echoed behind them. Then the sound of a cough echoed in three different tones simultaneously. "I may be able to help you," Niro said through his voice changer. "The island you speak of didn't have that name, but I've been exposed to it," he continued as he rolled up the cloth on one of his arms.

His veins were stained Cryos blue, which made it difficult for the others to focus on anything else. His covered face and smoky pupil-less eyes were focused on his arm.

Blague inspected it, "Your forearm is tinted the same wine red that Jason's whole body seemed to be."

Niro locked his eyes with Blague's, "I've endured

many years in the state that this man, Jason, is currently in. Each person reacts differently to it."

"This man fancies himself a god," Sabin said as he put down the radio.

Niro nodded, "I suppose that could happen. Memories that I had completely forgotten came back to me like they occurred just a moment ago. Time becomes incredibly warped in that state."

"Does one's intelligence rise in that condition?" Blague asked.

"Yes, unstably so. That island spawned from the quake years ago," Niro said with an echo, "It has been a hidden anomaly ever since. I suspect that the effect of that smoke will never truly leave me." Niro began to walk away, "But thankfully it does wane."

Everyone watched the strange man walk away with his cloth wrappings and old combat boots.

He turned his head, "I will accompany you, Blague, when you're ready." He turned back and continued to the stairs that lead to the roof.

Drino came walking up behind the remaining crowd, dragging a man by the hair. Drino stopped when he approached everyone and tossed the man to the floor. "This is the only pilot I can find, unfortunately," he said as he presented the disheveled man with his hand. The man rubbed the back of his head and hiccupped, looking angry. "This here is Oscin. He's a lousy cadet and an undisciplined shitbag, but apparently he can fly a jet."

Blague took a moment and then eventually nodded at Drino, "I guess he will have to do."

Drino nodded back, "I'm going to continue on with

my training session."

"Yes, carry on, thank you," Blague said dismissing him.

Lesh picked the thin man up by the collar with one hand and looked him in the eyes. "Pathetic. He's drunk during Drino's training and doesn't appear to have the strength to even push a lever on a jet."

Oscin swung at Lesh's face. She ducked it and punched him straight back to the ground.

"Well this is going to be an odd trip, it seems," Blague said.

"Are you sure it's a good idea to leave the mansion with two threats at large?" Cherris asked.

"For once, we are going on the offensive. I will entrust our home to the appropriate group in my absence, which includes the three of you. You must understand, my second in command is being held captive and we no longer have Briggs' expertise on our side. I have to keep the leadership of this group intact. I would do the same if it were any of you," Blague said as he extended his hand for Sabin to hand over the transponder. "Meet in my room for a strategic meeting in thirty minutes. After that, I'm departing," Blague finished.

Niro's demeanor is making it very hard for me to read him. At this point, I'm basing my faith solely on a good deed. He could be a part of Jason's crew, making him yet another mole within our ranks. My instinct says to trust him. Though, I wonder how much I can rely on such a feeling. Blague walked slowly up the stairs, his presence was felt as he passed through the civilians. *I'm without a doubt walking into some sort of trap by trailing Jason, but it's vital that I pursue this*

threat and return our commander to his home. Not an easy task
when a loved one bursts out of his past and begins trampling
over his present.

Blague's arm flexed at every grab of the railing, his
green eyes were in a thought-filled daze. He looked at the
mark on his arm, reminding himself that the Hiezers were
the bigger threat.

Jen beckoned Eugene over from the other side of the wall.

"Come on," Jen mouthed followed by a hand gesture.

Eugene quietly ducked down and snuck over to her,
holding a camera the size of his forearm. "I can't believe I'm the
camera boy for your suicide mission," he whispered to Jen.

She gave her usual big smile, her eyes lit up with
excitement. "It will all be worth it when I'm famous for
exposing these rats," she said quietly.

Jen kissed Eugene on the cheek and turned her head to
peek past the corner of the building. Hiezer guards were at
attention while a squad leader rambled on about purging Sins
who don't obey.

"A no tolerance policy is to be undertaken and a few
examples will have to be made in order to begin the
enforcement," the presenting Hiezer guard shouted.

"Are you getting all of this?" Jen asked.

"Just the audio," Eugene looked down at the video camera.

The buildings surrounding them were huge. The Hiezers
were gathered in an open street that was roped off from every
direction.

"Who's there?" a voice called from behind them.

Jen froze. Eugene put his camera away and drew a pistol.

"Jen!" Eugene hissed, "We have to move now!"

Jen remained frozen. Eugene shook her shoulder with his hand to snap her out of it.

"I heard something this way. Move," a voice said as it creeped closer.

"Jen!" Eugene said again.

Finally she jerked her head around one hundred and eighty degrees. Her face was a black shadow with no features. Eugene immediately backed away.

"No," he said to himself.

Jen's shadowed face became clear again, but appeared frozen with her mouth wide open and her teeth showing. Her eyes were large and unfocused; blood ran up and down her face. The sound of a scream shrieked, causing terror to flow through Eugene's body.

"Take them!" a voice said, only inches away.

Eugene turned around to the butt of a gun slamming him in the face.

He opened his eyes, gathering himself from the hazy memory. He felt the pulse of his temple beating, feeling like his head would explode. The jet hit some turbulence, causing Eugene's arms to pull in either direction.

I'm chained.

Eugene looked up to see his arms hoisted up, dangling. He looked back down to discover that he was shirtless.

Woken from another nightmare just to enter a living one.

A large metal door whipped open; Eugene caught a glimpse of thirty to forty people behind it.

Those few followers were Jason's back-up plan if things went wrong? I wonder how full of shit this guy is.

The lighting in Eugene's prison room was dim, although the whole room was visible. He woke up sweating from the nightmare; his dirty blonde hair was different shades of brown. He had a gash on the side of his head and some dry blood painted on his face. His small nose had sweat dripping off of the tip and his brown eyes looked pained as he tried to focus on Jason, Nemura, and Jen who just entered the room.

"Jen!" Eugene screamed in a strained voice. "We spent most of our adult lives together. How could you forget?"

Jen didn't flinch, her eyes remained dead. Nemura's devious smile widened as Eugene showed his desperation. He stood quiet as he watched Jason glide over to Eugene. Jason bent down and waved one of his hands around Eugene's face in an awkward manner. Eugene, already feeling dizzy, put his head down to keep from throwing up. Jason stabbed Eugene swiftly in the abdomen. Eugene gasped. The cut wasn't deep, but blood began pouring out of his stomach. Jason stared intensely with deep red eyes, cupping his hand to catch the blood.

"A message," Jason said while staring. He stabbed Eugene again, this time in the side. "You will be, a message," Jason said slowly. He shifted his blade vertically and stabbed a third time.

Eugene winced, trying to keep eye contact with Jason. He was starting to lose his vision again, but looked to Jen, who wasn't even paying attention to what was happening.

"Your eyes follow greatness, Eugene," Jason said. "She has been chosen as the next to be enlightened."

Eugene looked down at his three shallow bleeding wounds. The wounds resembled the symbol on their cloaks.

Branded twice in this life.

He looked up at his Cryos mark.

Both with no meaning.

"You're wrong. This mark has a purpose."

Eugene looked at Jason, shocked.

Did I say that out loud?

Jason stood up and pointed to Jen, who walked over and proceeded to cover the wound. The loss of blood mixed with the bash to the head drove Eugene to a new level of exhaustion.

"Look at me, Jen," Eugene pleaded, going in and out of consciousness.

Jen focused for a moment on Eugene's face.

She responded to her real name.

No sign of emotion was reciprocated. She rigidly bandaged up his abdomen and backed up, all while he was staring at her in disbelief.

"Your presence will not only increase the collective connection of Asura, but you will soon find your true purpose with her," Jason preached.

Eugene slowly faded out, losing consciousness.

Jeck and two other Hiezers followed behind Mulderan, walking hastily toward their facility in Faltier's Crest.

"Jeck, do we have an update on Blague's rebellion?"

Mulderan asked without turning his head.

"No, all has been quiet on that front, as expected. They were able to retain the Ayelan and our fortress. It seems they would have no reason to pursue us," Jeck replied.

Mulderan continued walking silently for a moment. He turned to Jeck, holding eye contact, "You haven't spent enough time with Blague yet to know we should have heard something by now?" Mulderan questioned pretentiously. "Something is off," he said out loud to himself.

"Would you like me to order another strike?" Jeck asked.

"No, I want them quarantined so they cannot expand further. We have to assume that his scientists learned to split the Ayelan at this point. With that assumption, we won't be able to bomb them, which would mean the loss of more men in close combat warfare. You're in charge of carrying out this order. Do not let them expand," Mulderan replied, locking eyes for a moment before facing forward again.

"Those Sins have the audacity to declare war on their providers," Jeck said with malice, "It will be my pleasure to stomp them out."

Mulderan raised an eyebrow, "The audacity comes from perspective and unfortunately, theirs is largely individualistic. To better their lives will not help our chances of survival as a race."

Faltier's Crest was the exiled continent that broke off from the Old United Kingdom. From the volcanic atmosphere, their boots became covered with black ash and dust as they proceeded to the remote facility, which was stationed far away from any Sin residents. In the distance, small houses could be seen lined up very closely to each other. Faltier's Crest was more developed than Senation; even within the classes, certain locations further separated the distribution of resources. Faltier's Crest had two volcanos in the horizon, accompanied by mountainous regions. It was ominously dark most of the time.

Mulderan turned to one of the Hiezers to the right of him. "Has my wife been adequately prepped for the procedure?" he asked.

"Yes, sir. Eldra is awaiting the shot as we speak," the Hiezer replied.

Mulderan nodded.

"Why don't we just cut off their food supply," Jeck thought out loud.

"I considered that myself," Mulderan stated, "but doing that will ultimately raise awareness and rally more Sins to Blague's cause."

Soldiers stepped aside as they entered the facility. Mulderan framed his eye with his fingers and the guards reciprocated. The facility appeared to be very high tech, with Hiezer symbols displayed throughout the rooms. A guard escorted them to a large open platform elevator, which lowered them underground. As they proceeded to their destination, guards quickly dispersed from Mulderan's path in a military fashion. Scientists were working on experiments in each room, mostly dealing with vials of different chemicals. The four Hiezers finally made it to the large room in the center of the facility. The room was molten orange to match the surrounding environment of Faltier's Crest. The ceilings were that of a cathedral, nearly sixty feet high; the golden Hiezer symbol of inverted waves crashing into a golden orb was at the center point of the ceiling. Mulderan's cloak swayed as he confidently and coolly approached his show. A woman was writhing with energy, trying to escape the machine that she was a prisoner to. She had mocha skin and a raging temperament.

"So is this how you get your kicks, highlord?" The woman said in a desperate, bitter manner.

Her British accent echoed through the room. Mulderan stared at her, unblinking and straight-faced. He shifted his gaze to his wife, Eldra, who leaned forward in a chair designed to administer the shot. She looked as if the process was taking too long, not at all phased by the twenty inch needle beside her. A scientist was swabbing her back.

"Eldra, are you prepared to take one step closer to immortality and to aid in preserving our species?" Mulderan asked very seriously.

"I'm prepared," she threw back in an icy tone.

"You're a sick bunch," the captive woman yelled out to them, still trying to break free from the contraption that kept her limbs stretched and spread out.

Mulderan nodded to the scientist next to the captive. The woman shook her head, experiencing the worst kind of fear.

"Don't murder me," she pleaded. Her Cryos mark shimmered on her thin arm. "I haven't done anything to deserve this."

Mulderan continued staring into her eyes, not shying away from his decisions. "It is your destiny to serve the greatest good, Melian," he said, unflinching.

The scientist next to Melian pulled the lever. A moment later she let out a blood curdling scream.

"Why? Stop!" she tried to form words through the agony.

Six needles punctured Melian's back, extracting her DNA and her life force. Mulderan showed no reaction to the woman's anguish. Eldra also leaned forward, emotionless. Her sniper rifle rested next to her, a black and gold masterpiece that was of high caliber and high quality grade. Eldra had long black hair and crystal blue eyes. Her skin was fair and her face was thin. Her exposed arms were thin, but toned. She was known as the Ice Queen amongst the lower classes. Her personality was befitting of Mulderan's. The cries of pain went on for another moment, making most of the Hiezers in the room uncomfortable. Finally the needles were retracted from Melian's back.

"It's over," she said calmly with a smile, gazing toward the ceiling.

She felt her heart cease and her vision went dark. Mulderan watched her head slump. He then shifted his eyes to the scientist and nodded. The scientist took the extraction and filtered what he needed in a connecting machine. He then took the vial of extraction to another platform next to the vial of Ayelan and began the synthesization process. Jeck was still uncomfortable from the moment past. He was headstrong and true to his beliefs, but still had somewhat of a conscience when it came to human suffering. Mulderan was so far removed from it all. He walked slowly over to his wife, his thin crown shining in the artificial, orange light. He held out his hand in a formal manner. Eldra reached out to grasp it, looking up at him without a smile.

"Join me in this extended quest. Don't lose sight of our purpose." Mulderan said, looking down at her.

His pauldrons exaggerated his regal image. A Hiezer scientist in a black robe walked up behind Eldra slowly. He held the twenty inch needle with a clear vial of shimmering, holographic Ayelan, mixed with the rare extracted DNA resting above it.

"The shot is ready to be administered," the scientist said.

Mulderan backed away, "Proceed."

Eldra didn't take her crystal blue eyes off Mulderan. The scientist jabbed the shot deep into her spinal cord. She let out a small grunt from the impact. A second later, her head jerked up and her eyes widened. Her blue eyes had orange iridescent light circling her irises. Her body then went limp.

"The process is complete," the scientist informed, "Long live the Hiezers."

Mulderan nodded and left the room.

Chapter 15

Blague walked confidently into his room, while his commanders, Cherris, Niro, and Oscin were all making their way to the fourth floor. He wore a tank top, exposing his bright, disheveled Cryos mark. He took a deep breath, formulating the best possible solutions for all of the mayhem that the group was experiencing.

I have to introduce some creativity to maintain the health of the Sins.

Blague unholstered his Desert Eagle and unsheathed his carbon blade. He set them down on the table and stood silently, waiting for everyone to arrive. Everyone took a seat around a large oval table made of rich, sparkling granite that was surrounded by leather chairs, all with gold designs imbued into the material. Niro walked in last; all eyes, including Blague's, followed him as he entered. He was by far the strangest of all of the eccentric personalities in the room. He walked toward the back corner behind Blague and leaned up against the wall, proceeding to clean his ancient rifle. Oscin held his head with one hand, struggling to focus on anything with the light beaming in his face. Drino pushed him from two seats over.

"Hung over or still drunk?" Drino asked, loud enough for everyone to hear.

Oscin shook his head, "You already called me out in front of the Sin fighters. Do you have to make your statement again, sir?" Oscin asked sarcastically.

Drino leaned back in his chair, "You should hope you don't make it back from wherever it is you're going, kid."

Lito, who was sitting between the two of them turned to Oscin with a smile, "Damn *mijo*, you should pick less deadly people to piss off."

Oscin glanced at Lito for a second, and then looked back down to continue holding his head.

Mars circled the table, gathering rubs from everyone who was seated.

"Whore," Sabin said as he folded his arms.

Cherris and Volaina laughed.

"Alright everyone," Blague said, holding back a smile from Sabin's comment.

"Where's Eugene?" Drino asked.

Blague held up his hand, signaling for him to hold off a minute. "My first in command has been drawn away and I choose these words very carefully. It seems we have a new threat that Lesh had forewarned may be coming," he gestured to Lesh who kept her eyes fixed on him. "Nemura, as most of you remember, has turned to the side of a new order, the Aura. This new order is led by a fanatical man who believes himself to be a god."

Cherris raised her hand.

"Yes?" Blague said.

"Nemura laughed at anything that was slightly farfetched, but he joined a group with a spiritual leader?" Cherris asked in a perplexed tone. "That doesn't add up at all," she continued.

"I agree," Lesh said, "but when I was chained up, listening to him and his crew babble about their beliefs, it became clear that Nemura believes in this man."

Blague nodded in agreement, "Both of your statements have truth in them. I have drawn a conclusion from Nemura's strange decision to join yet another underdog. This Jason Brink must have actually displayed some sort of supernatural power to convince his followers of whatever "truth" he preaches. I encountered him today and analyzed his behavior. He speaks in riddles partly to add to his mystery, but his motives are clear. He wants followers and a headquarters. That's one of the reasons he came to us today. He wants to recruit us for his cause. Knowing it was a shot in the dark, he opened up with his plan B. His plan A was to take a valuable commander of mine and begin the Sin group's descent into chaos," Blague said, addressing all members of the room by locking eyes with them. "Make no mistake; Jason Brink and the Aura are a secondary threat. Although we don't know the strength his group possesses, we can rest assured they don't have the resources that the Hiezers do. So, before I reveal my plan of action, I'd like to hear your thoughts on the situation."

Lito spoke up first, "When I went to patrol the back entrance to see if we were being ambushed, must've missed something. How the hell did Jason lure out a sniper from our roof?"

Sabin looked at Lito, brushing his beard. "It seems that the woman traveling with Jason and Nemura was Eugene's old girlfriend from when he was a Remdon. At least that's what I gathered from his crazed reaction," Sabin said shrugging his shoulders.

Lito shook his head, "So he ran into the enemy head on? Now he's their prisoner?"

Sabin nodded his head.

"Where do you think they went?" Cherris asked.

Sabin placed his transponder onto the table. "I tossed a tracking device onto the jet before they left," Sabin said turning his head to Lesh with a bratty smile.

Lesh shot back a look that could kill.

"It appears they're located near the mysterious island of Auront," Blague said.

"This is exactly what Nemura hinted at when he held me for dead," Lesh said.

Niro walked over slowly, his boots loudly thumping on the floor, looking at the transponder. "Those are the coordinates," Niro said, "They are undoubtedly on the island of Visitude." Niro stood next to Blague at eye level. "If you want your friend to remain in his current state of mind, I suggest you act quickly," he stared at Blague with his smoky eyes and then slowly walked back to his corner.

"Eugene coordinates many of our missions," Drino stepped in, "We need him back."

Blague stared at Drino, "Much like all of you, he is invaluable to me and more importantly, invaluable to the Sins."

Oscin chuckled quietly. Drino's nostrils flared and Lito's eyes widened as he smacked Oscin over the head.

Blague turned his attention to Oscin. "Speak up," Blague said.

Oscin coughed and pushed a few strands of hair out of his eyes, "How am I invaluable to you? I just got here."

Blague paused for a moment before responding, "It's not what you've done, it's what you're going to do."

Oscin looked down at the table, trying not to let the fear show.

"Alright everyone, unless anyone has further questions, it's time to reveal my strategy." The room was silent. "I will go through the plan in order of threat level. The Hiezers have been virtually silent for a few months. Although we aren't a high priority for them, we've successfully taken and held one of their fortresses; this means we're on their radar. Lesh and Volaina, you will infiltrate the Hiezers in Senation and acquire their plans from the higher ranks. Volaina, I want you to spy and Lesh, I want you to scout."

Volaina nodded.

"Ok, Blague, but we haven't gotten a chance to speak since my last scouting mission a day ago," Lesh said, tossing a recorder onto the table. "I have a lead into their plans," she pressed a button on the recorder.

"Why aren't we storming our facility and taking it back," one voice said through the recorder.

"Orders are orders, Rob. We can't let the Sins expand out further. So for now, we pick off any one of the Sins who thinks they can leave our fortress." The device blew some static and then stopped.

Blague looked down at the table for a moment, then looked up. His wavy, pushed back hair neatly stopped at his neck. The pupils of his piercing green eyes shrunk. "Mulderan knows my next step, but he doesn't know how we're going to achieve it. We must expand. Sins are still flocking to our cause and we must keep up the momentum."

Niro observed Blague from his corner, the cloth wrapped around his face rose on one side, mimicking a grin.

"So, Volaina, your mission doesn't change. Continue to spy. Lesh, you've already scouted it seems. It's time for you to clear a path so we can begin our expansion. The jets we've recovered from the Hiezers aren't safe to use yet, so I leave it to you to organize this mission."

Lesh didn't respond. The dark circles under her eyes made Oscin's glance at her short and fearful. Lesh eventually nodded at Blague.

"Ok, good. Now, for the Aura. I will lead the rescue of Eugene."

Cherris made a face, hearing the words again didn't resonate well with her. "You can't leave, Blague. We need a leader here in case of trouble," Cherris jumped in quickly.

"I entrust this room with collectively leading and maintaining our home," Blague responded. "My trip will be short. Drino, you will keep order amongst the Sin fighters."

Drino leaned back in his chair, "Of course."

"Cherris, you will keep the civilians calm and tend to their needs, as you always do," Blague continued.

Cherris gave Blague a worried look, but eventually nodded.

"Lito, you will keep our perimeters guarded and protected."

Lito nodded with a stern face.

"Sabin, you will ensure that overall operations are being performed accordingly."

Sabin raised an eyebrow, "If you say so, Blague."

"My missions will include myself, Oscin as my pilot, and Niro as intelligence," Blague said.

"Two wild cards to accompany you," Drino said, "That's very risky."

Niro didn't react to that statement.

"They are the best suited for the task at hand. I've already analyzed the risk I'm taking. Besides, I have full confidence in your collaborative efforts. Given Eugene's delicate emotional state, this mission has a strong potential to fail. Nonetheless, we must make an attempt. If nothing else, I will gain a clearer understanding of this new threat. When I return, we will gather all of the commanders, including the two in the field, and take vote to induct a new commander in an attempt to fulfill Briggs' role. Stay sharp, everyone. We will grow stronger from all of this," Blague concluded.

The jet landed harshly, jerking the corridor and jolting Eugene awake. In the distance, he heard footsteps exiting the aircraft. He felt like a truck had hit him, still woozy from the loss of blood. The large metal door swung open and in entered two familiar faces along with Nemura.

"Cut him loose and shackle his hands together," Nemura ordered.

Nemura brought his old crew into the Aura with him. I remember these guys from when they would stop by in between their scouting missions.

One looked at Eugene in fear, recalling his old commander. As the two henchmen got to work, Nemura paced back and forth.

"Intel has reached me, Eu," Nemura said, mocking Blague's nickname for him. His silver hair looked exceptionally wild. "A fallen Sin who you were pretty close with, I hear."

Eugene looked down and sighed, his face tensed up, feeling more pain.

"Briggs, that poor soul," Nemura said mockingly.

Eugene's arms fell to the floor as the men released his chains.

"I liked him better than you. It's a shame the Hiezers killed the wrong commander."

Eugene remained silent as the two men shackled his hands together in front of him with rope.

"Alright, you ex-military piece of shit," Nemura said, slapping Eugene's fresh wound. Eugene held back from grunting. "Let's move," he finished.

Jason pointed to Jen and named her as the next to be enlightened. I wonder if this has to do with what Lesh explained a few months ago. How much more can Jen endure? I already failed her once, leaving her to live the horrors of this world alone.

Nemura opened the door leading outside, the sunlight blinding Eugene's eyes. As they began to regain focus, a sea of hooded people came into vision. Jason was at the head of the group, displaying Jen as the next chosen one. Clouds of black and red smoke continued to rise into the air all around them. Eugene couldn't make out the words that Jason was shouting, but all of the followers raised their arms, reaching for the sky.

Nemura hit Eugene in the head, "Move it," he said, pointing to the stairs leading onto the stone terrain.

What a strange place this is, inhabited with even stranger people.

"Nemura," Eugene said in an exhausted voice, "this doesn't seem like your scene. I never took you to be this desperate."

"Hahaha, you'll soon see that Jason Brink possesses real power. Just wait!" Nemura replied excitedly. "You think he developed such a following by blowing smoke out of his ass?"

He does have a point. There must be at least five hundred followers crowded down there.

A brisk breeze hit them as they proceeded down the stairs. The air wasn't freezing, which was very odd considering they weren't too far from the South Pole. Eugene touched the ground with his hands; it felt like cement. The terrain appeared to be solid rock. The large group of followers lowered their arms and bowed. Jason promptly spun around, raised his cloak over his head, and began to drag Jen by the hand to the center stage. Eugene's heart began to race. No longer feeling exhausted, he stood upright, trying to nonchalantly keep tabs on the direction Jason was taking her in between the hundreds of hooded followers. They crossed what seemed to be a man-made bridge and shortly after disappeared into a massive cloud of deep red and black smoke. Nemura poked Eugene along, passing through the crowd of people. As he walked through, Eugene noticed the Aura symbol on everyone's cloak; what he didn't see was any signs of weaponry.

Is it possible they're unarmed? Maybe some kind of holy tradition? Where the fuck is he taking Jen?

Eugene, Nemura, and his two henchmen stopped at the head of the group where Jason and Jen were moments before. The surrounding followers began conversing with each other, exchanging thoughts and experiences about their journey to Auront. Eugene noticed that no one else had that odd red tint that Jason had. The group was a mix of all different types of people. Except for the hoods, they did not appear uniform or disciplined. Goosebumps ran up and down Eugene's arms as he heard a horrifying scream in the distance. He could recognize that voice anywhere; it was Jen's. This was the first time since he'd been reunited with her that he heard her voice. Eugene started to lose control, writhing in his rope.

Nemura pulled Eugene's hair back, "Calm down, she's not being tortured, too much." Nemura smiled and threw Eugene's head forward.

A second later, another loud shriek echoed through the group.

I can't let this happen again. I let myself think I was powerless in that situation years ago on that boat. Not this time. I got a second chance to make this right.

Eugene pulled the ropes back and forth with all his might, trying to loosen the knot. His face turned beet red as Nemura held a hand over his shoulder, reminding him that he's a captive. A moment later, a third scream radiated through the followers, making everyone uncomfortable. Chills ran down Eugene's spine; the sound of Jen's cries pushed him into frenzy. He thrashed until the ropes came undone, burning his arms as he wrestled free. He swung an elbow behind him, knocking Nemura in the face for the second time, and bolted toward the man-made bridge. Nemura held his cheek. This time he didn't laugh, realizing the gravity of the situation. Nemura's two henchmen proceeded after Eugene, who was now in full sprint.

Nemura yelled, "No! Do not enter the smoke of Auront; fall back!"

The two henchmen immediately halted, watching Eugene submerge himself into the cloud.

Lesh and Volaina began their mission together. They left in the midst of the night and wandered the far side of the rock path to avoid being scouted by Hiezer guards. The two of them trotted through the sand and gravel along the moonlit Atlantic Ocean, surveying for guards stationed to eliminate any Sins. The terrain was rocky, providing plenty of cover if need be.

"Do you have stories about quake?" Volaina asked in her Russian accent.

"I was dead when it happened," Lesh responded.

Volaina looked at her slightly confused. "That's an odd way to put it," she replied.

Lesh smiled in response.

I suppose I have to do my part in keeping the camaraderie up for Blague's sake.

"My late father shared stories when I was younger. That was the day that changed everything. The widespread panic brought out the worst in most people and the best in others. My father was one of the others." Lesh continued, her voice scratching along the way. "He brought in refugees to hide in the mountains, trying to gather food and support the helpless until the panic died down."

"Sounds like he was a good man," Volaina said sincerely, "I'm sorry for your loss."

Lesh shook her head, "He was a good man, but also a weak one. That weakness got him killed." Volaina stood silent. "My brother, who almost gave away our position back then, was cowardly enough to end my father's life. My father should have left my brother with tape over his mouth on the side of the mountain when he was born, but that life is dust in the wind now," Lesh said.

"I apologize to hear of such tragedy, Lesh. I've heard the stories from others," Voilana revealed, "but it carries real weight coming from you."

Lesh didn't respond to that. "What about you," Lesh said as she jogged, dashing in between the rocks.

"I was also dead when the quake occurred," Volaina said with a smirk. "Only by a few years though. My family was part of the war that erupted when the Hiezers assumed control. Half of Old Russia conformed, the other half were too prideful. It took the Hiezers ten years to fully occupy their power, longer than it took them to conquer any other continent," Volaina said.

"It sounds like you share that pride," Lesh said turning her head to look Volaina in the eyes.

"Heh," Volaina laughed, "I guess some Russian pride rubbed off on me. My family was captured and sent off to exile amongst different continents. I've been alone in Senation ever since. I was lost until Blague found my crew and I. That man's sense of purpose is infectious," Volaina said.

"Can't argue there," Lesh agreed.

Lesh slowed to a walk and put her hand out to slow down Volaina. Lesh pointed as she ducked down behind a rock. There were three Hiezer guards on the high ground with binoculars; the moonlight shimmered off the lens.

"Is your rifle silenced?" Lesh asked.

"Of course," Volaina replied.

Lesh motioned for her to hand it over.

"Please keep one helmet intact. That's my ticket into this unit," Volaina said.

"Their armor seems slightly different from the norm," Lesh said.

"These are elite guards," Volaina confirmed, "They have authority to kill on sight."

"That makes this decision even easier," Lesh said as she aligned her eye with the scope. "Let the expansion begin," Lesh beamed a flashlight behind her, signaling to her crew. Moments later, a team of Sins ran up behind them as Lesh took aim.

The smoke blinded Eugene for a moment, taking time for his eyes to adjust. Everything around him was shrouded in a deep shade of red. He began to feel lighter.

Something doesn't feel right. I'm losing feeling in my fingers.

Jen's scream echoed in Eugene's ears. He tried to follow it, but then the scream repeated as if the sound was being produced right next to him. Eugene fell to one knee and held his head.

What the hell was that? Am I hearing things?

Another shriek vibrated his entire body. He held his chest as he felt his heart beat through it. His whole body reverberated what felt like an earthquake.

I have to fight through this. I have to find Jen before it's too late.

Eugene stood up and proceeded forward. Another scream echoed from the east. Eugene changed direction and headed forward. Stone bannisters appeared on either side of him. He squinted, trying to see past the smoke. He attempted to grab onto one of the bannisters, but couldn't tell for sure if he was holding it. At this point, he completely lost feeling in his hands. His head felt as light as a cloud.

Am I hallucinating now?

The land in front of him began rising and falling like waves rippling through an ocean; the ground rose and fell ten feet high in a fluid motion.

Yep, I'm hallucinating.

Eugene walked forward slowly, trying to determine whether or not the ground was actually moving in front of him. His foot began to rise, so he jumped back. Jen's voice projected another scream. The voice echoed what seemed to be hundreds of times within just a few seconds.

Eugene's adrenaline was refueled by the thought of Jen's desperation. He sped forward, trying to time the movement of the ground in an attempt to not be thrown into the air. He found himself running downhill, just a few feet away from the moving mountain in front of him. He tried to concentrate on keeping pace, but mistakenly looked down to find faces on the floor staring up at him, with red eyes and deep frowns. Eugene lost his footing and toppled over. The downhill quickly morphed into an uphill. The swift movement of the ground launched him into the air. His face was covered in the red smoke. He floated for what seemed like minutes, not being able to find solid ground. Noises were constantly sounding in his ears. It sounded like flies buzzing and random xylophone tones speeding up around him, driving him mad. Eugene rolled on his back in midair, clenching his head with his hands, squeezing his eyes tightly shut. When he opened them, he saw Jason's face and upper body exposed; thin red capillaries and veins decorated him. His eyes were bloodshot and bulging, and his expression was psychotic.

He bared his teeth, "You are in my world now, Eugene," his voice echoed through him. "My eyes are on you. I am omnipresent within the smoke of Auront. The universal force has chosen me to connect the worthy, to create harmonious thought. That is the next evolution of this race."

Eugene stared up at the floating body in disbelief. Jason's neck extended forward.

"Now stop interfering!" Jason shouted, the wind from his voice pushed Eugene back to solid ground. "Your connection with Asura will be renewed in time,"

Jason said sternly. "Now, sleep."

Jason jutted two fists forward. What looked like capillaries flew toward Eugene and rained down upon him. He covered his face and found himself passing out while being punctured by countless needles.

This is all an illusion. It's just a chemical, just a drug. Snap out of it Eugene, snap...

Blague boarded one of the Hiezer jets that they were able to restore from the battle. He watched Oscin proceed to the cockpit, while Niro stayed toward the back of the plane and watched them both. Oscin felt right at home as soon as he sat down in the pilot's seat. He seemed to operate the plane's equipment intuitively.

This kid's confidence seems to be somewhat justified. Another calculated gamble.

Blague turned to Niro, "This operation is going to be carried out under your directive. You're the only one who can navigate this island."

"It's far more complicated than that," Niro responded. "You have to survive the island without losing your mind," he continued through his voice changer.

Niro looked down, recalling the horrors he had experienced. Blague took some time to digest that. Oscin took flight, lifting the Hiezer jet straight up. Blague looked out a window, seeing his commanders conversing as they watched the departure.

I've inspired confidence in them to lead in my absence. They won't let me down.

A faint sound passed into the darkness, drowned out by a deep sleep.

Get up, Eugene, get up!

As the sound of a woman's scream intensified, Eugene's eyes quickly opened. He tried to get up, but realized he couldn't move his body. He then tried to move his head, but couldn't.

Sleep paralysis. This smoke is poison.

Another murderous scream pierced through him like a knife. Frustrated, Eugene concentrated on moving one limb at a time. He saw cloudy spirits colored bright red fly by him. Lightning flashed just a few feet above him, causing his body to jerk.

"Eugene!" The loudest of all screams reached Eugene's ears.

Jen had called out his name. His thoughts became still, his focus was sharpened, and his anxiety subdued. He struggled to get up and eventually gathered enough energy to sprint toward the cry for help. The air he ran through made red waves, as if he were swimming through water. The red shadows his body cast glowed around him. The smoke in front of him began to solidify and fall to the ground like glass. In the distance, he saw a red silhouette of two bodies. As the smoke fell around him, he felt the pain of glass slicing his arms. The smoke cleared in the distance, as if he was reaching the end of a tunnel. Eugene slowed his sprint to a cautious walk, as he saw Jason hold Jen's head into a live geyser. The ground around it rumbled and smoke spewed from its center. Jason flexed his arm and held Jen's face close to the precipice of the geyser, fighting the force of the blasting smoke. Jen screamed as loud as she could. She tensed her arms and held on to the outer points of the spout. The flow of smoke stopped as Jason pulled her head back and tossed her to the floor by the hair.

"It is done, Asura. Awaken in your new form," Jason said in an ominous tone.

Eugene lunged forward, but at that point, Jason had already faded away into the smoke surrounding the geyser. Eugene slid over to Jen and held her. He lifted her head with his hand, gazing at her, looking at her scars and the deep red tint that was now painted onto her body. Her veins were jutting from her neck and temple, reflecting the trauma she had just endured.

"Jen! Wake up, Jen!" Eugene cried in desperation. He put his head to her chest and checked her pulse. She was alive, but unconscious. He shook her gently. "Come on, Jen. We have to get out of here. Wake up!"

Eugene looked around to see if he was still hallucinating. Shapes were forming in the smoke and everything around him was swaying in unison. Jen moaned slightly and eventually opened her eyes. To Eugene's shock, they were bloodshot and now brown mixed with a deep red hue. She put her hand up to Eugene's face and held it.

"Eugene," she said smiling, "every bone in my body is saying that I've missed you, but I can see in my mind that we were just together, chasing Hiezer stories and living together," she said.

A tear escaped the corner of Eugene's eye. He hugged her tightly, "I've missed you too, Jen," he said tensing up from the rush of emotions. "Do you remember our quarters? Do you remember cooking dinner and enjoying our life together? Do you remember when we first met?" he asked.

"Of course, Eugene, but are we not still living that life? Didn't we just have breakfast this morning?" Jen asked, confused.

Eugene looked puzzled.

Please don't tell me this is a dream. She's right here in front of me, I can feel her.

"Jen, what did Jason just do to you? He kept speaking about becoming enlightened."

Her brow tensed for a moment and she tried to stand up. Her blonde hair now had wine red tips, and her hands, now a shade of deep red. She held her head in pain. "It was agonizing. He held my face in the center of a smoking hot geyser and let it erupt over and over again. Now everything is different. I can't explain it," Jen said.

"Try to relax," he said, "I'm not going anywhere without you."

Jen flashed a pained smile at him and put her arms out for a hug. Eugene reciprocated and lifted them both up to stand.

This moment is surreal. I never thought I would be able to feel this way again.

"I'll never let you go again, Jen," Eugene promised.

"Why are you saying these things? It's ok, I'm right here," she replied.

Eugene looked down at her.

She seems not to remember much of the current chain of events.

Just then, Jen pushed Eugene back and grabbed her hair. She fell to her knees and moaned. Eugene reached forward, but she shook her head. Eugene looked at her with terror in his eyes.

What the fuck is happening now?

Jen moaned again and then screamed frantically, "Get off! Get the fuck off of me!"

Oh my god, she's reliving the nightmare Nemura told me about. Fuck, I was hoping that wasn't true.

"Ahh!" She kicked and yelled frantically. She looked up at Eugene with her bloodshot red eyes, furious. "Why are you letting this happen to me?" she screamed at him.

Fuck, there's nothing I can do. It's inside her head.

"Eugene, how could you?" she moaned and screamed and tossed around the floor.

"Jen, snap out of it! That happened long ago!"

She got up and ran as fast as she could into the smoke; she tore at her body to get rid of the feeling of unwanted hands touching her.

Eugene ran after her, "Jen! Don't go that way!"

I can't let her run back to Jason.

Chapter 16

"The radar shows a large group of people gathered on the northern part of the island," Oscin said as he displayed the populated area on the map to Blague.

Niro slowly walked over to the cockpit.

"Do not let them hear or see our jet. Take the longest route to circle the island in order to get to its southern side," Blague said as they both gazed out the front windshield. He turned to Niro, "I need your guidance on a safe landing point that's out of their sight."

Niro looked at Blague, "The central geyser is the key to this island and it's located northwest of here," Niro said pointing to the area on the radar map. "We want to land on the western side if our enemy is on the northern. Be prepared. It's a different world down there," Niro warned.

"I'm prepared to deal with this island," Blague said.

"We will see," Niro responded.

"Annnd what will I be doing?" Oscin questioned.

"Keep the gatling guns on this jet armed and defend the jet with your life," Blague said.

"With my life, huh?" Oscin said sarcastically.

Blague gave Oscin a grin as he leaned toward him, "Maybe you didn't learn from Drino's beatings, which is fine, but I understand how people think and what makes them tick," Blague continued as he reached to the inner side of the pilot's seat. "If you're not with us, Oscin, just let me know and I'll drag you out onto the island at gunpoint and leave you there," he said calmly as he pulled out a flask of booze that Oscin was hiding.

Oscin sank down into his seat.

"You'll get this back eventually," Blague said as he stuffed the flask into one of his pockets. "I'm not asking you to respect authority. I understand that it's not in your nature to do so. A mutual understanding between us is all I need."

Oscin hesitantly looked over at Blague, whose hand was extended.

"We both want to strive for a better life, right? Why else would you have sought refuge with our group?"

Oscin eventually nodded and shook Blague's hand. "Prepare for landing, you guys," Oscin said, reeking of alcohol.

Niro gazed out of the window, mesmerized by the familiar terrain and the endless clouds of smoke. "Get ready, Blague. I can already hear the screams," Niro said.

Oscin flipped a lever and guided the jet to a precise vertical landing.

Before hitting the ground, Niro swung open one of the gates. "Let's go," he said, seemingly in an intense rush.

Blague jogged over just as Niro jumped from the jet. His cloth wrappings flapped in the wind as he dropped thirty feet to the ground. Without flinching upon landing, Niro began sprinting toward the smoke. Blague waited another moment for the jet to land and then raced to catch up with him. As he began running, he could hear the echo of a thousand screams. The climate was as confusing as he expected. The brisk breeze was masked by an odd humidity. Niro passed into the smoke, fading away as he entered. Blague had his reservations, but couldn't let them hold him back. As Blague submerged himself into the smoke, Niro was standing there.

He put a hand on Blague's shoulder, "In here everything is different, Blague. It seems the man you spoke of has taken control of this island by embracing its power. Let me deal with him. Whatever you do, find your friend and get him to the jet," Niro's voice changer echoed amongst the screams; they sounded like the cries of spirits rising to the sky, dispersed in every direction.

Blague stopped to analyze his surroundings. A red haze filled the air, clouding his vision. He stared at Niro's smoky pupil-less eyes and eventually nodded. Niro plunged forward, disappearing into the smoke. Blague attempted to follow, but sinkholes began to form, shrinking the ground around him. He found himself cornered by large, gaping holes of nothingness. He dove to the remaining land mass in front of him, which began to spin. Blague closed his eyes for a moment, understanding that it was all a hallucination. He reopened them with a tense brow.

I've already experienced hell. It doesn't matter what new form it takes, I can get through this.

Blague walked forward into the nothingness, not letting his mind accept that the ground disappeared. He didn't fall. As he tried to concentrate on maintaining his grasp on reality, spirits began rushing past him. Their faces were decrepit and distorted. Blague did his best to ignore the incoming attacks. The spirits slashed through him, fading into the air behind him. One spirit stared him in the eyes, smiling with sharp teeth. As it grabbed Blague's attention, it then slashed his right arm. Blague looked down in shock to see blood exit from the wound, but then float upward into the air. Blague drew his carbon blade and met the distorted figure's next strike.

This isn't real, don't give in. The more you participate, the deeper your mind will succumb to this illusion.

The spirit struck low; Blague met the strike out of instinct and slashed its face. A shrilling scream echoed in the distance.

That sounded real. That's where I should be headed. I'm on my own now, since Niro faded onto his own path.

Four more spirits charged out of nowhere. Blague extended his arms to either side and didn't brace for impact, convincing himself that it was all falsity. He saw a bluish glow emanating through the smoke. The glow became brighter as a figure began to materialize, charging straight at him. Startled, Blague raised his blade and began to swing, only to hold back at the very last moment upon seeing Eugene's desperate face charging at him. Blague side stepped and tripped him.

Eugene caught himself on what seemed to be air and sprung himself back upright. Staring at Blague in confusion, "Another hallucination?" Eugene asked himself out loud.

Blague sheathed his blade and grinned between the mist of red smoke. "Not this time, Eu," Blague said.

He has no rifle and seems as confused as I am. That's enough to convince me that he's not an illusion.

Blague put his hand on Eugene's shoulder, "I've

come to bring you home."

Eugene looked down for a moment. Blague immediately knew what Eugene was about to say.

Eugene looked up, "I can't go home yet. I've got to save Jen. Every moment I stand idle is too long," he said in despair. "Your fight is my fight, Blague. You know this, but right now I have to get Jen back."

Blague gave a nod, "The Sins need you. Let's get your partner back and get the hell out of here."

Another shrilling scream echoed past the both of them.

"Is that her?" Blague questioned.

Eugene nodded.

"Ok, this way," Blague said.

In the dark, Milos sat in Cherris' wagon. His arms rested over his knees and a small puddle of blood formed in front of him, dripping from his knuckles. Cherris opened the curtain to see that Milos was the only kid left sitting there.

"Let me take those broken shackles off of you," Cherris said as she took a step into the wagon.

She was startled when she noticed the blood, but tried not to react.

"No," Milos responded curtly, "they are a reminder that I'm weak and not at all ready."

"Ready for what?" Cherris asked kindly.

"To fight," Milos said looking up at her.

Cherris knelt down next to him, "There's more to do than fighting."

"I used to think that," Milos responded politely, "but ever since that day, it seems that all we do is fight or get ready to fight."

"I know it might seem that way, but life is so much more than fighting the next battle. Just promise me you won't lose sight of having fun and being a kid once in a while," Cherris pleaded.

Milos sat silently for a moment. "Do you have tape for my hands?" he asked.

Cherris looked worried, "Sure."

Milos got up and followed her. She wrapped up his knuckles, and then he proceeded up the stairs to Lesh's empty room. Kentin watched Milos from the main floor as he walked up the stairs with his head down and his fists clenched. The severed shackles rattled with every step. He slammed the door shut and started whaling away at the punching bag, focusing his thoughts on every time Lesh had knocked him down.

I have to get stronger. I can't let anyone else die.

He hit the bag harder, wildly swinging his fists. Tears began to well up in his eyes from the pain, blinding his vision.

"I love you Milos," his mother's face appeared in his head, followed by her warm embrace.

The image was fleeting, the winds of his mind were blowing it away. He began to calm as he recalled his training with Lesh; his punches started to become more intuitive and accurate. The tape now had red stains plastered all over it. He imagined an adult body and began to strike it effectively.

Lesh said that I have to make up in precision what I lack

in strength. When she comes back, I'll be stronger.

A knock on the door was drowned out by his thoughts. After a few minutes, the door swung open. Kentin walked in and shut the door behind him.

"Why didn't you show up to my dad's funeral?" Kentin asked.

Milos stopped hitting the bag and looked at Kentin; sweat was dripping down his raggedy hair. Thoughts from every angle were racing through his head for the past few months, but none of Kentin and Briggs.

Milos paced over to Kentin slowly with his head down. "I'm sorry, Kentin. I haven't been ok since what happened with my mother. And I've been feeling even worse since what happened with Felik."

Kentin walked closer to Milos and gave him a hug. "I know how you feel. It's ok," Kentin said. "It's been years since I've seen my mom. I forgot how sad it is to lose someone," Kentin said before breaking the hug. "We have to help each other, Milos. Neither of us have anyone anymore."

How is Kentin able to talk so much and remain upbeat after his father died?

Milos put up a shackled fist and said, "Deal."

Kentin met his fist with his own and smiled.

"Lesh has been showing me how to defend myself. Do you want me to teach you?" Milos asked.

Light returned to Kentin's eyes. "Yes!" he exclaimed.

Kentin's brow tensed for a second and his eyes looked fearful, "Wait, did you say Lesh?"

Milos nodded.

"She is frightening," Kentin recalled.

"She's mean, too. Don't worry though, you won't have to deal with her. I'll just show you when she's not around," Milos responded. Milos put up his fists, "Let's begin."

Maybe I can still be the conqueror one day. Maybe I'm not rotten.

Lesh crawled to the top of the sand hill and carefully slid the Hiezer bodies down the slope. She had to time the shine of the lighthouse patrol; the semi-circle swing of the light included a sensor that could register any motion. Volaina grabbed the bodies at the bottom of the hill. She quickly mix-and-matched undamaged parts of their armor and equipped herself. Lesh beamed her flashlight to the rogue team taking cover behind the rocks. They began to advance through the beach to the next checkpoint. Lesh ducked the light that shined past her as Volaina ran up the hill to meet her.

"Godspeed," Volaina said as she extended her hand to Lesh.

Lesh reciprocated, "Good luck. I'll be careful not to radio you and break your cover, but let me know if they're on to us."

Volaina nodded and sprinted off to infiltrate the guards. Now that Volaina was on her way, Lesh realized that the mission had just evolved into a speed operation. She became more focused, analyzing the Hiezer patrols ahead.

I have to lead this group to the transport jet before the Hiezers notice something's amiss. Time to ramp this mission up.

Lesh slid halfway down the hill and began to sprint at an ungodly pace. She beamed her flashlight for the team to keep up. A group of shadows emerged from the rocks and proceeded down the beach. Lesh spotted the next group of guards and sprinted back up hill. She dislodged two knives from her ring and kept them between her fingers. As soon as the light from the lighthouse passed, she flipped over the top of the hill with one hand and swung the two knives with deadly force. Before they could land, she unsheathed two more knives. A knife connected; one of the guards grasped at his throat. The sound of gurgling alerted the two other guards of the threat. She hurled another knife, piercing a guard right below the neck. She spun to gain force and flung another, piercing his heart. Without skipping a beat, she sprinted over to the remaining conscious guard who was desperately reaching for his radio. Lesh took a step and lunged toward him, stabbing him in the stomach. She stared him in the eyes while digging deeper into his flesh, the lesion causing the radio to drop from his hand. As soon as it did, she flipped her legs around his neck and snapped it for good measure. Noticing the patrol light was quickly making its way back toward the top of the hill, she flipped off of the dead guard, reclaimed her knives and kicked the bodies down the slope. She saw her shadow rapidly changing direction, and so she dove off the cliff a split second before the light shined on her. Lesh hit the gravel, rolling into a graceful summersault, and quickly regained her footing. She beamed the flashlight toward her team and continued sprinting as if nothing had happened. Lesh continued a similar routine three more times. She regrouped with her team before proceeding to the lighthouse. She took a quick scan of the group, noticing most of them were out of breath.

Is this fear? Or just poor physical condition? Drino has to continue toughening these people up.

"Listen up, everyone. I don't usually carry out my operations with a team, but this is a special circumstance. Once we shift west around this lighthouse, the transport jet hanger is about ten miles into Clestice. Once we're in the city, the Hiezers will not suspect us as part of Blague's group, so long as we stay scattered. Everyone has a map, so stay on course and protect the builder," Lesh said as she pointed to him. "I'm responsible for getting you in the air. You're responsible for following my direction. Let's go," she finished while turning around and sprinting off.

She began climbing the rocks, dashing from one to the other, making her way to the front of the lighthouse. She looked back quickly.

How does Blague deal with this shit? They're moving like snails.

She looked forward to see two heavily armed Hiezer guards protecting the entrance. She knew that she would have to make quick work of them before her team fumbled to the entrance. Lesh gripped two spread out rocks with her hands. With great force, she propelled herself upward, drawing the attention of the guards.

"There! An intruder!" a guard shouted in the distance.

Lesh threw a knife straight from her ring, impaling one of the guard's legs. Gunfire erupted; the guards struggled to pinpoint their target. Lesh leapt, extending one leg over her head, planting her foot on the rock wall next to her, and pushing off. Her trajectory was arced as she side flipped in the other direction. She reached toward her knife ring, swiftly releasing two knives while in mid-air. One of the guards grunted as he lost his footing and toppled over at the same time Lesh landed. The other was trying to steady his aim with a knife sticking out of his side. One of Lesh's squad members, who finally made it to the top of the rocks, crouched there, watching her in action. As Lesh landed from her flip, she unsheathed another knife from the top of her ring and flung it overhead, cleaving the guard's skull. His head jerked back as his hands went limp, causing his gun to drop. She dashed around to reclaim her knives. She then tossed one of the guard's guns to the member who made it to the lighthouse entrance.

"Try to keep up," she said, as she sprinted off again.

The Sin fighter was stunned. Lesh gazed into the distance as she ran as fast as she could, noticing the rundown huts that populated Clestice. She put her hood up, preparing for the journey into the city.

Blague and Eugene wrestled through what seemed like endless smoke. The screams echoed in every direction as Blague attempted to follow the source. The sound of chanting filled the air. Eugene extended his hand to the floor, trying to keep his balance as his surroundings continued to change. Blague looked back at Eugene and motioned forward, noticing shadows in the distance. The two men stumbled forward and came to a stop, both of them breathing heavily from their struggle through the distorted island. To their dismay, Jason was floating in the air, tilted toward Jen, who had her hand up. She had fallen to the stone floor and lay there with one hand up, pleading for Jason to stop. Jason's red eyes were glowing. He was shirtless with the same bulging red veins and capillaries as when he first appeared in front of Eugene. Jason's full head of brown hair was thickly clumped into large strands, all with deep red tips; his features were oddly exaggerated in this form.

"You have been enlightened, Asura. Our minds must merge to increase our collective being. We must create a harmonious thought. Evolve with me," Jason preached.

His mannerisms looked as though he were experiencing a hallucination as he continued to preach. Eugene ran forward, charging Jason, and Blague ran toward Jen. Eugene jumped and tried to grab Jason out of the air, but it was no use; it was as if he were a mirage. Eugene flew right through him, scraping himself on the floor as he landed. Jason projected his veins toward Jen; they crawled off of his body in rapid motion. His eyes rolled to the back of his head and he bore his teeth. Jen screamed as his veins pierced her, but no blood was drawn. Blague drew his Desert Eagle and fired at Jason's image. The bullets whizzed through his smoky body, creating holes that quickly closed. Immediately realizing it was pointless to fight Jason in his current state, Blague scooped up Jen and headed toward Eugene.

"Eu, get up. We have to get out of here now!" Blague

yelled.

Jason's body shifted towards them, as he whipped his red veins at them, which were glowing with energy. The sounds they made were loud and debilitating. One whip wrapped around Blague's arm. He drew his carbon blade and attempted to cut it. His swings past right through the phantasmal strings, still grasping firmly onto his arm.

"They're all hallucinations. We just have to run and get away from the smoke!" Blague shouted at Eugene.

Jen shrieked in agony, feeling impaled from Jason's spikes. Jason began to advance closer to the three of them, who were all quickly losing stamina. As Jason reached for Blague, a flash of light jerked everyone back. Jason let out a deep scream as his veiny, red arm fell to the floor and dissolved into the smoke. Niro appeared in front of them. His smoky eyes were wide and his clothes were different than the norm. His cloak was now black with strange designs embroidered into the cloth, which covered most of his body. He turned away from Jason and in the blink of an eye, Niro slashed all of the energy whips with one swing. The sword he wielded appeared to be from ancient times, similar to his rifle. Niro quickly faded into the smoke as Blague stared at him with intrigue. Another flash of light lit up the sky. Niro fell from thin air, his cloak rippling in the wind, as he slashed Jason's shoulder at lightning speed, tossing him to the ground.

Niro landed and dashed to slice Jason again. He then turned to Blague and Eugene, "This is all just Jason's projection, using the winds of this island to gain control over you. Run."

Niro turned to Jason, who was now recovering from the wounds.

"Another test of chaos. How amusing," Jason said as he let the veins from his torso shoot at Niro.

Niro faded back into the smoke, dodging the incoming projectiles. Eugene threw Jen over his shoulder and began to follow Blague back to the jet. Niro reappeared behind Jason and slashed him from the neck down to the hip, and then faded back out of existence. Jason screamed as he was cut down.

As Eugene and Blague ran for the jet, Eugene turned back when he heard the scream, "Glad to have him on our side."

Blague's eyebrows went up, "Definitely. He's obviously been here before."

Eugene nearly tumbled when a stone wall rose from the ground to block their path. Another wall shot up from behind them.

"This way," Blague said, trying not to let the obstacles slow them.

In the distance, Blague saw what looked like Elaina, reaching for him. Blague's brow tensed.

Don't be tempted, it's all hallucinations.

Blague shook his head and continued on, the image of her floated away from him, breaking into a thousand pieces. A third wall shot up, enclosing the pathway they were treading on. Blague's parents materialized in front of it. A shadow of his mother opened her arms for a hug and his father smiled like he did every time he saw Blague. Eugene slowed down, but Blague sped up.

"It's all a facade," Blague said to himself as he

charged the wall.

"What are you doing?" Eugene screamed. His voice tapered off in the distance as Blague sprinted ahead.

Blague put one shoulder forward and broke straight through the wall. The pieces fell up into the sky instead of to the floor. Confused, Eugene shrugged and kept running. Oscin quickly dropped his feet from the dashboard and screwed back the top of yet another flask. He fired up the jet as soon as he saw Blague, Eugene, and Jen emerge from the smoke. Jen snapped back to consciousness and violently clawed at Eugene's back. Eugene held on tight, wincing as they made their way to the jet. Oscin lowered the entrance dock so that they could board. Jen flipped off of Eugene's shoulder just a few steps away from the jet. Her eyes were unfocused as she stared at the sky. Eugene reached for her, but she clawed him away and backed up.

She looked up at him with red eyes and an angry face, "You can't take me, Eugene. I'm not yours to take!"

"Come home, Jen," he begged, "We can figure it out there."

"You, Jason, and Nemura will all die at my hand," Jen said, staring at him with angst.

Blague remained silent on the jet's loading dock, witnessing more of the psychosis that Auront had to offer. She screamed and held her head, then looked back up at Eugene with recognition.

"I'm sorry. We'll find each other again," Jen said, then turned and sprinted back into the smoke.

"No!" Eugene shouted, running after her. "Blague, I'm sorry, I can't come home."

Blague gazed into the opera that was playing out in front of him.

This is Eugene's path. I understand now.

He turned away as the jet entrance closed. Blague entered the cockpit and put a hand on Oscin's shoulder. "We have to wait for Niro."

Oscin looked at him, drunk and confused. "He got here before you did," Oscin said as he pointed to the back of the jet.

Niro was posted up against the wall, his smoky pupil-less eyes darted back and forth. He remained in a trance as the jet took off.

Until we meet again, Eu.

Lesh perched up on the roof of a tall hut, hooded and hidden from sight. The windy city was quiet, making the operation more difficult to complete unnoticed. Lesh counted her team members as they passed by, spread out and on a path to the transport jet. She leapt to the next hut roof, swiftly climbed down into an alley way, and dashed through the garbage and homeless people. She slowed her speed as she reached the sidewalk, falling in line next to a hooded ally.

The cloaked man turned his head, "You put on quite a show back there, sweetheart," Morn said, "You got the people glad they're on your side."

"So glad I can inspire," Lesh said sarcastically.

"Heh, you really think this plan is going to work?" Morn questioned.

"These are the next steps. I trust Blague's judgement

and you should too," She said.

Morn chewed on a toothpick and swung it to the other side of his mouth, "I reckon that guy has done alright by us so far."

Lesh didn't respond to the obvious. "Did you pass your old store?" she asked.

Morn looked down for a moment, "Yeap, it was all boarded up. I guess the owner wants too much rent for a new one. That dumb prick ain't got no sense. He's missing out on coins every day."

"If this expansion works, you can start trading among the Sin community again," Lesh said.

"I'm counting on it," Morn agreed.

"We have a mile or so until we reach our destination. Is the terminal usually heavily guarded at this time?" she asked.

Morn shook his head, "No, but we've put the guards on high alert, so we should expect the unexpected."

"It's only a matter of time until the Hiezers realize that a quarter of their elite guard is missing, unless Volaina can stall," Lesh said. She picked up her radio, "One mile due south is our destination. Once the jet hanger becomes visible, take position to fire. And protect the builder at all costs," Lesh said releasing her finger from the radio button.

"I hear the two scout commanders are being pulled from the field," Morn said.

"That's true," Lesh responded, "You'll meet them when we get back."

"Lesh, we have trouble at the gate," her radio went off.

Lesh and Morn exchanged a look before they sprinted to the terminal. Lesh broke away from Morn and flipped onto the side of a building, scaling the roof to get a clearer view. Morn took the back alley in an attempt to stay hidden.

"I know you're here," an Australian accent amplified through a megaphone. "We've got one of your rats!" the voice boomed, "A Sin rebel. Can you crawl any lower?"

From the roof, Lesh had a clear view of a young Sin fighter fidgeting, while one large arm was wrung around his neck and a pistol held to his head.

"Are you scouting?" the voice asked, waving the megaphone from left to right to project his voice as far as possible. "Or are you planning a takeover?"

"It's just me," the captured fighter said, grasping for breath.

The Hiezer guard knocked him in the face with the megaphone. "Shut up, boy," the guard said.

All of Lesh's squad members got into position, silently aiming their weapons, waiting for orders.

The guard put the megaphone back up to his mask. "You know being a Sin rebel is punishable by death, right?" The guard's accent projected as he cocked his pistol and repositioned it on the young fighter's temple.

Morn's face turned red as he kept his eyes on the young fighter. "Those pieces of dog shit," Morn said out loud to himself, spitting as he spoke.

Lesh faintly heard Morn speaking from the building beside her.

That southern idiot is losing his temper at the worst possible time.

"Hold your fire," Lesh whispered through the radio.

Morn stomped forward to the front gate with his revolver drawn and his face beet red and shaking. "Hey! Hey, guard!" Morn said, waving his gun in the air.

"Stand down," Lesh said through the radio.

Lights shined on Morn's face, highlighting his greasy, curly hair. "Take me, you pussy!" Morn yelled in his southern drawl, "He's just a fucking kid!"

"That's the jewelry store owner," another guard said to their sergeant.

The guard acknowledged as he held on to the squirming boy. He pressed the button on the megaphone, "Shouldn't you be in bed, hotshot?"

"Let the boy go!" Morn yelled, ignoring the guard.

"This here is a traitor," the guard said, pressing the pistol to the boy's head.

The jet hanger was visible in the distance, beyond a dirt road. Hiezer guards were lined up in front of a few transport vehicles, guarding the area. Lesh stalked closer on all fours, moving seamlessly to try and get within throwing distance to save the fighter.

"Swap the boy for me!" Morn demanded again.

"You mean nothing. This boy is part of an uprising and my orders are now to kill on sight! And since he seems to be alone, I have no more use for him."

The guard looked at the fighter while his trigger finger tensed. Morn raised his revolver to point at the sergeant. In an instant, twelve guns were aimed at him, the sound of gun metal echoed.

"I just got an idea," the guard said "How about a public display of authority, to show you that this isn't a playground anymore?"

Morn's face was boiling with rage, his hand holding the revolver was shaking. The guard turned to face Morn as he pulled the trigger of the gun, blowing the blood and brains of the young Sin fighter all over the ground.

"Fire," Lesh commanded.

From all angles, Sin fighters opened fire, causing the Hiezer guards to lose their focus and aim. Morn dove while firing rounds of his revolver, screaming in disbelief at the cruelty he just witnessed. He crawled, avoiding ricocheting bullets in his path. Lesh silently hopped the gate, chasing after the guards who tried to get away. Lesh put one foot on a nearby rock and pushed off of it to get a clear shot of the sergeant and his two soldiers attempting to flee. She tossed two knives with intense force. She summersaulted forward back onto her feet and sprinted toward the sergeant. One soldier limped away with the knife sticking out of his oblique muscle. The other was writhing on the floor from the knife sticking out of his back. The sergeant spun around and opened fire, causing Lesh to dive to the side. She flipped herself back onto her feet and swung her arm with brutal force. The knife whipped as it soared through the air to pierce the sergeant's calf, immediately tripping him on impact. Lesh sprinted to the limping guard and kicked him to the floor, puncturing the back of his neck. She wrapped her arm around his gun and fired toward the sergeant. She saw a splash of blood and heard a grunt. As she crept closer, she watched the guard pathetically crawling, using his back to try and gain a few inches, staining the cement floor as he moved. Lesh looked fierce in the shadows. Her sharp face, flowing hair, and the points of her knife ring created a deadly silhouette.

"The Angel of Death has finally come," the guard said to himself.

Lesh leaned down on one knee, unsheathing a knife from the lower part of her ring. "I'm no angel," Lesh said, as she dug the knife into his throat.

She stared into the guard's eyes as the blood spewed down the man's body. She stood up, looking back to see her fighters advancing toward the jet. Two fighters were guarding the builder, who was safe. She realized the mission was a success and headed toward her group.

"Where's our pilot?" Lesh asked.

The fighter pointed to a cuffed Hiezer guard. Lesh nodded and continued to the gate. She walked past the young Sin fighter who lost his life. She gave a long stare as she walked by, and then turned to face Morn, staring at him coldly in the eyes. Morn was ashamed, now that he had cooled down from his rage.

Lesh slapped him in the face, "You almost jeopardized the mission. That boy's death is on your hands. How can I trust you if this is how you're going to act?" she asked.

"I didn't think they would actually murder the boy in cold blood," Morn defended himself.

"Don't pull that shit again," she responded, pointing a knife at his head.

Morn bit down on his toothpick and gave a curt nod.

"Let's wrap this up," Lesh said as she turned back to her team.

Chapter 17

Sabin walked down to the main floor alongside Lito, both of them staring at Lito's device. Lito still had his dingy goggles on from the work he performed outdoors. He extended a dirt encrusted finger, pointing to the locations that were ridden with landmines.

"As you can see, the perimeter is secured. The families can rest easy because no one is getting in here on my watch," Lito said.

Sabin nodded while looking at the device. "Yes, I'm sure the mommies are happy that if one of their kids strolls outside, they may explode," Sabin said jokingly.

"Come on, *mijo*. They're all remote detonated!" Lito said while he showed the trigger device in his hand. "Seriously though," Lito put an arm around Sabin, "When I was setting up outside, there have been times when I spotted Hiezer guards snooping in the distance. What if they set up sniper patrol that kills on site? It seems like the war is escalating in that direction."

"I know," Sabin said, "Half of me wants to quarantine the kids to the mansion for that reason, but that would be living in terror again. We have to have faith that Volaina or the scouting commanders would have intel on that before it happens."

Lito made a face and nodded while pulling his arm

off of Sabin. Sabin looked down to pet Mars.

"We have concerns that are piling up," Sabin said looking up as Lito removed his goggles. "Communications have been spotty. Every time there's been an issue, it takes way too long to fix. Someone has to step up," Sabin said.

"That's probably what Blague had in mind when he spoke about inducting a new commander," Lito said. "I miss Briggs. He was my *hermano*."

"We all do," Sabin replied.

"Speaking of which, I'm going to go hang out with Kentin after we speak with Cherris. Mind if I take Mars with me?" Lito asked.

"Not at all," Sabin said while he patted Mars' side.

The two men perused the main floor. The environment was positive; kids were playing, adults were conversing while working, cooking, or cleaning. The issue with Jason Brink was contained to the fighters and the expansion threat of the Hiezers was not yet an issue within the walls of the mansion. Blague's grand scheme was beginning to come together. Sabin and Lito spotted Cherris speaking among a group of women.

Lito turned to Sabin and gave him a look, "Maybe we should wait?"

Sabin smiled and walked past the group of women. Cherris made eye contact and nodded. The topic of conversation was streamlined education for the growing number of children within the mansion. A determined woman with long, auburn hair and glasses was speaking articulately about education in general.

"It doesn't matter what living conditions this group

is currently experiencing. Whether a given day consists of a battle to defend our new home or a quiet warm afternoon, we must have a system to educate and make sure that system is effectively running through either of those situations."

Cherris smiled as the woman spoke, "I admire your enthusiasm, Teles, and you're right about further prioritizing the growth of our community now that we're settled. Please choose a team of two and come see me so we can start implementing our ideas."

Teles sat down and quickly began writing in her notepad. Sabin observed the other side of operations, with a greater appreciation for Cherris. He and Lito sat back a few feet away as they waited to speak with her. The group of women noticed the two commanders waiting. They exchanged looks between each other and slightly altered their behavior. Rank and position was starting to carry additional weight now that the Sin population was gaining civility. The meeting eventually concluded and the group dispersed.

Cherris stood up and turned to the commanders, "I'm assuming you want to speak about the scientists?" Sabin nodded. "Endok came to me earlier this morning with a report about Ayelan splitting," Cherris continued, "They are confident in their ability, but have stumbled upon many new questions about the chemical. Seeing that they used to work closely with Briggs and Eugene, they don't really know who to turn to, so they're requesting a meeting with Blague."

Blague and I had this discussion months ago. It seems the time may be coming to discuss the chemical in depth. I hope it doesn't cause too much of a stir.

"Ok, we will set something up as soon as he returns. On a similar note, it seems the builders are making great progress on the two new fortresses adjacent to this one. Considering they haven't been bombed, Blague's prediction was probably correct. The Hiezer's believe we have already split the Ayelan and placed it within the skeleton of the new buildings," Sabin said.

"That's a pretty big bluff," Lito responded.

"It is," Cherris said as she looked at Lito, "but it's necessary. We're a few days away from the reality and only the commanders and a few other trusted sources know the truth. We just have to hope that the intelligence doesn't leak."

All three of their radios buzzed at once. "Blague's jet is incoming. They're due to land within ten minutes," the radios echoed.

"Did anyone debrief Lesh and Morn?" Cherris asked.

"Lesh briefly mentioned that she carried out the mission and promptly slammed the door in my face after that," Sabin said while shrugging, "Every bone in my body said that it wasn't the time to ask any more questions."

Lito laughed, "Good move."

Cherris raised her eyebrows and nodded, agreeing with Lito.

"Let's get to the roof," Sabin said.

The jet soared in, reducing speed only a half mile

away from its landing. The sleek black jet had silver rotating thrusters that shifted vertically to properly descend for a secure landing. Blague viewed the skeletons of the two future buildings, admiring the progress. The landing platform was lowered as soon as the jet landed on the roof. The jet engines slowed to a stop as the flame from the thrusters diminished. A few moments later, Blague emerged, his stifling Cryos mark brightly lit his arm and reflected on the side of his face. His strong body ached from wounds that he wasn't sure were real or not. His combat gear was torn up from the sharp terrain on Auront. The commanders were hoping for a victory in the form of Eugene's face, but unfortunately he never showed. Sabin ran up to Blague and hugged him.

"Don't ever leave me again!" Sabin said jokingly.

The other commanders laughed as the wind from the jet died down.

"Wait a second," Sabin continued, "Where's my best friend?"

Blague's grin turned straight-faced. "Eu has a different path unfortunately. We couldn't recruit him back."

Sabin's face became serious, "I'm sorry to hear that, Blague."

"Me too," Blague responded as he descended down the landing platform.

Oscin held on to the side of the railing with his head hunched over. He wiped his mouth with his free hand. Obviously somewhat dizzy, he walked down the platform in a staggered line. Oscin didn't appear out of it though; he seemed very comfortable in his relatively continuous drunken stupor.

He stopped in front of Drino, "I guess I'm back under your command, sir."

Drino nodded. Neither of them made any harsh remarks, considering the solemn environment around them. Niro appeared last. His body was illuminated from the Cryos stained veins on his exposed forearms. The parts of his uncovered wavy grey hair flew in the direction of the wind as he descended down the platform. The sound of his heavy combat boots clanking against the metal floor forced everyone to turn their eyes to him. The numerous cloths wrapped around him from his face to his shoulders, draped unevenly around his torso. He scanned the roof with his smoky eyes as he slowly walked past everyone. Without addressing any of the Sins, he was the first to exit the roof. After

Blague's eyes stopped following Niro, he turned back around to Sabin, "Bring me to Lesh."

Volaina studied the elite guard as she joined in with one of the squadrons.

"Squad T-Nova was decimated three clicks north of the lighthouse," Volaina said, masking her voice as a man.

"That's outside of their patrol range," the squad leader said.

All six of the Hiezer guards had their rifles drawn, but facing down. They were a mobile scouting guard; their armor was leather and their masks were lightweight. The sand and gravel in Clestice covered the ground around them. Volaina met up with this squadron about a mile away from the city's population.

"We were chasing a potential threat. We didn't get eyes on any of them. The crimes were committed by a group of snipers," Volaina lied, projecting a firm and confident voice.

"And you got away completely unscathed? How?" the guard asked.

"I guess I'm the messenger. They left one of us alive so that I can spread the word." Volaina continued.

She knew that one stutter would mean her cover was blown. She had to keep sharp and confident, masking her accent as well as her gender. The leader of the squadron nodded to another guard, who promptly radioed T-Nova.

You're obviously not going to receive an answer since Lesh impaled them all.

The guard continued flipping through transponders, until finally Volaina's went off.

When it did, she raised her hands to either side, "Are we done wasting time here?" she asked.

The main guard was satisfied, "Let's move to Clestice headquarters. We should report this in person."

Volaina held her side pretending to be injured in hopes that the other guards would leave her alone and not give a second thought if she was out of sequence.

These guards aren't traveling in formation. They are much less uniform than infantry. I wonder if they're awarded more freedoms for being the elite class.

"Did you hear about Old New York?" one of the guards said in earshot of Volaina.

"Yea, I heard it sank forty something years ago," a

guard with a dark red visor responded, making himself laugh.

"No, asshole. Apparently, the highlords ordered a station to be built where outsiders would least expect it," the guard said, swinging his gun onto his shoulder to reposition it.

"That would be brilliant, because I don't even believe you when you say it. I'm sure a terrorist would just laugh," the red visor guard responded.

Old New York? Why? There's nothing left there but water and waste. The Hiezers wouldn't need a secret hiding spot, unless other uprisings are starting to overwhelm them.

They continued to walk a few miles away from the huts, approaching a building with cathedral type architecture. Long black straps fell from the sides of it, making whipping sounds in the wind as they flapped. The six of them trekked through the gravel toward the headquarters, all with slender leather armor and lightweight helmets, creating haunting silhouettes as the patrolling lighthouse beam flew past them.

"Hey," Volaina said to the talkative guard, "which threat are the Hiezers hiding from?"

Three of the guards looked at Volaina for a good five seconds without saying anything. Her heartrate began to rise, goosebumps rose throughout her entire body, but she kept a cool exterior.

"I've been on duty for weeks, I'm out of the loop," she said.

"You really haven't heard?" the talkative guard said.

Volaina shook her head.

"A movement that originated at the Templos level

has grown and organized attacks on the estates of the Dactuars. Mulderan himself even took one of his jets off course to defend a Dactuar estate," the guard said as they entered the headquarters.

Volaina made sure not to enter first, preparing to make her move if the required scanning item wasn't located on her armor.

"Mulderan's squad decimated the threat by tactical ambush. I guess he likes to meet his enemies face to face," the guard finished.

The guard with the red visor nodded in agreement. The commanding elite guard stepped forward and placed his feet shoulder-width apart. As a light shimmered beneath them, a metal door unlocked and slid open.

Their boots have the scanning device? That's the last place anyone would think to look. I hope I have two boots from the same guard on.

When it was her turn to step forward, she hesitated for a moment, noticing slightly different marks on both boots. Her heart began pumping rapidly again, her adrenaline rising. The threat of being caught could be seconds away from becoming reality. A couple of seconds passed as Volaina's thoughts raced, scrambling internally for options to avoid getting caught. She turned around quickly to get a glimpse of the guard with the red visor. An immediate sigh of relief came out when she noticed each of his boots had slightly different designs. Volaina stepped forward onto the scanning platform. She held her breath in anticipation, staring down at her boots with one hand in position to draw her rifle. The illumination of blue and white light shot up from under her, scanning to finally admit her into Clestice headquarters. The lighting of the building was dim before entry, making the cement and metal surroundings barely visible. The light around the accepted guards' boots shined blue and gold.

Once the main door opened, everything was different. An immaculately clean main floor was decorated in a very matter of fact, militarized fashion. Different forms of liquid replenishment supplies were placed throughout the quarters, along with a functional automated meal service. Guards pressed a button indicating their desired choice and a plate of food delicately lowered down through a glass tube from an upper level. Guards of different ranks were conversing and spread throughout the floor. There were separate rooms where strategies were discussed. The headquarters was meant strictly for business and operations. Volaina was thankful that a lot of the guards remained in full gear. The commanders and other notorious members of Blague's Sin group were all on a defiler list, which demanded capture dead or alive. The elite guard with the red visor flipped his mask up. A clean shaven man in his mid-thirties put out his hand.

"I'm Ronnie Stenner, elite guard for four years," he said to Volaina.

Volaina stuck out her hand to meet his, "I'm Trevor," she said with a disguised voice.

I have to remain somewhat meek if I'm to retain my cover.

"That hammerhead over there is Gus. I swear, we can't trust that man with any bit of important information," Ronnie said. "He's probably the main reason classified intel falls to the lower ranks," Ronnie continued, pointing at Gus who looked over at them, while stuffing his face with food.

Jackpot.

His mask was pushed up to his forehead as he waved at Ronnie and Volaina; Ronnie turned his point into a wave and flashed a fake smile toward him.

"If he wasn't so damn spot on with a rifle, he never would have made it into this guard," Ronnie finished. He pulled his mask back down since there were guard leaders walking around. "Smart, Trevor," Ronnie said pointing at her head, "No need to disturb the leaders."

Gus walked over to them with a stuffed face and carried an overflowing plate.

"Fhhdge miug gorsh," Gus said.

Ronnie slapped his helmet off of the top of his head.

"Hi, I'm Gus," he said smiling, trying to swallow his food. "You should join our squad since you lost yours," Gus suggested sincerely.

Well, Gus just gave me the card I'm playing for the rest of my stay.

"Thank you," Volaina said while looking down.

"Give the guy a break," Ronnie said to Gus.

"What?" Gus responded, "I'm sure he just wants more vengeance on the terrorists. Just helping him out," he said while taking another bite of bread, "We're going to war soon anyway."

Ronnie slapped his leather armored chest.

"What do you mean by that?" Volaina asked.

"You're very curious," Ronnie said.

Volaina paused for a moment and started to sweat inside the suit, thinking this could be her last moment.

She was dead on sight if she was found out in these headquarters.

"What?" Volaina said cool and disguised, "T-Nova was not nearly as informed as you are."

Gus loved the compliment. Ronnie shrugged.

That's the last probing question for a while it seems.

"All of the highlords are gathering near the New York operation I told you about. Somewhere up in the mountains where the flooding is stagnant," Gus continued.

Ronnie threw his hands up in the air.

"Oh, shut up," Gus said slapping Ronnie back, "We should help out our future teammate."

"Sounds serious," Volaina chimed in, "Wonder if it's the Sin threat or the Templos threat they're going to wipe out."

"Well, the Sins have our Ayelan and I don't think we have intel on the Templos threat hideouts, so it's anyone's guess," Ronnie said.

When are the highlords going to meet? I just need to know when and I can slip out of here.

"Oh shit," Ronnie said, "our squad leader is beckoning us from the third strat room."

Gus finished shoving food into his face, grabbed his mask, and put it on. "You should come, Trevor. Let's get you acclimated to the quartermaster."

Volaina's gut instinct told her to get out of there.

"I've called a meeting with all of the commanders,

including the scouts," Blague said to Lesh, Sabin, and Cherris. "I've made a decision while returning to Senation. We're going on the offensive against the Hiezers. It will be the only way to distract them from our inevitable expansion," Blague continued with an even tone. "I have a lot to inform everyone about, but first, please update me," he finished.

Sabin and Lesh looked at each other.

"I'll begin," Lesh said, "The mission was ultimately a success. The builder and the Sin fighters have a pilot hostage who is escorting them to Bulchevin, in hopes to gather supporters to our cause and create a base within the vicinity of its Hiezer fortress. I lost a young fighter within the operation partially due to lack of discipline. I take full responsibility for that," Lesh finished.

Blague stared at Lesh for a moment, folding one hand over the other on the marble table they were sitting at.

"Please have someone make arrangements to inform the fallen fighter's family and to arrange a proper burial," he said calmly.

Lesh nodded.

"Your mission was a success. I'm glad to hear one of the two were."

"What happened to Eugene?" Lesh asked.

"He's chasing a ghost from his past," Blague replied. "It's a legitimate chase though. Some form of his partner from a past life still exists here today. That's his path now," Blague said somewhat disappointed. "There are some positive aspects to my failed mission. I've learned and experienced the island of Auront, which was as much of a hazy acid trip as you might expect after encountering Jason. Furthermore, I learned that Oscin can in fact pilot a jet," Blague said.

"That's good news," Sabin said while petting Mars.

Blague held his finger up, "That's not all. We have one hell of a strange asset in Niro. That man has experience that reaches far beyond our reality," Blague continued.

Sabin looked surprised, "For you to say that, he must have pulled some impressive stunts."

Blague looked at Sabin in the eye, "He did."

"I wouldn't be sitting with you here today if not for him," Cherris added.

They heard a knock on the door of the laboratory room.

"Come in," Sabin said.

The large metal door swung open and in walked Lito and Endok.

Blague stood up and extended his hand, "Endok, you've been making great strides with your work, which is allowing us to continue living in some semblance of peace. I thank you for that."

Endok walked over and stuck out his hand to meet Blague's.

Endok pushed his thick glasses up, "It's an honor. Besides, you've allowed my team to experience experimentation with the rarest chemical on this planet," he said with excitement.

Sabin held his head up with two fingers, not sharing Endok's enthusiasm on the matter.

"Your success with Ayelan splitting is a great step

and strongly displays your capabilities," Blague said as he motioned for Endok to have a seat next to him, while Lito and Blague exchanged a quick greeting.

"Yes," Endok said, "we are about a day away from carrying out a live split. My team is getting everything in order."

As everyone sat, Blague slowly took a seat.

"As we advance toward our enemy, we should try to understand their complexities, including their strengths, weaknesses, and motives. I trust all of you in this room and that is why I want you to stay for this conversation. Some of you," Blague gestured to Sabin and Endok, "know more than others about me, but by the end of this conversation, you should all be on the same page," he said while looking around. Blague shifted his attention to Endok, his deep set green eyes were intense. "I've been consistently experiencing vivid thoughts that are not my own."

Endok looked confused. Sabin propped himself in his chair while Lesh, Cherris, and Lito leaned forward.

"Sir," Endok said, "are you sure I'm the right person to be talking about this with? Maybe you need to see a shrin..."

"Yes, Endok, I'm sure," Blague cut him off with a grin. He stood up slowly from his seat. "I need answers. I'm confident you are the only one who may be able to provide them." He walked into the shadow of the room, pondering as he spoke. "These thoughts are connected to something I experienced long ago."

Blague took off his shirt and stepped into the light. His intensely muscular, vascular body was decorated with scars. The commanders and Endok had no idea what to expect next. Blague's demeanor was unchanging as he spoke.

He threw his shirt on the table and exposed his back to the group, "Tell me what you make of this."

Chapter 18

Volaina meekly followed Ronnie and Gus into the strat room, pondering ten different potentially fatal outcomes all at once.

The quartermaster probably has a greater sense of the members that make up each squad. I have to choose my words carefully based on the Hiezer intel I gathered from previous missions.

"Was the sniper part of Blague's rebellion?" Gus asked, turning his head slightly to hear Volaina's response.

"Hard to say," Volaina said in a man's voice, "Based on the placements of the wounds, the only thing I can confirm is that the shots didn't originate from our fortress. But considering their hideout is so close, it's probably them."

Gus nodded in agreement while Ronnie opened the door to the strat room. The quartermaster stood waiting with his arms folded. His mask had a roaring lion artfully etched into it. If that wasn't intimidating enough, he was about six feet five inches tall, towering over the three of them.

"Your squad leader informed me of your situation. It seems only one of you have actually witnessed the event, so speak up," the quartermaster opened with a deep, punctured voice.

Gus and Ronnie turned back to look at Volaina, who stepped forward with her hands behind her back.

"Trevor reporting from Squad T-Nova," she said confidently, "My squad was decimated by one or more snipers within a fifteen second period."

The quartermaster lifted his mask, to get a better look at the distressed soldier.

"The shots were fired ocean-side. This seemed to be an attack without a mission, the purpose of which was to eliminate Hiezers," she continued.

The quartermaster took a step forward and looked down upon Volaina, "And how would you be able to make such a determination with the twenty seconds you were exposed?"

"Because, sir, none of our bases have been taken and it seems the other elite squads are still functional," Volaina replied.

Take the bait, take the bait, tell me if they made it.

The quartermaster backhanded her after pausing for a moment. Volaina tightly held on to her mask as she whipped herself back into upright position. Her heartrate began to rise again, as her body tensed up for whatever was to be thrown at her next. One slip and she'd be killed; there was no way she could take out all three of them in the confined location.

"Elite guards have to learn harsher lessons if they're to one day lead the Hiezer Protective Order," the quartermaster said.

Ronnie and Gus remained silent for a moment, obviously uncomfortable.

"Don't make a rash assumption like that again. A jet was taken just an hour ago in the Clestice hanger," the quartermaster said.

Yes! Lesh made it! He took the bait.

"Sir!" Gus said as he stepped forward, "Trevor has lost his entire squad and is far from his home station. We request that he be assigned to our squad, Balista."

The quartermaster remained unmoved for a moment.

"C'mon Wes," Gus pleaded.

The name Wes, a group of guards mentioned him a few missions ago. Wes Howard. The guards rumored that he runs into battle heavily armored with no weapons. I better not fuck this up.

Wes waved his hand, "Yes, he may join your squad temporarily."

Gus' smile grew ear to ear behind his mask. You could almost hear the smile forming.

"Ronnie, you're quiet today," Wes said with confusion in his voice. He then turned to Volaina, "Have a seat. Where did you say your home station is?"

Volaina's legs shook under the large, plain marble table; Gus noticed, but didn't think anything of it.

"I was stationed in Verleice for twelve years, since the day I was accepted into the Elite Guard."

The pressure was starting to get to her, the sweat inside her suit made her fidgety.

This cover was a longshot. Pretending to be a normal guard made it easy to blend in, but the elite guard is too risky. Calm down, remember your training.

She began to relax, anticipating Wes' next question.

You've done this a million times before.

Wes nodded his head and folded his huge hands.

Ronnie nudged her shoulder with his, "You can ease up. Wes isn't going to kill you."

Volaina nodded and sat back.

"So, Mr. Howard, do we get to go to Old New York next month?" Gus asked.

Oh you stupid son of a bitch, Gus, I love you. Now I just have to get out of here as soon as possible.

"The enlisted squads are confidential, even I wasn't told yet. Apparently, this meeting is to determine the priority focus of the highlords," Wes continued.

"Mulderan and Eldra have a lot to reveal, I'm sure. I remember being on protective watch for them. They were eager to march on the front lines whenever we were assessing a threat. It's as if they have no fear," Gus said.

Ronnie turned to Gus, "I remember fighting alongside Eldra. She's incredibly resourceful and ruthless. It kind of gave me the chills being around her."

"I see what you did there!" Gus laughed hysterically.

Even Wes chuckled.

"I didn't mean to, I swear!" Ronnie said.

Hmm, must be an Ice Queen reference.

"Alright gentlemen, you're dismissed. I have work to do in assessing this new threat," Wes said.

All three of the elite guards stood and gave a Hiezer salute and turned for the door. Wes put a large hand on Ronnie's shoulder as he lifted his own mask. Wes had brownish grey hair and a large scar down his right eye. He had a defined crease on both sides of his face, starting by his nose and ending by his mouth.

"Watch your back. This threat seems serious," Wes said.

"I will, sir. My squad has my back," Ronnie replied.

"Blague, that's the same translucent mark that the spy had on his back," Endok said.

Cherris gasped, "That's right! The boy, or man rather, Felik." She looked down for a moment.

Lesh was staring intensely at Blague, while Sabin sat back and watched the story unravel.

"So," Cherris said, "you received an Ayelan shot."

Endok was using a microscope to inspect the holographic scar.

"Yes, a lifetime ago this shot was forced upon me," Blague said with his back facing them and his head turned, somewhat pained.

"You've brought me here to inspect this for a reason," Endok said as he fixed his glasses. "The cocktail that is the Ayelan shot includes the DNA of another," he continued. "Are you suggesting…"

Lesh interrupted Endok, "How old are you?"

Blague turned completely around. Endok turned with him as if he were glued to his back.

"Approaching a century," Blague said as he stared at Lesh.

Cherris gasped again. Lesh's eyebrows raised.

Sabin smirked with his hands behind his head, "Our fearless leader is an old man!" he said as he laughed.

"I always knew something was off about you," Lesh

said, "but oddly enough I don't trust you any less."

Blague gave a nod of appreciation. His shredded, scarred body didn't at all correspond with what he just revealed.

"The time has come to reveal the truth. We've fought and bled together long enough for you all to know my true motives in your own minds. My past is a dark place, but my vision of the future is bright," Blague stated.

Endok cleared his throat and Blague turned his head.

"As I was saying," Endok interrupted, "You explained that some of your thoughts weren't your own. Are you suggesting that the DNA shot into your spinal cord years ago contained memories of the person to whom the DNA belonged?"

"At first, I thought it was ridiculous," Blague said, "but I'm now fairly certain that these visions are memories, not manifested thoughts."

"How could one be sure of such a thing?" Endok asked in a skeptical tone, as he pushed his glasses back into position.

"Because, the DNA implanted with the shot belonged to my wife, Elaina, and I know the events leading up to her death, but I wasn't there for it," Blague said.

Sabin almost fell back in his chair. "What? I never knew that! That's crazy!" Sabin shouted.

"That sounds bizarre," Endok said.

"Yes, I'm aware," Blague replied, "But is it possible?"

Endok paused for a moment, his curiosity stirring, "Of course it's possible. Anything is possible."

"That's what I thought," Blague said, "I've chosen the right person to investigate this."

"Who administered the shot?" Lesh asked.

Sabin turned in his seat to look at her, "It gets worse," he said.

"Mulderan Grenich," Blague responded, "my half-brother."

Eugene was gasping for air as he dropped to his knees. He had searched the smoky areas of Auront in hopes of finding Jen. His pants were ripped from his constant battles with the strange, ever changing terrain. Eugene stopped to rest on a concrete spike, allowing himself a moment to catch his breath. He scanned his surroundings and realized he had discovered an exit in the distance. Re-motivated and desperate, he sprinted toward the opening of light until the smoke was finally behind him. In the far distance he saw the Aura huddled in a giant circle, most likely surrounding Jason.

I need to arm myself if I'm to survive another day in this nightmare. I also need to eat, I have no idea if I actually ingested that food inside the smoke. Jen can't be in Jason's possession yet, the group wouldn't be so calm.

Eugene gathered himself before making another move. He sprinted toward the back of the jets to get out of the Aura's line of sight. He still had no shirt on from when Jason had stabbed him. The bandages that Jen wrapped him in were layered around his waist. He looked drained, as though he hadn't slept for days.

Which jet did Nemura drag me out of? Think, Eugene,

think.

Eugene plodded forward, grabbing on to anything he could as support. As he got closer to the Aura, he recollected a similar view to when Nemura escorted him off the jet.

This must be the one. I need to regroup and get back to finding her.

With the last of his strength, he climbed the back of the plane's staircase, grabbing on to anything he could find to hurl his way up, making as little noise as possible. His arms were shaking from exhaustion. The mix of frigid wind blanketed by strange humidity blew his dirty blonde hair all around. When he got to the top, he quickly attempted to swing himself over to get into the door. He gained momentum, but couldn't reach the ledge to swing himself upright. He made a grunt as he scraped for the ledge, his body swinging wildly.

Fuck, I can't make any more noise. There must be guards on board.

A flash of Jen's scarred face and the echo of her screams in Eugene's head gave him a burst of adrenaline. He swung again, this time more forcefully, finally gaining the momentum he needed to grasp the ledge. He pulled himself to the top of the stairs and dove into the front entrance of the jet. To his shock, there was a body lying bloody on the floor. He followed the footprints of blood with his eyes to discover a distraught Jen holding her shaking head with both of her hands. Eugene quickly charged over.

"Jen!" he shouted in a loud whisper.

"Eugene," she said back in between her sobs, "I

knew you would be here, I saw it in this goddamn head," Jen slammed her fist down onto her own skull. She looked up at him with tears flowing down her scars. "What's happening to me, Eugene?" she asked as she held up her red tinted hands. "I want to go home!" she pleaded.

Eugene tried to reach for her, but she swatted him away.

"What made you kill that patrol guard?" he asked.

"I didn't," she said, shaking her head violently, "He was dead when I got here."

Holy shit, she's lost her mind. Her hands are soaked with his blood.

"Jen, snap out of it, please!" he pleaded.

Jen stopped shaking and looked up at Eugene with familiar unfocused dead eyes.

"You let them do this to me! How could you just stand there and watch? For days, Eugene? How could you betray me like that?" she said in a deep, scolding tone.

Defeated from the madness, Eugene let himself fall on his ass across from Jen.

"It's over, isn't it?" Eugene said out loud to himself, "There's no escape."

Jen crawled over and put her hand on his. He turned his head downward to face her, surprised.

Her face was twitching, "Don't give up," she said in a soft voice.

His arms filled with goosebumps; the tone of her voice immediately brought back memories of them being together in their house.

The memory faded from his vision and he grasped her hand with both of his, "I won't give up. We have to make it past this. I've been given a second chance to save you and I'm not passing it up. You can bet my life on it."

Jen struggled to keep her attention honed on what he was saying. She smiled and then immediately curled up into a ball, screaming in excruciating pain. She kept violently tearing at her hair and hitting her head. Eugene hastily ran over to carefully shut the front door of the jet. He ran back to her as quickly as he could, frustrated, not knowing how to help her.

"You have to get this under control somehow," Eugene said hesitantly.

"My name is Asura!" she screamed back. "You lost me the moment you let that scum have their way with me. I'm no longer yours!" she screamed.

Maybe the effects of that geyser depend upon the mental state of the person.

"Eugene," she said softly, moments after the screaming, "I see scenarios playing out in my head. One of them ends with Jason murdering you and enslaving me."

Eugene shook his head, "Pick a different one."

"This doesn't make any sense," Jen said, "It feels like I met you yesterday, but I have a lifetime of thoughts racing through my head and you're in so many of them."

"I heard Jason babbling about similar feelings through Blague's radio back in Senation," Eugene said. "He seems to have embraced this feeling. Maybe you should try doing the same," he continued.

Jen continued to hold her head, "I can feel Jason's thoughts. He's finishing up a speech as we speak."

Is this it? Has she lost her mind?

"I think that geyser connected us somehow," Jen said.

She let out another scream and slammed her head onto the metal floor. Her blonde hair made a small puddle on the floor around her. Eugene ran over to the dead body, and scrapped his clothes, and started dressing himself with what he needed.

"Eugene!" she screamed. "What if Jason can feel my thoughts too?"

Just then, they felt the vibrations of a large group walking in unison. Eugene rushed to a window to see the entire Aura surrounding their jet. His eyes widened and Jen stood up, her eyes completely unfocused. She slowly walked over to Eugene, who was scrambling to take the dead guard's weapons in hopes of making a final stand.

This is it, this is how it ends.

Jen walked up behind him with a gash on her forehead from when she slammed her head. Eugene tried to turn around, but she already had her arms firmly around his neck and head, strangling him.

"This is squad leader. When you're done stuffing your face, meet us at coordinates 65, 146; the lighthouse entrance. We're investigating an ambush as directed by the quartermaster," both Ronnie's and Gus' radios projected at the same time.

"I guess he's referring to me," Gus said while laughing.

"Wes seemed a little worried to me. That's very

unlike him," Ronnie said, hoping for a response from Gus.

I have to make my escape somehow. I have all of the information I'm going to get.

"Ready for your first mission as a Balista, Trevor?" Ronnie asked, patting her back.

"Affirmative, I need to avenge my squad," Volaina said.

"Careful," Ronnie said, "make sure you keep your head on straight. As you know, elite guards have no room for error."

These two are good people. It's a shame that we view the world so differently.

"Hey! Go easy on him. He knows the ropes. He just lost his second family," Gus said. He then turned to Trevor, "I know you're motivated to kick ass on our next missions, but you could lay low and follow along until you're acclimated."

Volaina put her head down, "I'll see how I'm taking things as they progress."

Gus nodded and turned back around. Ronnie stepped ahead of Gus and they each headed single file toward the exit of the main quarters, back into the scanning room.

"The snipers are still out there," Ronnie said, "Stay alert."

The three of them ducked forward and began running toward their next mission.

This is always the worst part of my line of work. I wish I was a sociopath and could detach from emotion or rationalize hatred. But unfortunately, that's not me and this is reality. I've seen too much to think that I'm on the wrong side.

"Slow down," Volaina said, "I see something far ahead."

The three of them stayed low to the ground, but decreased their speed to a slow walk. Both Ronnie and Gus were trying to analyze what Volaina saw. They lifted their masks to get a better look. She slowly pulled out a silenced pistol, lifting her mask to reveal her strongly defined, but attractive female face.

"I'm sorry," she said in a sincere voice, no longer masking her gender.

Ronnie was clearly shaken, as he slowly turned around and reached for his weapon. Volaina's bullet pierced through the back of Gus' head.

Had to take out the marksman first.

She turned her pistol to Ronnie as they made eye contact. He swiftly tried to lift his rifle, but he knew it was already over for him. Volaina fired one shot to his forehead. A tear escaped her eye as she did it. She stood on the pathway between the Clestice headquarters and the lighthouse. At least a mile in between stood nothing but gravel hills. The silence became eerie, as it mostly did in these situations. Volaina extended her arm and looked the other way, pulling the trigger as she aimed at the wound she had just created; she tried making the bullet hole bigger so that it would look like a sniper rifle made the shot. She then dragged Gus' body about twenty feet ahead and did the same to his corpse.

She reached for Gus' radio and masked her voice, "The sniper got Ronnie and Trevor! I'm making a break for the lighthouse! Get inside!"

Hopefully the disappearance of "Trevor's" body gets lost in the chaos of the numerous Hiezer elite guard deaths.

Volaina reached for her Sin radio, "Blague, mission accomplished. I'm heading home and I have intel."

Chapter 19

"Elaina, once we deliver this last piece, we can focus on your work for the rest of the year," Blague said, while keeping his eyes on the road.

They were traveling west, admiring the Manhattan skyline in the distance.

"I know. You've worked very hard to make your dream a reality. Just focus on accomplishing this last task, then the rest is in his hands," Elaina said.

Blague paused for a moment, "You know, my father was right. The business world I was once a part of was fruitless. The sense of accomplishment was purely individualistic and selfish."

"You could say that, but it pushed you in the direction that led you to me and your new purpose. It gave you the confidence to aspire to something greater. Not to mention, it gave you clarity on what you didn't like," Elaina said with a smile.

Blague drove silently for a moment. "Hah, if nothing else I guess working with those assholes taught me how to handle myself differently. Maybe it wasn't all a waste," he said looking over at her.

"It wasn't, Blague. I've been with you for a long time, trust me on this one."

"What about you? Do you regret spending so much time in college pursuing a PHD?" Blague asked.

"Of course not! I now know what it takes to do something great!" she exclaimed. "I obviously didn't stop there," Elaina paused for a moment, "It's been years since anyway," she said while smiling, thinking back to her past life.

Blague glanced over at her and thought to himself, "Her ambition keeps on growing. I hope we can continue banking off of each other's drive."

They drove silently for a while. Elaina had the passenger's side window open, letting her long brown hair dance in the wind. She was thin and of average height. She had illuminating energy; you could almost see her thoughts creating her actions. Blague admired everything about her, from her beautiful features to her ability to reinvent herself, constantly pursuing change and growth. It certainly kept Blague on his toes.

"I'm worried about Orin. He has his hands full with your brother. Maybe we should reconsider our trip until things are straightened out," she said.

"Mulderan's peculiar way of operating led him down a very dark path. But I don't think he would actually act in a way that would harm people," Blague responded.

"I don't know. You have too much faith in him. His ideologies are a little sociopathic," she said while laughing nervously.

"I know, that's why I've detached from him for the most part. And you shouldn't worry about my father. If there's one thing that man can do, it's handle himself," Blague responded.

"From a son who believes the end of the world is coming?" Elaina fired back, "And that anyone not pulling their weight should be killed?"

"Hah, you know Mulderan was never known for his heart," he said.

Elaina paused and looked down for a moment, "I want to

ask you a question that I haven't asked in years," holding and then breaking eye contact.

Blague looked over for a moment, "What is it?"

"Have you still given up hope on the rest of your family?"

"Yes, dear," Blague said trying to keep the conversation light. "I didn't grow up in a nurturing environment. You know it's only natural for me to continue on my own path without looking back," he finished.

"But aren't you curious?" Elaina asked, "Hell, I'm curious for you."

They both laughed, knowing the conversation wasn't going to go any further. Elaina looked at the dashboard and tensed her eyebrows, watching as it began to shake violently. A second later, they felt the entire car bouncing back and forth.

"What the fuck is going on," Blague said.

As they continued forward, the ripples beneath the ground caused everything to tremble around them. In the distance, a skyscraper toppled over.

"Did you see that?" Blague screamed.

Elaina held onto the dashboard as her whole body tensed.

"Are we under attack again?" her shaky, terrified voice asked.

"No," Blague said while calming himself, "this is something else."

Another building imploded and fell vertically, lifting a huge cloud of smoke into the sky. The ground wildly started to crack around them. Piles of cement and rock were tossed in every direction.

"An earthquake?" Elaina screamed in terror.

"This isn't like any earthquake I've ever experienced. Everything is happening so fast," Blague said while slowing down the car. "Elaina, look at me," he grabbed her shoulder, "I love you," he said as he closed his eyes and gave her a kiss. "Listen to me, we both know I'm trained for survival, but judging by the intensity, our living through this is largely up to chance." Blague put his hand behind her head, "Ok?"

Elaina bit her lip as the tears flowed down her cheeks. She eventually nodded, "Ok, I love you too."

She leaned in for a hug. Blague hugged her back and then swiftly reached for his bag in the back seat.

"Follow me," he said.

Their surroundings appeared as if a tornado was forming of rock and terrain. Banging as loud as thunder sounded right at their feet.

"What the hell is that?" Elaina screamed while holding her ears.

Blague grabbed her hand, "Run now, ask later," he shouted through the clamor.

Blague was clean shaven in a seemingly expensive suit; his wavy hair was pushed back.

He looked around frantically, quickly deciphering the best route to take, "Water. We need to get to a small body of water or a small brick shed."

Blague gripped the bag tightly with one hand and grasped Elaina's hand with the other. People were abandoning their cars and running frantically through the streets. The poor souls who decided to hide out in their basements were crushed by toppling houses. The quake wasn't sluggish or predictable. The damage was occurring devastatingly fast. Terrain was whipping out from under them, launching people into the air as the cement flew, and crushing others as the blocks of asphalt fell. Blague sprinted only enough so that Elaina could keep up. They hopped fences in a residential area in Queens, New York, trying desperately to get to open ground and minimize the chance of *being hit by flying debris.*

Could Mulderan have been right? His theory that Earth's aging core would shoot flares that would eventually tear the earth apart from the inside… could this be it?

Blague spun around and grabbed Elaina, pulling both of them to the floor, ducking a massive boulder that flew past them.

Blague's radio went off snapping him back to reality. He looked up while the pupils within his green eyes became constricted. He was still sitting at the table where he revealed some of his past to his team. Endok and a few of his scientists remained, studying the puncture on his back.

Blague picked up his radio, "Lito, gather all of the commanders and meet at the front entrance."

Mulderan and Eldra walked at the head of a group of highlords and high council as they approached a giant black marble roundtable. Mulderan remained standing as the others proceeded to sit. The highlords elegantly tucked their cloaks as they sat. Mulderan's Hiezer cloak continued to ripple as he stood still. His cold stare passed through all of the participants as he observed his audience. He slowly took a seat, keeping his elbows on the table and folding his hands close to his head.

"Is everything in position for Old New York?" he questioned.

One of the highlords spoke up, "The gatekeepers of the new fortress are awaiting our arrival."

Mulderan nodded, "Then our departure will be one

month from today," he said with no room for debate.

"What is the purpose of this gathering, Mulderan?" another highlord probed.

Mulderan turned his head and coldly stared at him, "To ensure the next stage of our survival."

The highlords began conversing with each other, trying to decipher what that could mean. Eldra and Mulderan sat back silently and exchanged a look. Another question rose above the chatter.

"What about the current uprisings among the Templos and Sin populations?" a highlord asked.

Mulderan backhanded the air, "Trivial in comparison. We will address that here. It's part of the agenda."

A highlord with thick black hair sitting slightly over his face leaned forward. His robe had additional cloth hanging over the sleeves of his cloak.

"The assault on Dactuar estates is unacceptable," the man said in a British accent.

"Alek, you can't possibly be serious," Jeck said. "The Sin threat took over our Senation fortress and what's worse, they are in possession of Ayelan," Jeck continued, "Your cousins are Dactuars, so your motive is personal."

Eldra leaned forward, both Jeck and Alek shifted their eyes hesitantly to her. The icy stare from her crystal blue eyes was enough to divert anyone's attention. Her pupils were unusually small, making the crystal blue shine that much more noticeable.

"The Sin threat is currently contained to the exiled continents. The Templos threat is crossing borders and gaining ground. Regardless if it's personal, Alek is correct;

we must stomp out the Templos threat first. I've proposed a means to do so," Eldra said as she slid a device to the middle of the roundtable.

A picture projected out of the device.

"The three names listed above are the drivers of the Templos movement. We have the means to capture their immediate family members and use them as leverage to prevent their expansion. If they don't comply, we will execute each of the hostages until they do. This process will allow us to gain intelligence as to their motives and goals, at which point we will find their weaknesses and exploit them. The Sin threat will remain secondary so long as they remain contained. Remember highlords, there is an impending matter that takes priority over all of this," Eldra said.

Alek nodded, content that her long winded declaration swayed in his favor.

"With all due respect," Jeck said, "you haven't considered the rate of growth of the Sin uprising. I've resided among them. Blague is extremely capable and determined. This will bite us in the end," he warned.

"My brother's capabilities have been noted, Jeck," Mulderan interjected, "The fact is that the Templos uprising is better equipped and more likely to interfere with our research progress. As of this moment, that threat is on hold."

Jeck reluctantly nodded and sat back.

"Your promotion to high council may be short lived if these failures continue," Mulderan said in a cold tone, "it was your responsibility to prevent the Sin expansion."

Jeck clenched his jaw and broke eye contact with

Mulderan.

"As a more economical matter, the funding toward the earth's core drilling has reached its goal," a woman with long light brown hair stated. Her dark brown eyes scanned the room for a reaction.

"Great," Alek blurted out, "then we should begin drilling immediately."

"You should consider all the facts first, Alek, when you have them," Mulderan said in a cool tone.

Alek looked annoyed, "Well, in the interest of transparency, perhaps you should enlighten us."

Mulderan's long flowing hair fell over to one side as he shifted his head, "The matter is top secret. The information must be handled delicately. I'll be confident relaying the information in our New York fortress. So be patient and trust your leader."

Alek leaned back and mumbled, "How can I trust someone who sentenced his own father to death?"

The highlord next to him kicked him under the table.

"Careful, Alek," the Ice Queen warned.

"Let's be realistic," the brown eyed woman said, "We wouldn't have made it this far without Mulderan's guidance. I, for one, plan to continue to respect his wishes."

"Out of fear!" Alek said, raising his voice.

Mulderan shifted his gaze to Alek, analyzing him with an emotionless face.

"Out of loyalty," the woman responded.

The room was silent except for the slight echo of the woman's last words. Alek took the moment to regain his posture.

"Prioritization of the significant threats, phase of the drilling development, and the announcement of the gathering date," Mulderan announced with a still voice. "I have one more matter of discussion before I open the floor to any other topics. Eldra has served humanity with expert war strategy, heroic battle participation, and overall stellar performance measures. With this in mind, it's my pleasure to introduce the newest recipient of the Ayelan shot. On behalf of the continued survival of humanity, may her vision never dim," Mulderan said, presenting his wife, who stood confidently.

The roundtable of highlords and council all framed their eyes with the Hiezer Salute. Eldra took a seat.

"The floor is open," Mulderan said, while gesturing with his hand.

Blague and his team waited in the front of the mansion to welcome his scout commanders home. Volaina was beside Lito and Sabin, still dirty from the mission she just returned from. Sabin held out his hand low for Volaina to give him five. She looked at him, smiled and slapped his hand.

He leaned over to her, "You know, if they don't figure out that there was a spy among them, you may have just scored us one of the most valuable ambush opportunities," Sabin said.

"I hope you're right. If we take hold of a fortress in Bulchevin, that may be another turning point for us," she responded.

Lesh and Blague faced straight ahead as a diverse group of people were admitted past the breach point.

"Niro is nowhere to be found," Lesh said to Blague.

"I figured that would happen sooner or later," Blague responded, "He's not the type to participate as a commander."

Lesh scoffed, "Neither am I."

Blague let out a small laugh, "Are you defending him?"

She raised an eyebrow and didn't say anything.

A man covered in rags led the incoming group. He walked with a limp; his short, black hair was parted down the middle, greased to either side. Pigeons circled him, one of which decided to rest on his shoulder as he walked. He appeared to be in his late fifties sporting a large, sharp nose and a goatee. When he saw Blague, his eyes teared up.

Blague stepped forward and gave him a hearty hug, "Good to see you, Telfice."

"I miss him already, Blague," Telfice said as tears fell from his eyes, "To not see him standing with you, waiting to greet us, made it all the more real. Briggs was the best of us. No offense," he said as he lightly hit Blague's chest twice, releasing from his hug.

"None taken," Blague said with a grin.

Telfice sniffled and his pigeon cooed. He then extended a dirty hand behind him, "This is my lot. They serve me well and have been great scouts within the exiled continents." He raised a finger to Blague and looked at him suspiciously, "You know what I always say?" Blague looked at him with his eyes nearly closed.

"Communication is key," they both said at the same time.

"Hah," Telfice let out a laugh, "That's why you're our leader."

He put a hand on Blague's shoulder and walked over to greet the other commanders. Lesh eyed the pigeons circling above Telfice, itching to take them out of the sky. Telfice's scouts respectfully nodded toward Blague as they made their way toward the mansion.

"This man has more connections than that bastard, Nemura," Sabin said loudly, letting out a hearty laugh as he hugged Telfice.

Blague turned his attention ahead, awaiting the other man he was curious to see again. The man slowly walked forward, taking in his surroundings. His very dark, smooth skin radiated a richness about him. He wore a fitted black cloak with sapphire stones as buttons. His shaved head reflected the sun.

"Biljin!" Sabin shouted, "Any slower and I'll be dead by the time you get here!"

Biljin paid him no mind. He approached Blague and stuck out his hand. Blague extended his to give the formal handshake that he expected.

"Good to see you, Blague. You haven't disappointed. We are successfully reducing the Hiezer control. I'm glad I bought into your vision."

"The information you've been providing has been invaluable. You're one of the only eyes we have in the upper classes," Blague said.

"I've ascended quickly," Biljin responded, "I'm to be accepted into the Dactuar class within months."

"That would be a game changer," Blague said happily.

"Indeed," Biljin responded, "It took great lengths not to be followed. You should see the rags I left at the entrance."

Blague didn't respond to that comment.

"I know we don't see eye to eye on everything, but tyrant control is one thing we both know has to change. I've lent you my intellect and you've used it so I could climb these arbitrary class ranks. I'm a forward thinker; let this meeting show me that I haven't spent all this time for naught."

Blague stared at him for a moment, remembering the distaste he had for his arrogance. "You're free to go on your own whenever you please, Biljin. it's your choice if you want to remain with us. Although I appreciate your great contributions, I would never beg for your services, let alone alter the group's meetings for your individual preference."

Biljin had a look of disappointment as he looked Blague in the eyes, but eventually backed down and gave a slight nod.

"I'm assuming that genius intellect figured out that the goals of our big picture outweighs that ego of yours," Blague said somewhat lightly.

"I suppose it has," Biljin responded.

"The candidates are ready in room 1B2," a voice said through Blague's radio.

"Let's proceed to our induction," Blague replied as he led the line of commanders toward the front door of the mansion. "Before we join the civilians and general public, I have an announcement to make," Blague said as he turned to face his most trusted group. "Due to Volaina's stellar infiltration of the Hiezer elite guard, we have intel that the Hiezers have built a fortress in upstate Old New York. The highlords will gather from around the world to meet in about one month. This is our chance to go on the offensive. There is a large risk in doing so, but it's necessary to draw eyes away from our inevitable expansion. We will discuss logistics and strategy after the induction, but I wanted this news to begin sinking in now," Blague finished as he turned back around to open the door.

Blague walked to room 1B2 with his entourage behind him. He met with Cherris, who was standing at the doorway.

"Niro has vanished. I know you wanted to thank him. I'm sorry," Cherris said while looking down.

"That's alright. I have a feeling we will see him again one day," Blague said as he entered the room.

The commanders walked in, each with their own swagger, not two of which were remotely alike. Five candidates stood in their assigned spots, ready to be judged for a promotion. The commanders took their seats facing the candidates. Blague sat in the middle and began the induction process.

"Ladies and gentlemen, you have incredibly large shoes to fill. Briggs was exceptionally resourceful: a master of communications and an elite solider. We sit here today to judge whether any of you has the potential to be half as great as he was. Drino," Blague said as he motioned toward him, "please begin."

Drino stood up from his corner seat and, in a militaristic fashion, walked over to the first candidate. "This here is Airos, born into the Sin class. He has an extreme drive to turn this world upside down in order to improve the living conditions for his mother, wife, and soon to be child. Airos has been the sergeant of Squad X and is nothing short of a war hero. Do you have anything to say for yourself before the commanders comment?"

Airos stepped forward, "Blague, I've been with you since the inception of this group. I will follow you into the deepest layer of hell if that's my duty."

Airos followed his speech with a pound to his chest. Blague gave an old fashion salute back to him.

"I admire this man's drive and previous service, but this position isn't set for a war hero," Blague said.

"Airos has served me diligently. He's more than capable to fulfill the role," Drino rebutted.

Lito shook his finger at the candidate and shook his head, "That man right there, he is not a communications expert. And this room knows, we need to improve our communications."

"I wouldn't toss away a veteran so quickly," Telfice said, "He may be exactly what this leadership needs."

Blague put his hand up. Drino promptly walked over to the next candidate.

"This here is Kenna. She has been coordinating the civilian home assignments and also has been elected to manage the budgets for the new buildings. She is as ambitious as she is vivacious," Drino said, obviously pained in reading the words that she drafted for him. "Do you have anything to say for yourself before the commanders comment?" Drino asked.

"My résumé speaks for itself," she said confidently.

"I like her," Biljin said.

Sabin laughed, "You would."

"We need more brass and brain in this cohort," Biljin replied.

"Coordination does not necessarily translate to technology. Not to mention she has zero experience on the battlefield," Volaina said.

"I concur," Blague said.

Sabin raised his hand, "We could use an official coordinator. Our group is rapidly expanding, so things may get out of hand soon."

The commanders conversed, some agreeing with each other. After a moment, Blague raised his hand and Drino walked over to the next candidate.

"This here is Rodest. He was Briggs' understudy in communications. He is incredibly talented with technology and has been vouched for by Briggs himself on multiple occasions. Do you have anything to say for yourself before the commanders comment?" Drino asked.

Rodest stepped forward, "I am the missing link in your leadership. I don't mean it arrogantly. I mean it in the sense that Briggs was like a father to me. I was with him through every mission and have a knack for technology. Outside of that, I'm as adaptive as I must be to fulfill my role. I stand before you to continue to lay my life on the line in order to see that the vision of our people becomes a reality."

He then stepped back into position.

"This kid has what it takes and his expertise is

needed," Telfice said.

"I like him, too. I've worked alongside this *mijo* a bunch," Lito said.

Biljin leaned forward to analyze him, looking him in the face "He doesn't have the confidence of a leader and I'm not so sure that's something that can be learned."

"Hah," Sabin said, "He's not squirming or cowering in fear as you rip him apart. That should count for something."

Blague raised his hand and Drino continued on.

"This here is Oscin. He's a very talented pilot and is a whiz with communications and technology. The catch is, this kid is a raging alcoholic and a smart ass. Do you have anything to say for yourself before the commanders comment?" Drino asked.

Oscin stepped forward, pulled out a flask, took a swig, and stepped back.

"A wildcard! I like wildcards," Sabin said. "You got our leader back in one piece from flying in a Hiezer jet, so that's gotta count for something," Sabin added, excited to see what the others had to say.

"I can whip this guy into shape," Lesh said, "If you believe his talents are worth it, that is."

"Are you kidding? He's the most disrespectful candidate so far. This kid is years of discipline away from being worth anything," Drino said while pointing right at him.

Blague raised his hand and Drino advanced to the last candidate, scoffing at Oscin as he walked by him. Oscin tipped his flask and gave Drino a smile.

"This here is Morn. Up until recently, he sold jewelry

in Clestice. He has developed useful connections over the years and has proved to be resourceful throughout missions and within the mansion. The downside is his hot temper. Do you have anything to say for yourself before the commanders comment?" Drino asked.

Morn stepped forward with his tanned trench coat, boots, and curly salt and pepper matted hair.

"It's an honor, commanders. If ya decide I'm worth your time, I'd be happy to contribute at a higher level," Morn said.

He stepped back and gave a look to his competition.

"He's a hothead that almost jeopardized the mission, but he's since been reliable and has proven to be resourceful," Lesh said.

"He's been able to survive with you know who," Sabin said motioning to Lesh, "He must be a tough customer."

Lesh rolled her eyes.

"I'm not sure his general resourcefulness will be enough to adapt to a group of roles he's had no experience with," Blague said as he raised his hand.

The room became louder as the last candidate stepped back into position.

"Thank you, candidates," Blague said, talking over the crowd, "You're dismissed."

They walked out of the room in a single file as the commanders continued to converse with each other.

"Commanders, take a half hour and submit your votes. Majority vote wins. If there's a tie, the two candidates with the most votes will be voted on again. After the voting has completed, we will discuss the strategy of our upcoming invasion and induct our newest member," Blague said.

Eugene woke up in a daze, his eyes unable to focus. He heard Jason's voice as if he were underwater. He quickly realized his hands and feet were tied. He twitched spastically, scraping his bare arms on the cement floor.

"Cut it out, jackass," Nemura's muffled voice warned, followed by a backhand to the face. He then pulled Eugene by the hair, "Can't you see the boss is speaking?" Nemura asked with a grin, staring him in the eyes.

Eugene's eyes still struggled to focus as they kept rolling to the back of his head every few seconds.

"The Aura grows!" Jason's voice carried through the air.

When Eugene regained his focus, he could see the entire Aura gathered around the jets. They all wore hooded half cloaks, except for Jason and his new prize who stood next to him, Jen.

"We've been blessed by a higher power. This island has given us the ability to evolve. We would be foolish not to embrace it," Jason said staring at the smoke-filled sky.

He awkwardly extended his left hand, reaching for Jen who was a few feet away.

"Asura and I are now connected. We will soon learn how to operate through one mind. I can already feel her thoughts. You will all experience this in time," he promised.

Jen stood unsteadily with her head tilted toward the ground. The scars on her face were wine red. The effects of the geyser had begun to settle in.

She seems calmer, at least for the moment. I thought she was going to kill me.

Eugene took in his surroundings. He watched as Nemura re-cloaked himself, trying to regain his focus on Jason's speech.

By some stroke of luck, we're both still alive. Well, I know why she's alive, but why me? Is it because I'm to be used as some sort of message?

Jason tilted his head to the side, letting his eyes roll to the back of his head. He lifted both of his arms. "My loyal servants, brace yourselves! This is the beginning!" Jason shouted.

Not a moment later, Jen let out a terrifying scream. She dropped to the ground and stared at her hands, all of her muscles were tensing. She clutched at her chest and shrieked again. Eugene tried to stand up to get a closer look. Jason stood with his arms raised, unmoving, showing no reaction to her cries. The ground around Jen's hands and feet cracked as the members around them bowed. Eugene noticed something odd. They weren't bowing to Jason, they were bowing to Jen.

"Asura," they began to chant.

Jen jerked her head up, whipping her hair back from her bulging reddish eyes. The smoke surrounding Auront began to move in their direction. Jason was concentrating, but it didn't seem like he was controlling what was occurring; Jen was responsible for it. Some sort of power was obviously emanating from her. The deep red smoke started to close in on them as if an avalanche was chasing them. Jason gently lowered his arms, with limp wrists and a smug face. He slowly opened his eyes and smiled at Jen.

"Asura, welcome to God. You and I will be the first to achieve harmony. But first, please," Jason motioned with one hand, "release your chaos," he said smiling.

Jason put both hands behind his back and leaned in, staring at Jen with half opened eyes. A long black lock of hair with a deep red frosted tip fell over his face. Jen's face was full of rage. Eugene attempted to peek over the heads of the group in front of him, trying to see through the hooded crowd. The smoke was moments away from approaching.

"Rise, Asura," Jason said still bent over. Jen unsheathed a knife. Eugene recognized the blade, taken from the guard that she had murdered.

What is going on? Why are these people so calm?

The smoke rapidly engulfed Jason and Jen first; Eugene saw Jen charge Jason as the smoke consumed them.

As soon as the smoke consumed Jen, she felt unstoppable, like a rush of adrenaline and power overtook her. She stomped the ground, to see it crack around her again. A funnel of smoke cleared within a small radius around her. There Jason was, ten feet taller than just a moment ago. Jen felt the tangle of fifteen unwanted hands grasping at her body, causing her to further enrage. She charged Jason with her knife.

He laughed at the sight, "Cause your chaos, Asura," he antagonized.

The smoke followed her as she sprinted toward him, the radius closing as she whipped around him, slicing at every exposed limb. She spun around his huge body that was now decloaked, and leapt toward his stomach, stabbing his abdomen with all of her might. She used her free hand to grip his chest and flung herself higher to slash open his throat. Red smoke poured out of Jason's open orifices, as he smiled at Jen with no emotion or reaction to the attacks. When Jen hit the floor, the smoke swiftly pulled back, rewinding to its normal state.

The Aura looked on calmly. Eugene was freaked out, trying to get a handle on what had just happened. His eyes widened when he looked over toward Jen. Jason had fallen to his knees, with blood pouring out of multiple wounds. His neck was slashed, but his face remained calm, even as blood spewed from his mouth. Jen stood next to him, breathing heavily with her fists clenched. She tossed the knife to the floor, her rage noticeably leaving her body. Slowly, her demeanor changed.

"Eugene!" she screamed. She looked at her blood soaked hands, "What's happening to me?" she whispered to herself.

Out of pure panic, Eugene wrestled free from his rope shackles and punched Nemura in the face.

"You piece of shit!" Nemura yelled.

The rest of the Aura bowed down to their only remaining god, Asura. Eugene pushed Nemura's face onto the cement ground, tying his hands behind his back.

"You're so lost," Nemura said, laughing at Eugene.

Eugene took Nemura by his wild silver hair and slammed it into the ground.

"Hahaha," Nemura laughed, "Your precious girlfriend is now our leader. Give it up, old buddy." He spun around to look at Eugene, "Do you know what Jason Brink said before he was slashed bloody?"

"What?" Eugene asked with little patience in his voice.

Nemura lifted his scraped face and said, "Follow Asura in my absence. She will end this life of mine, and until I return, she will continue the Aura's evolution."

Chapter 20

I've lived a youthful life longer than any man should. I've seen the world in two completely different states and lived with strong purpose throughout it all.

Blague looked at his hands.

I haven't aged in over forty years. I don't deserve to wake up young for the better part of a century when young men and women are dying before thirty in this sad excuse for a life. If this is my last battle, I have to make it count. I have to do it for the people who haven't yet lived.

Blague looked up; his Cryos mark was stifling, leaving a heat trail emanating from his arm. Blague stood on the roof of the mansion, observing as the final preparations were made to the jets.

He turned to Lito and put a hand on his shoulder, "This battle may become intense. With all of the highlords in one place, you can expect the protection to be ironclad. I need you to promise me something, Lito," he said.

"Of course, anything," Lito responded, bowing his head to listen more intently.

"Don't jump headfirst into battle. Your role is expanded now. As soon as the battle looks like it's going in our favor, you're to take a fighter jet and a pilot and get your ass over to Bulchevin to oversee our expansion. Is that clear?" Blague asked.

"*Comprendo*, boss," Lito responded.

"I'm serious, I can't have you dying on me," Blague said.

Lito lifted his head, his green mohawk slightly blowing in the wind, "I hear you, I'll be careful."

Blague stared at him for a few moments and eventually gave a nod. Lito jogged off toward one of the jets and spun his finger in the air, signaling to the others to get things moving. Blague heard a bark and turned around. Sabin strutted confidently over to Blague with Mars at his side.

"This is going to be like old times, old friend," Sabin said smiling.

Blague flashed a half smirk back, "How do you figure?"

"Oh come on," Sabin said, "I'm riding with you, aren't I?"

Blague didn't respond for a moment.

Sabin held up his stringed blades, "You know I prefer close combat and I know you're the one expecting to pay your brother a personal visit," he said excitedly.

Blague nodded, "You were coming with me from the start."

Sabin's golden eyes lit up. "You hear that, buddy?" he said as he kneeled down to pet Mars, "We're flying with the boss today."

"Hah! Have you asked out your love yet?" Blague asked.

Sabin waved his blade by his own neck, signaling for Blague to stop talking. Blague then recognized the sound of Lesh's footsteps walking up from behind him. He couldn't help but laugh. Sabin, not taking himself too seriously, also burst out laughing.

"You two are laughing like little school girls," Lesh said.

"We have to enjoy ourselves sometimes, even in the face of death," Sabin said in between laughs.

"Ok, try me. What's so funny?" she asked.

Blague looked over at Sabin to let him respond.

"Sorry babe, girl scout secret," Sabin said as he smiled.

Lesh rolled her eyes and turned to Blague, "Am I in the longview command post with Drino?"

Blague nodded.

"Are you sure you don't want me in close quarters combat?"

"I want you in both, Lesh," Blague responded, "I'll let you choose. You'll sway whichever squad you're in to our favor," he continued.

"I'll decide how dangerous the longview command is once we get there," she said without reacting to Blague's compliment.

"You two be careful once we get there. We're now fighting for more than that small group that we started with," Blague said.

Sabin nodded while Lesh stood there, contemplating the best course of action.

"Alright, I'm going to make sure Cherris is prepared to hold down the fort. Please excuse me," Blague said.

"How's that boy that you're training doing?" Sabin asked.

"What the hell? Are you spying on me?" Lesh asked.

Blague smirked as he trailed away from them.

Today may change everything. If we can disrupt the highlord meeting, we can stall their plans and buy us time to take a second fortress. Mulderan won't retaliate against our home because he still believes the Ayelan chemical to be too precious to risk destroying. This attack may drive him to a breaking point, though.

Blague walked through the large crowd on the roof; people bowed out of his way as he headed toward Cherris.

Even though that bastard was right one day years ago, it could never justify mass murder. Even if he believes in his calculating head that he's preparing us for survival. He's playing God by the judgements he passes. He had this day coming to him.

"Blague," Cherris said with her arms held out for a hug.

Blague walked right in and hugged her back.

"Keep things in order while I'm gone," Blague said, "We have intel that the meeting is to begin shortly."

"You're leaving me kind of thin on protection," she said while giving him an impatient look.

Blague stared back reassuringly, "Telfice and his crew will be patrolling the perimeter. You will be protected. Besides, Rodest has been ordered to stay by your side as he manages our communications and Volaina will be close by as well."

Cherris nodded, "It's been a month. He's picking up quickly. It seems you all made the right choice inducting him."

"I'm glad you approve," Blague responded, "I'll see

you soon."

"Be careful. This is an aggressive assault you're pulling. Just don't forget the hope you've instilled in all of these families when you're out on the battlefield. Try not to get killed," Cherris said.

Blague nodded and turned to head toward the jet. The roof was packed with Sin fighters readying for battle. They sprinted in every direction, scrambling to prepare for the assault on the flooded wasteland of Old New York. Blague wore light combat wear all in black, with a deep blue tank top under his vest.

Briggs, Eugene, my old friends… how I could use you now.

Blague walked onto a recovered Hiezer jet infused with the advanced technology needed for a surprise attack. He watched as the coordinators signaled for the jets to take off.

Elaina, if there's some semblance of you that lives within me, hear this: I would give anything to connect with you again.

Blague looked up as the landing platform lifted. Anger began to flow through him yet again.

Mulderan, you've caused enough suffering for one extended lifetime.

The highlords sat at an oval, black marble table, decorated with golden candles and a large Hiezer symbol in the center. The facility was immaculate and new, with a unique architectural design. The structure of the building was centralized around the meeting room, the ceiling of which extended thirty feet high, ending with a sharp point. The secret fortress was intertwined within a mountain, sitting about thirty feet above a large body of water. The view from the other end of the building consisted of about two miles of flat land extending into more hills and mountains in the distance. The foundation of the fortress was made up of long pillars that firmly anchored into the water, similar to the foundation of a bridge. The secondary support included contraptions built around the mountain to firmly secure the portion of the building that was suspended in mid-air. The roof had several cathedral-like points, portraying a regal and rich ambiance. The fortress had an additional circular structure jutting out from the backside, floating over the body of water. It acted as a landing pad for Mulderan's jet, which was still steaming from its earlier landing. Hiezer elite guards were stationed within close vicinity of the fortress, followed by a few hundred infantry. Mulderan stood at the head of the table with his head turned to the elite guard at the door.

"The perimeter has been swept. We're all clear," said the six foot five inch Protective Order guard, who was equipped with a machine gun.

Mulderan nodded and faced forward with Eldra by his side. The guard left the room to safeguard the doorway.

"Full disclosure," Mulderan said, "before we begin, a quartermaster from Clestice believes that there's a slight chance that the location of this fortress could be compromised. We have taken precautionary measures and pulled an additional hundred guards from the field as protection," he assured.

"We are the world's protectors all sitting in one room, Mulderan. How could this meeting be called with even a slight chance of the location being leaked?" a tall tanned skinned highlord asked.

"There is always that risk, Veer," Mulderan replied, "This knowledge is urgent and is worth that risk. We have one bit of news before I begin." Mulderan motioned to Eldra.

She stepped forward to her seated audience and slid her device to the middle of the table.

"The leader of the Templos movement has been silenced, by way of our successful apprehension of his son and daughter. Though it is rumored that a man who hides in the shadows supersedes this leader, the attacks have ceased since we captured his offspring. If further attacks on Dactuar estates are reported, we have decided to set loose Dendrid on the rebel group," Eldra said.

"Releasing Dendrid is something that should be subject to a unanimous highlord vote, considering the damage he's done," an older blonde woman said.

"Hah, it would be more ethical to execute the kids," Jeck said out loud to himself.

Mulderan raised an eyebrow as his eyes shifted from Jeck to the center of the room.

"The kids are additional leverage," Eldra said while leaning on the table with both of her hands.

Veer raised his hand and stood, "Forgive me for being stationed on the other side of the world, but isn't that the man who carved out his brother's eyes and set his parents aflame when they came to his aid?"

"That would be him," Alek said with his arms folded,

sitting back in his chair. "If that's not bad enough, he was eleven when he did it," Alek continued.

Eldra put up a hand, "Enough."

Veer took his seat.

"We will place a tracking signal in his spine that will shock and paralyze him with the press of a button, if it even comes to that point," she said.

Mulderan stood quietly. His long, silky black hair did not match his stern face. His cloak flowed with a unique, regal Hiezer design, as it was stitched more elaborately than his fellow highlords. Eldra took her hands off the table and sat down.

"The matter is settled," Mulderan began. "The attacks have ceased and we have a plan if they resume. There's little room to debate that matter. On the other hand," he said while pacing slowly around the room, "the microdrill reached its destination and surveyed the earth's core. The outcome is as I predicted: seismic activity is becoming more frequent due to the erratic temperature changes within the inner core. The drill transmitted temperatures ranging from six thousand to ten thousand Kelvin. In other words, the core is heavily unstable and at any moment we can have a reoccurrence of the quake in 2022."

Chatter broke out among the lords.

"Fortunately," Mulderan said as he held his hand up for silence, "we have been preparing for this for over forty years. To start, all Hiezer fortresses are completely quake resistant, using an expanding cohesive that can adapt to rapid change in density. Second," he said while almost completing a full circle back to his chair.

A rumbling interrupted Mulderan's presentation and

alarms rang throughout the building. The highlords began to panic. Mulderan and Eldra remained calm and exchanged a look.

"Was is worth it?" Alek shouted to Mulderan in between the chaos.

Mulderan stared at him with a straight face and paced over to him calmly.

"I've just given you the most delicate information in this world," Mulderan shouted for everyone to hear. "Take it and flee. Be responsible with it, as the continued survival of humanity depends on your ability to react."

Mulderan motioned for Eldra to join him as he moved toward the exit.

"Head to the highpoint of the valley about six hundred feet west," Mulderan told Eldra, "It will act as a fine sniper's nest."

"Where are you going?" Jeck asked.

"To handle the threat," Mulderan replied.

Blague stopped running and held his knees, out of breath.

"You're out of shape," a man with golden eyes said, smiling.

"I came as fast as I could, Aldarian," Blague said as he held out his hand to reveal an Onyx imbued key.

Aldarian grabbed and inspected it.

"We're too late, my good man, although this key is beautiful," he said.

Blague looked around at the weathered tent that he had just sprinted into.

"Listen to me," Aldarian said as he put a hand on

Blague's shoulder, "Society N vanished after the quake. We don't even know if any of the members are still alive. This world is growing cold and cruel by each passing day. I'll take this key and continue our search, but if I don't make it, promise me one thing."

"Sure, Al, anything," Blague said as sweat dripped down his forehead.

"Reach out to my son and look after him for me."

Blague stood silent for a moment, taking in the reality that he may lose another dear friend. Eventually, Blague gave a curt nod.

"Thank you, old friend," Aldarian said as he patted him twice on the shoulder. "Now, let's have a drink and we shall toast to the end of civilization!" he shouted.

Blague couldn't help but smile back.

At that moment, he returned from his world of thought, standing in the jet hanger with Sabin in his line of sight. Blague looked at his hand, realizing he hadn't aged since that time long ago.

"Your father would be proud," Blague said to Sabin.

Sabin looked up a bit startled, "Are you reminiscing in that brain of yours again?"

Blague shrugged a shoulder, as if to say, do you have to ask?

"Thanks, Blague," Sabin finally responded. Blague looked out the window, noticing the longview squad jets already landing on the other side of the fortress.

"You know, my father left me a series of notes, one of which said, 'trust Grenich.' He really should have put a first name on that sheet of paper, because you're kind of an asshole, and I think I picked the wrong one," Sabin could barely finish the sentence without cracking a smile.

Blague let out a laugh.

"You two are jackasses," Lesh said, standing behind Blague.

Moments later, the jet began to shutter as they boldly landed eighty feet from the fortress, just out of range of their anti-aircraft defenses. Blague's tone became very serious.

"Get ready, Sins," Blague said as the veins jutted from his neck, "This battle ensures another day of safety for our families at home. Think of them when you give the Hiezers hell today."

Blague slammed his chest and an echo of beats followed.

It was a cloudy day in the wasteland that was Old New York. The body of water surrounding the top of a mountain made for a surreal scene. Drino pulled up on the far side of the flat land at the same time the jets made their landing. Drino docked the recovered Hiezer boat, which the Hiezers had used to storm the mansion months prior. He took with him a small army consisting of multiple squads. The side of the boat lifted, allowing the masses of Sin fighters to unload onto the land and meet with their comrades who poured out of the jets. Drino, who was equipped with a minigun and two rifles strapped to his back, ran to Lito's jet.

He was aware of Lito's orders to head to Bulchevin, "Let's get you out of here as soon as possible."

"Aye, *mijo*, but not yet. We got work to do. I have the

medics and nurses setting up in that area," Lito said as he pointed to a partially blocked off corner where the jets had landed. "There isn't much cover here and that's a lot of guards prepping in the distance," he continued.

"My squads are setting up as we speak. They're flanking behind the west mountain," Drino said, "We just have to stall as much as we can."

A bullet whizzed above Drino's head, hitting the ladder of a jet.

They both ducked, "They're closing in," Drino said as he turned around and stood tall.

"We have to give Blague cover, now!" Lito said.

"Soldiers!" Drino roared with a stentorian voice, "Attack! For the Sins!"

Drino let two shielded soldiers ahead of him and then sprinted, hauling his minigun. Lito dashed to the edge of the mountain closest to him, carefully plotting his strategy to bomb the Hiezers. He took a quick survey of the layout of rocks to use as cover. Back on the flat land, a mix of Hiezer elite and infantry guards aggressively ambushed the Sins, unleashing hell in the form of bullets. Their ferocity was stemmed from the Sin's audacity to attack them at their own headquarters.

Lito picked up his radio, "Snipers! Aim for the departing jets in the distance! Those bastards must be the highlords."

"Roger, commander," a Sin sniper replied.

A wave of high caliber bullets clanged as they punctured steel jets attempting to take off. One jet faltered since the pilot panicked for a moment, reducing the thruster speed as it lifted vertically. The pilot recovered and quickly sped off, leaving a trail of smoke from behind.

"Adjust!" the sniper yelled as he repositioned.

A second wave of bullets crashed into the next departing jet, this time hitting a vital fuel pocket. The jet caught fire and spun back down toward a group of Hiezer guards, knocking up the terrain as it swiped the ground. The guards and fighters who were mid-field opened fire, which erupted into an intense, high velocity battle. Both sides of the mountain had enough rocks to take cover, but the land in between was flat and open. The only cover provided was whatever bullet-proof vests and shields the soldiers had equipped. Some guards continued charging as others remained prone, unleashing havoc with their rifles. Sin fighters fell around Drino; their bodies jerked from the impact of bullets. His jaw remained tense while he quickly assessed the situation. He was sandwiched behind two fighters, who were desperately pressing their shields onto the sides of his minigun, trying to deflect the incoming barrage of bullets. Drino pulled the trigger; the engine of the gun revved for a second before the bullets shot out. Drino let out a roar as he swung his gun to take out the closest advancing troops. Blood and falling bodies painted the canvas around them.

A Sin fighter quickly dropped to the floor and took aim at a guard who was getting into position. He fired and watched the guard stumble and fall to one knee, desperately trying to close the wound in his arm where blood poured out. The fighter stood up to get a better shot and finish the guard, but a bullet kicked his head back as it pierced his forehead. His body fell backward and landed contorted.

"We have at least one highlord still on the premises," Lito yelled through his radio, "He's limping out of the fallen jet."

Lito put his binoculars away and pulled out a mortar stand from his backpack. He bobbed his head, unable to contain his excitement. He spun the lever a few times to calculate the precise angle. He then took a moment to witness the chaos of the two forces clashing together; the firing match had now developed into a tangle of close combat warfare and ranged assault. He dropped a mortar down the shoot and fired toward the back of the Hiezer army. Bodies were thrown all around from the blast. Anxious to change his position, Lito quickly dropped another mortar down the shoot. He ducked behind a boulder, noticing a few soldiers shift their rifles to his location. Lito's short, green mohawk barely stuck out above the rock. The guards advanced toward Lito very low to the ground.

"These dudes are more adaptive than the other Hiezer guards I've faced," Lito said out loud to himself. "I wonder if they can adapt to these," he said as he reached in his bag and pulled out two hand grenades.

He pulled the pin and hooked one over the rock, past the guards. Lito peeked out, watching the guards' necks turn to follow the grenade lobbed overhead. Lito rolled the next grenade on the ground toward them before they could react. He then sprinted back toward the Sin camp. Lito plugged his ears while the explosion tore their bodies to shreds.

"Now!" Drino yelled into his radio before a pack of

advancing Hiezer guards tumbled onto him.

Drino's coordinated squads flanked from the southwest, emerging from the rock path with ferocity. Squad X positioned themselves midrange, unleashing a storm of bullets toward the advancing guards' backside. Lito took a glance and although the struggle was violent, the battle now appeared to be moving in the Sin's favor. A guard lunged, desperately reaching his blade toward Drino's neck, in an attempt to take a top commander's head as a trophy. Drino was overwhelmed with three bodies sprawled around him, pushing him to the ground. Time slowed for a moment; he sat back dazed as gunfire and explosions lit the air above him, deaf to all of the insanity. After a brief moment, his hearing came back and his adrenaline released him from the daze. Drino lifted his head to see the guard about to slice his throat. He wrestled one arm free by flipping a body off of him and snapped the guard's swinging arm. He closed his fist around the blade to prevent it from cutting his throat. He then jerked the blade, quickly twisting it free, and snapping the guard's shoulder right out of its socket. Blood dripped from Drino's hand as he released his grip on the blade. The cuts were deep, but there was no time to even consider them; he was overcome with bodies desperately trying to make it out of the dogpile alive. Drino cracked another guard's mask with his brass-knuckled fist. He then used his arms to pull his legs out from under a limp body. Without taking a moment to recover, he dove to save a fighter's life, by strangling a guard and repeatedly smashing his temple. Lito, still sprinting for the medic wedge, noticed three slim elite guards run past the crowd. All of them seemed to be equipped with explosives, sprinting at high speed.

"Snipers, focus fire on the three elite guards heading toward the jets!" Lito shouted into the radio.

The snipers, who were covered by rock, adjusted their aim. The guards began to close in on their target. A sniper fired, nearly blowing off one of the guard's arms. The force of the bullet spun him to the floor. The other two snipers fired. One of the guards dashed and flipped as soon as he heard the gun shot, barely dodging both bullets. The guard regained his speed as soon as his feet hit the floor. A sniper let out another high caliber bullet. The bullet hit one of the grenades attached to the other sprinting guard's hip, ripping her to shreds. The other elite guard pulled a grenade from his hip as he approached his destination. He flung it into the landing platform of the jet and sprinted to the next. The mid-section of the jet exploded, damaging it beyond repair. As the guard approached the next jet, a man jumped high from the landing platform, tackling the guard before he could pull the pin on his next grenade. The Sin fighters that spotted the guard were hesitant to shoot, considering he was full of explosives and infiltrated the camp. Chella ran up to get a closer look. The man who tackled the guard was Oscin. She almost couldn't believe her eyes; the thin, drunk man apparently found an ounce of courage in him. Chella gathered herself after realizing that Oscin was losing his heroic fight. The elite guard had both of his hands wrapped around Oscin's neck. She ran over and as Oscin kneed him in the groin, Chella knocked him in the face with her automatic rifle and shot him in the head.

Oscin struggled to catch his breath as Chella reached out her hand to lift him up. After ten seconds of coughing and heavy breathing, Oscin finally reached out.

"That was very brave of you," she said.

"What choice did I have?" Oscin asked as he wiped the dirt off of him. "It was either stop him or blow up in a jet," he said, his breath reeking of alcohol.

Chella smiled at him and jogged after Lito, who was approaching.

"Hey, thanks for the save," Oscin said.

Chella turned back and nodded. Oscin headed back toward his jet. Bullets whizzed in all directions. The flank carried out by Drino's squads noticeably turned the tide of the battle. Lito jogged up to Chella, when a loud noise echoed through the air. Oscin turned his head to see six Hiezer carrier jets pull up to the fortress. Lito and Chella's faces turned tense, realizing this was an awful turn of events.

"They wouldn't bomb our camp, would they?" Chella asked as the noise of the jets died down.

Lito shook his head, "They have to assume we carry Ayelan with us wherever we set up a base. At the same time, we shouldn't use our jets for combat either, in case they get blown up. Then we be sitting ducks for their reinforcements. Blague assured that the warfare would remain traditional because of this. Smart man, that boss of ours," Lito said while tapping his finger on his head.

Chella raised her eyebrows and nodded.

"Pull the reserve fighters and send them in under my order. This does not look good," Lito said.

Oscin ran up the landing platform in a panic and

tried to shut it. A moment later, the jet's engines fired up.

"No! That *pedazo de mierda*!" Lito shouted, turning back to see a rising jet. "Get back here, Oscin! We need every resource we can get!" Lito shouted through the radio.

The jet took off and headed westbound.

Chapter 21

Is this a brotherly feud? No, it's more than that. Blague is genuine and he's always been. It seems like his brother may have just pushed him over the edge. Backed him into a corner, with nothing left to do but fight. No, that's not it either.

Lesh walked beside Blague and Sabin, as she twirled a throwing knife on her finger. The three of them, along with fifteen top Sin fighters stormed the fortress head on as the battle raged on outside.

He wasn't backed into a corner. He just had nothing more to lose. Elaina and his father were taken from him. He saw the layers of hell within this world and this man had enough courage to try and change it.

"It's too quiet in here," Sabin said, with his string blades out and Mars by his side.

Lesh analyzed the area while determining her next moves. Blague confidently led the group, taking note of their surroundings.

"We're going to find what we want in here. All of the highlords couldn't have had enough time to escape, but rest assured, when we find one, that person will be heavily guarded," Blague said.

The long, prestigiously decorated hallway seemed endless. There were three separate doorways at the end of the hall creating a fork in its path.

"I heard something," Lesh said.

As they slowed their pace, the muffled sound of a loudspeaker echoed through the room.

"Blague," Mulderan's distinct voice came through the speakers, "how curiously aggressive of you to barge in on my progress."

Blague drew his Desert Eagle, fully aware that the trap had sprung. The eighteen of them heard the front door slam shut behind them.

"Your interference has so little purpose. You couldn't be more ignorant as to what lies ahead of us. Now, you've forced my hand. You will have to hear your friends die with no help from their leader," Mulderan stated, annoyed at the attempted ambush.

Blague's radio went off a moment later, "We're being overwhelmed Blague! Phase two is not a go. I have to stay put, we may not make it!" Lito shouted over the chaos in the background.

Sabin clenched his jaw and turned to Blague, "They knew about the ambush?"

Blague shook his head, "If they knew for sure, they wouldn't have come. They might have had a hunch though, judging by the level of protection."

"What are we waiting for?" Lesh interrupted, "We have to get on with this if we're going to save the fighters outside." She sprinted ahead.

Blague looked at Sabin, "She's right, let's move."

Sabin swung his arm for the team to follow. Lesh flipped upward to the ceiling, hanging upside down from its ledge. She took out a small device made by Rodest and flashed it by the control panel next to the metal door. The door immediately opened. She quickly peeked from the top of the doorway and got a glimpse of the soldiers taking cover in the next room. The room was large and filled with thick pillars from the floor to the ceiling. Lesh dropped to the floor and slipped in. Blague followed with his gun pointed toward the floor. They both took cover behind the first large pillar to their left. The door shut behind Blague, locking them in the room. Another one opened near where Sabin and the remaining fighters were standing in the hallway. A huge elite guard swung a giant fist in through the doorway, smashing a Sin in the temple. Sabin fell back for a moment from the shock.

"Charge the left door!" Sabin shouted as he held Mars by the collar, preventing him from leaping at the guard.

Sabin's half cape flapped in the wind as fighters sprinted past him.

"Fire!" Mulderan commanded in the distance.

"He's close," Blague said.

Lesh nodded, "No time to waste," she said before dashing in between the pillars on the left side of the large room.

Two Hiezer elite guards revealed their position and opened fire. Lesh flipped high into the air and flung two knives, impaling one of the guards in the shoulder and neck. Blague pushed forward as the attention was on Lesh. He opened fire on the second guard, hitting him in the thigh and stomach. The guard groaned and dropped his assault rifle. Lesh looked behind her and noticed Blague's rage beginning to manifest. She sprinted toward the dead guard and retrieved her two bloody knives. She saw four more guards break their cover and open fire.

Her evasive tactics made her a very difficult target to nail. Not losing an ounce of momentum, she ran two steps up the wall closest to her and kicked off into the air, becoming visible to the guards. She tossed a bloody knife into a guard's eye. Screams and curses came out of him as he dropped his rifle. The other guards ran to where they thought Lesh would land, only to find a Desert Eagle waiting to claim them. Blague fired four shots, fatally wounding the three of them. Blague lifted his gun upright as he saw Lesh fly through, landing on her feet from a long backflip.

"He's here, Blague," Lesh said, "I got a glimpse of him."

They both ran toward the next room, strafing back and forth, advancing through the elite guards set to protect Mulderan. Lesh's deadly knives stuck out of each guard only for a second before she recycled them to her next victim. Blague provided protection to Lesh and smoothly switched to the lead in between her kills. They poetically made a mess of the fortress, leading all the way to Mulderan, who fearlessly stood in plain sight. His black cloak extended to his shins and his regal shoulder guards and crown shined in the light. His long flowing hair made it seem like he never tasted battle before. Lesh swung two knives at him, each soaring at just under a hundred miles per hour. Mulderan unleashed his black and gold bow and deflected them effortlessly; knocking one into the wall and one back toward Lesh. Blague rushed out and opened fire. Mulderan took cover before the high caliber bullets could penetrate.

"It looks like this is it for me. It's been a pleasure

serving with you all," Drino's struggling, spotty voice came through each of their radios.

Lesh took a deep breath and Blague's rage grew stronger.

He ran over to Lesh and looked her closely in the eyes, "Go, save our friends. I'll take it from here."

Lesh nodded and sprinted back for the door.

Drino held his stomach as the blood poured out of the bullet wound in his abdomen. His brass knuckles were dented and covered in blood. He fell to his knees and grimaced in pain. His free hand fell on the assault rifle of a fallen fighter. Twenty guards marched to snuff out his flame.

The reinforcements, they were so close to the fortress. They had to have known.

Squads X, Y, and Z were commanded to retreat back to the camp on Drino's orders. The reserves and fighters also regrouped at the camp to await their commander. Few fighters remained on the battlefield after the reinforcements wiped out most of the front lines. Medics ran to the field to save who they could.

If we stay, this could turn into a massacre. I hope Lito makes the right call.

The twenty guards ceased their march a few feet away from Drino and the wounded fighters on the battlefield.

"Cleanup," Drino said out loud to himself, coughing.

They raised their weapons, each taking aim at the survivors. Three of the guards were fixated on Drino, who exuded strength, even with a bullet in him.

"Ready!" the leading Hiezer guard shouted.

The sound of tensing muscles inside leather armor carried through the air. Drino readied himself to die fighting. A moment later, an explosion shot scrap metal through the air where the reinforcement carrier jets had landed. A jet then slowed its speed and unleashed a barrage of bullets upon the unsuspecting Hiezer cleanup crew.

"You're not going down like this, commander," Oscin said through his radio.

Drino grinned at the unexpected save. He drew the weapon from under his free hand and swung his arm with the last of his strength. A trail of bullets from the automatic rifle finished off the cleanup crew. He dropped the gun and fell to his knees when he saw the last guard fall. He stared at the wound for a moment as the blood poured down one of his hands. He looked up to the sky, just before a determined medic hooked him from under his arms and hoisted him onto a stretcher. Oscin's jet slowed and landed back at the Sin camp.

"I have to stay out there," Drino yelled at the medic, with a strained voice, "There're still at least five hundred Hiezer reinforcements to our two hundred remaining fighters!"

The two medics carrying his stretcher ignored him as they lugged him back to the camp. He reached for the stained battlefield as it faded into the distance.

One of the rooms in the fortress erupted into a bloodbath. As the Sin fighters entered, gunfire spewed from both sides. Sabin fired careful shots with his long barrel pistol, waiting for the right time to unleash his blades. He ordered Mars to stay in the hallway until the gunfire died down. The elite guard with a roaring lion etched into his helmet ravaged through the fighters; his steel breastplate fended off incoming bullets. He lunged forward, unleashing deadly force in the form of heavy, brutal punches. The fighters were focused on the incoming fire, while Sabin diverted; he noticed how much of a threat the weaponless colossus was.

Volaina mentioned this one. He must be Wes Howard, the guerilla warfare nutjob.

Sabin saw the open creases in his armor and quickly let a blade fly. Wes lifted his leg, causing the blade to bounce off of his steel armor. Sabin whipped the blade back, catching it with his metal glove. Wes lunged at another fighter, shattering ribs with one punch to the gut.

"I knew you pieces of shit would show up," Wes roared as he spun to uppercut the next fighter, snapping his neck.

Only a handful of guards and fighters remained. Sabin jumped behind a pillar to avoid incoming gunfire, but had a clear shot at the charging beast wreaking havoc. Sabin threw his blade and used his other arm to adjust the tightening string. He guided the blade upward, slashing Wes' skin right between his forearm and bicep. Sabin whipped the blade back as Wes groaned. Wes focused his attention to Sabin.

Oh shit.

Sabin kicked off the pillar and dove out of the doorway, as Wes ran in his direction. Mars was anxiously waiting behind the door, obedient to Sabin's orders. Mars' ears tensed as Sabin flew out of the doorway. He whipped his blade toward Mars, timing the shot perfectly. Just as Wes charged into the hallway, Sabin's blade slashed him right behind the knee. Wes grunted, while Sabin whipped the blade back to his hand. He simultaneously threw the other blade toward Wes' neck. Wes caught it midair; his hand spewed blood from the deep cut. Wes yanked the blade as hard as he could, jerking Sabin to the floor.

"Now, Mars!" Sabin shouted.

Mars lunged from his position, tearing at the exposed flesh between the back of Wes' knee and calf. Wes cursed, swinging wildly behind him with his free hand. Mars took another ferocious bite. The giant's strength didn't falter. Wes jerked his leg, sending the wolf flying into the wall. Mars yelped upon impact. Wes turned back to Sabin, now bleeding from multiple wounds. He pulled Sabin into his hands with two tugs at the wire and lifted him by the neck. Sabin kicked spastically, unable to catch his breath.

"You giann pfffor shtttt," he mumbled, while gasping for a breath.

Wes released one hand to remove his mask so that he could take a closer look at the man he was strangling.

"Golden eyes," Wes said curiously, "Where have I seen those before?"

Wes re-tightened his grip. Sabin tried to jab at the man's face, but quickly reverted back to trying to pry Wes' fingers from his throat. Just then, the middle door opened behind them. Lesh flew out like a bullet, tossing a knife into the elbow crease of Wes' armor. She removed the knife, flipped over the tall man, and then sprinted toward the front door. Distracted and in pain, Wes loosened his grip. Sabin fell to his knees as he tried to catch his breath.

"We're even!" Lesh yelled as she sprinted for the front door, flashing a grin at Sabin.

Sabin took the blade that was still tumbling on the floor and slashed into Wes' exposed skin near his shoulder. Wes' blood puddled onto the floor from all of the fresh, open wounds.

"What I was trying to say is that you're a giant piece of shit," Sabin said as he kicked Wes to the floor.

Sabin quickly ran over to Mars, who was breathing, but in terrible pain.

"You're alright buddy," Sabin said as he inspected his best friend, "It's just a bruise."

Mars was dazed from the impact, so Sabin pet him delicately and then went to go check on any survivors in the other room. Two Sin fighters were left trying to keep a third fighter alive, putting pressure on a deep stomach wound. Sabin shook his head and wiped off the blood on his blade.

He picked up his radio, "I need medics in the fortress. The front hallway is clear," he said as he walked back to tend to his wolf.

Blague shot at the pillar Mulderan used for cover.

"Is this really your path, Blague?" Mulderan questioned.

Blague shifted to the next pillar and let out three more shots.

"Stopping someone from achieving something great?" Mulderan questioned again as he shifted his position to shield himself, "What would Elaina think of you now?"

Blague dipped his head, the memories rushing into his mind as fast as the blood flowed through his veins.

"Murder, Mulderan. Murder is all you have accomplished," Blague said with strain in his voice, dragging his words out.

"For humanity, brother," Mulderan shouted as he shifted pillars, letting out a spray of bullets from his rifle, "There's nothing greater than that."

They continued to exchange shots as Blague retreated into his head, his thoughts racing.

"You could have been a great contributor, Blague," Mulderan said as he held down his distraught brother.

Blague was still sickened from the murder of Elaina just an hour earlier.

"You fail to see the truth, just like our father," Mulderan mocked as he unclamped one of Blague's arms. "Now hold still while I sentence you to banishment."

Silent tears escaped Blague's eyes, digesting the reality of another fallen loved one.

"You could have been the greatest Hiezer of all," Mulderan said as he lowered the Cryos needle.

Blague transcended human strength as the needle engraved the Sin mark onto his arm. He twitched and broke through the steel clamps and knocked Mulderan ten feet back. His mark was a mix of Cryos blue and blood; an unfinished, smeared mark unlike those of his new Sin brothers and sisters. Blague got up and charged his smiling brother, getting a few rage induced smashes to Mulderan's face.

Mulderan laughed as the guards forcefully restrained Blague, "I'm actually remorseful I wasted the preservation of life on you, a defiler. Get him out of my sight," Mulderan said, waving Blague away.

Blague shifted pillars and gripped his gun. He aimed his last shots at the low ceiling of the room. Mulderan was forced to strafe in Blague's direction to avoid the falling debris. Blague took the opportunity to kick the rifle out of Mulderan's hand and swing for his face. Mulderan spun and reached for his staff, as Blague unsheathed his black carbon blade. Blague lunged forward, slashing twice. Mulderan flipped his staff artfully, blocking both of Blague's advances and kicking him back. Mulderan unclipped his pauldrons and shrugged them off; they hit the ground hard and his cloak followed to the floor. Mulderan's tall and lean figure was more apparent in his fitted, rich garb of black and gold. He flipped his staff to show off before attacking Blague, whose Cryos mark was glowing through his bloodied arm. Mulderan attacked three times at lightning speed with his staff. Blague parried with aggression and held the third clash, pushing his brother back and indenting Mulderan's staff with his blade.

"I've always enjoyed this more," Mulderan said, leaning in to closely stare Blague in the face, "It's much more personal than pulling a trigger."

"When have you ever identified with any emotion?" Blague asked as he pulled back the parry and slashed toward Mulderan's face.

Mulderan evaded and slammed the bottom of his staff into Blague's shin.

"On the contrary, why would I fight so hard for humanity if I didn't have my own memories I thought were worth fighting for?" Mulderan asked rhetorically while swinging his staff and pushing Blague into a corner. "Every unfortunate life that I had to take was backed by the thoughts of my experiences and how billions of potential lives may have experiences of their own in the future. Why am I the only one with the fortitude to make the ultimate sacrifices?" Mulderan asked as he swung his staff harder, causing Blague's parries to jerk closer to his body. "Why am I the only one who can see that a billion lives are worth a few sacrifices? It's my curse, and indirectly your curse too. But it's to humanity's gain," Mulderan finished.

Blague lunged forward and kneed Mulderan in the stomach.

"You truly are lost. Your obsessiveness and obscurity has made it impossible to reason with you. That fact has remained unchanged since we were kids," Blague responded as he stabbed and slashed, aiming to kill.

Mulderan ducked and parried, guiding Blague's blade in different directions.

"I always knew you were meant for something greater. I just didn't realize what that was until now," Mulderan said as he motioned to the scientist to proceed. "Goodbye, Elaina. I'm sure Blague will miss you."

Tears fell as she remained silent, staring at Mulderan. She knew it was useless to try and reason with him.

Blague's green eyes turned bloodshot from his rage. He swung with a wrath that Mulderan could only keep up with for a few seconds. The carbon steel blade clashed against the metal stave, causing sparks to fly. Blague spun and slashed wildly, splitting open Mulderan's garb and slicing his chest. Before Mulderan could look down, Blague dashed and jabbed a fist into his face. Blague let out a roar as he gathered momentum to elbow him in the temple. Mulderan stepped back, dazed and barely able to hold on to his staff. Blague was focused and his strength was beyond his normal limits. Without giving Mulderan a moment, Blague tackled him straight through the door leading to the outdoor landing pad. Blague lifted himself and flipped the blade in his hand to face the floor, in position to stab Mulderan.

"Forgive me father, I couldn't save him," Blague said as he stared into Mulderan's hazel eyes.

Elaina, I should have done this a lifetime ago.

Blague's arm descended with force as Mulderan grinned, staring back at his brother. Just before the knife plunged into his heart, a spear punctured Blague's shoulder and sent him flying back, slamming his back on the ground. He grabbed the spear with both hands, realizing it was lodged deep. The sound of guns loading echoed. Blague lifted his head to see an elite guard flipping spears around with both of his hands, followed by twelve soldiers with assault rifles coming his way.

"Did you really think I would leave this battle to fate, Blague?" Mulderan said, brushing off the dirt from his fall. "My mission is as large as this earth, while your rebellion is as insignificant as a grain of sand," Mulderan said as he kicked his staff back into his hands. He turned his back to Blague, waved his hand, and calmly said, "Open fire."

Eldra fired at a Sin fighter who attempted to flee the scene. The Sin reserves took cover behind shields and jets on the other side of the battlefield; Eldra made it a point to help clear both. Her sword rested on the side of her belt as she lay prone on the floor, adjusting her aim for her next shot.

"The battle has turned in our favor," Eldra proclaimed loudly to her Hiezer cadets. "We have to crush their morale before the retaliation begins. If another jet takes flight from their camp, focus all fire on taking it down."

We have the numbers and the momentum. I have to keep the upper hand.

She kept a keen eye on the chaos in the middle of the field. Her scope crossed a medic, who was desperately trying to save a fighter. She took aim and pierced the medic's brain in an instant.

Of course!

Eldra moved her face slightly away from her scope, focusing on her epiphany.

The medical station.

She jumped up confidently, holding her rifle in one hand. Her crystal blue eyes were radiant in the cloudy, grey atmosphere. Her long, black hair waved as she quickly advanced toward a higher sniper's nest. She wore light-weight black and gold combat attire that allowed her to move swiftly, as a sniper should.

"Follow me," she said loudly.

Bombs and screams sounded loudly in the distance, even though the mid field battle was coming to a notorious end. The Hiezer cadets shot up from their positions and fell in line behind her.

"Take out the civilians. This attack will cut their lifeline and their morale with one swipe," she said with a smirk.

"The queen is ruthless," she heard a cadet whisper; she pretended not to hear.

A bullet whizzed closely behind the advancing snipers. Eldra repositioned herself, resting her pristine rifle over the ledge of the cliff. She had a clear view of the hardworking medics stashed away in the far corner of the field. Without hesitation, Eldra fired on the first unsuspecting victim. The bloodied medic groaned in agony, wondering how the battle could have stooped to this level.

There are no rules in war. There are only the victorious and the dead.

She fired again, taking out another. Eldra then shifted her aim. She aligned her crosshair with a frightened nurse with a nose ring, who struggled to stop the blood of a wounded fighter. Narene took her last breath, sensing that she was next. The wind blew Eldra's silky hair all around her as she tightened her finger around the trigger. Eldra heard the sound of a bullet piercing through the air, before hearing her scope crack; one of her eyes went dark. She found herself sliding down the sniper's nest. She screamed an explosive battle cry as her sniper cadets flew back from their positions, each with their own high caliber bullet wounds.

Distressed, Lito ran over to where he saw an unknown jet hover for a moment, before it unloaded bullets onto the field. Bodies decorated the ground around him. The outlook of the battle seemed grim as only sixty or so fighters remained. He walked to the top of the hill, ready to pull the pin of a grenade. Lito froze in position before pulling it; he discovered a familiar sniper who was creating harrowing screams from his victims.

"Eugene!" Lito's voice was full of hope as he ran over and hugged him.

Eugene sighed, "We have work to do. Get off of me," he said with a smirk.

Eugene took aim to finish off the last Hiezer sniper. He pulled the trigger as multiple jets approached the vicinity. The jets dispatched members of the Aura, who promptly helped wounded and demoralized Sin fighters back to their feet.

"You came back," Lito said in shock, "And even better *mijo*, you saved us."

Eugene turned to look at Lito, "I haven't saved anyone yet," knowing that there was still work to be done.

Stray Hiezer soldiers attempted to flock to the queen, responding to her cry. Eldra somehow got back to her feet. She ripped a piece of cloth from her sleeve and wrapped it around her head. Her one crystal blue eye darted around with a lust for revenge. Lesh ran after her, as she whipped knives into the air. She punctured the back of each Hiezer guard that stood in her path. Lesh then flipped high into the air and threw a knife, aimed straight at the Ice Queen. Eldra quickly unsheathed her curved sword and deflected the blade into the air. Lesh kicked off of a falling Hiezer, drew two throwing knives, and spun them between her fingers.

This bitch is living up to her name. That wound on her eye is fresh; how could she possibly have the energy to fight?

Lesh leaped a third time, now within close combat range of Eldra. Lesh spun on her way down with the two knives in hand. Eldra slashed her sword, meeting with one of Lesh's blades, which caused her spinning motion to cease. Lesh quickly jumped back and shifted her momentum forward again. She slashed high with one arm and Eldra dodged it. Eldra had to hastily adapt to her newly impeded vision, her depth perception was lacking. Lesh spun again and swung low with her other arm. Eldra met Lesh's knife with her blade.

The Ice Queen, her reputation precedes her.

Eldra advanced forward as she swung her sword at Lesh; Lesh parried some, but dodged most. Eldra's long blade was easier to evade than to deflect. Lesh back flipped onto a fallen Hiezer's back to reclaim her knife, which jutted from his corpse. Eldra became further agitated by Lesh. She slashed her sword more violently, as blood drops seeped out of her mostly covered eye socket. Lesh saw a brief opening and took it, parrying Eldra's blade and guiding it to the floor. She then stepped on top of the blunt side of the blade with one foot and jerked her body, creating enough force to kick Eldra across the face, throwing her onto the floor. Hiezer guards flocked to her aid in the distance. Lesh took notice and rapidly tried to end the duel by throwing a knife toward Eldra's forehead. Her expression hardened, her icy blue eye pierced through Lesh's as she still managed to deflect the knife with her sword. Stray bullets ricocheted around Lesh. She looked back and decided it was time to flee. She gave Eldra a cold stare back, as if to say, 'we'll finish this another time.'

Jets piloted by the Aura continued to fly overhead, aiming to take out the Hiezer reinforcements. The Aura began to march onto the battlefield, all with hooded half cloaks and large rifles. With their large numbers and fresh spirit, they helped to turn the tide of the battle, once again. Jen walked up to the medic center. She was impossible to miss with her deep red hue and the slight trail of red smoke that followed her.

"But Eugene," Lito said, still surprised by Eugene's return, "How did you know? How did you find us?"

Eugene looked over at Lito in between shots and gave him a look, before giving him an explanation.

Blague looked forward at his reapers as they took aim.

My Sin brothers and sisters, you can take it from here.

Elaina's smiling face came into vision before everything turned white; all he could hear was a strong ringing in his ears. Blague thought that this was what the final moments before death felt like until a few moments later when his vision returned to him. To Blague and Mulderan's surprise, most of the Hiezer guards toppled over from the bloody slashes delivered by a man sheathing an ancient blade.

It was a flashbang, I'm not dead yet.

Blague tried to sit up, grimacing from the spear impaled near his shoulder.

"Niro," Blague shouted with a strained voice.

"You've got it backwards," Niro responded, emitting three different tones from his voice changer.

A spear flew in Niro's direction. He side stepped and caught it, using the momentum to swing it back to the elite guard who threw it. As the spear reverted back with swift speed, it barely shaved the guard's arm as he evaded the attack; he lost his balance and fell thirty feet into the body of water. Mulderan pulled out a pistol and aimed at the odd man, firing rapidly. Niro's riot shield expanded from the block of metal strapped to his arm, deflecting the full clip of shots. Niro then kicked the shield in Mulderan's direction, causing him to strafe out of the way. Niro advanced toward Mulderan, while he reached down from the bottom of the largest of his cloths, gripped the end of it, and pulled it over his head. All of the cloths and his voice changer fell to the floor behind him. Blague's eyes widened and Mulderan dropped his gun. The older, fit man with smoky eyes and Cryos blue veins walked forward, unsheathing his ancient sword again.

"Father?" Mulderan said as his voice trembled. "I watched you die!"

"Apparently, not closely enough," Orin's exceptionally deep voice projected.

His wavy, shoulder length grey hair blew in the wind. "I've watched you for nearly a century," Orin said as he slowly walked toward Mulderan, who drew his staff.

Orin suddenly moved so swiftly, it was as if he appeared in front of Mulderan out of thin air. Orin swung and Mulderan blocked, holding both hands on opposite sides of his staff to resist the pressure. Orin quickly slid his blade down one side, slicing open one of Mulderan's fingers.

"You speak of the greatest good," Orin said as he sliced again, pushing Mulderan back. His deep voice rang through Mulderan's ears. "Such a noble cause, but every action you take contradicts this notion," Orin continued as he slashed again. "Every thought stemming from you is evil."

Orin kicked Mulderan backward.

"That's not true," Mulderan said, flipping his staff and attempting to advance.

He swung wildly, as he struggled to mentally grasp this evolved version of his father.

"Neither of you could ever understand my vision; it's the ultimate sacrifice." Mulderan swung hard, but Orin guided the staff down with his blade and quickly spun it, slicing Mulderan from his abdomen to his chest. The wound was shallow.

"You have much to learn, my son," Orin said as he sheathed his blade.

He reached for Mulderan's stomach and tightened his grip around the fresh wound with one hand and reached for his neck with the other. Mulderan dropped his staff.

"I should take you out of this world, for I'm responsible for unleashing you unto it," Orin said as he lifted Mulderan off his feet. "Look around you. Look at all of the anguish that you've caused," Orin said as he stared up at his son with his smoky eyes.

He released his hand from the wound and drew his blade, grazing it against Mulderan's neck. Mulderan stared back with cold eyes, as the air was being crushed out of him. Orin flipped Mulderan to the floor and cracked him in the temple with the hilt of his sword.

"I suppose I'll let the others, whom you have caused so much despair, pass judgement on you," Orin said as he looked down on his son with a glare of disgust.

He dragged Mulderan's unconscious body by his hair and walked over to Blague. He picked Blague up by the collar, ripped the spear out of his shoulder, and tossed it. He then wrapped the wound with one of his cloths.

"Never give up, my son," Orin said.

Blague was conscious, but in tremendous pain. He stared at his father, still dumbfounded that he was watching over him for some time now; he was pronounced dead all of those years ago. Orin's exposed skin was tinted wine red.

He hasn't aged since the quake. He must easily be the oldest living person on the planet. He guided me through the most difficult parts of this world.

"Thank you," Blague said.

Orin leaned him against the wall. "Elaina would be proud, and I am too."

Orin picked up his riot shield and grabbed Mulderan by the hair again. Blague's radio went off.

"It's over, boss. Apparently, we have allies," Lito said.

Blague looked down and covered his face with his good hand, taking all of this in.

"We have to get out of here before reinforcements come to wipe us out," Lito finished.

After a long pause, Blague picked up his radio, "Copy."

Orin and Blague remained for a moment, enjoying the unique view of the mountaintop in front of them, with water surrounding it. Blague struggled to get up. As tough as he was, he was fatigued from the wound and spent from battle. Orin remained silent, feeling that he said all he had to say. He watched Blague get up and walk back. He followed closely behind.

Chapter 22

Blague walked through the crowd of the mansion with a sling, as he escorted his shackled brother to the newly constructed prison. The prison was designed with reinforced steel and twenty four hour surveillance, compliments of Rodest. They both walked with an obvious struggle in their steps. The crowd of civilians kept their distance as they passed, emitting mixed emotions. Some offered angry gestures to Mulderan, while others bowed down to their leader who captured the enemy. Blague approached the cell slowly, contemplating the recovery period to come. Mulderan's generally pristine face and garb remained bloody and ragged.

"This is a dire mistake. You don't have the ability to understand what's coming. You may despise my methods, but you will be begging for guidance in the near future," Mulderan warned.

Blague looked over, "Perhaps, or maybe you're just bluffing because you're backed into a corner."

Blague threw him into the cell and locked it, leaving him next to a critically injured Wes Howard.

"Do you know why I chose you for preservation, Blague?" Mulderan asked.

Blague stood silent.

"Because, in the grand scheme, it doesn't matter if we're at odds. You will aid in humanity's survival," he finished.

"Until next time," Blague said as he turned away.

Sabin looked around the room, "Cheer up, guys! The ambush was successful! We've just ensured our future, kind of!"

The other commanders conversed, although most were fatigued from battle. Telfice joined in on trying to comfort the others. Lesh cleaned the blood off of her blades and Orin stood in the corner without his rags. His arms were folded and his smoky, pupil-less eyes darted back and forth.

"Who the fuck is that?" Sabin said to Eugene, pointing at Orin.

Eugene couldn't help but laugh at Sabin, "That, my fellow jackass, is the man who saved all of your lives. Who do you think sought us out to save you?"

Sabin squinted for a moment and knelt down to stare at him, with Mars at his side. "Is that Niro?"

Mars barked and Eugene nodded.

"Yep," Eugene said, "without all of the cloths."

"So we're all standing here now because of him? Maybe I should go give him a hug?" Sabin asked Eugene.

"I wouldn't," Eugene said with a grin.

Two nurses walked a crutched Drino through the door.

"Dude," Sabin said, "you just got shot. What. Are. You. Doing?"

Drino waved at him to shut up. Blague walked in last. As soon as he passed through the door, a low clap followed. The group did not want to dishearten all of the families who lost loved ones in the battle. Blague smiled at his commanders and hugged Eugene first, then looked over to Sabin and included him in the same huddle.

"Thank you. Thank you all. I would be nothing without you," Blague said. Most of the commanders gave a nod or a bow.

Lesh rolled her eyes, "No need to get sappy, Blague. You're going to ruin your tough image or something." The room laughed.

"Or something," Telfice said, "hah."

Blague walked over to Orin, "Thank you, father."

Orin awoke from his deep trance after he heard his son's voice through a muffled thought. As Blague came into Orin's focus, he nodded with pride for his accomplished son. Blague then walked over to Drino and stared.

"Now, this is one tough son of a bitch," Blague said.

Drino, who was sitting there wrapped in bandages, flashed a half smile.

"I just don't get how he had time to fix his hair," Sabin said.

The room laughed again. Drino held his stomach from the pain caused by the laughter.

Blague walked back over to Eugene. "Is Jen stable?" he whispered.

Eugene nodded, "She killed Jason Brink while she was unstable though."

"Oh," Blague said as he scratched his head. "Does

that make the Aura our ally now?" Blague asked.

"For the time being, it appears that way," Eugene said.

"And you?" Blague asked. "To be the right hand commander of the Sins, if you'll have me," Eugene said.

Blague put a hand on his shoulder and nodded, "We'll figure out the details later. Come take a walk."

Cherris stood over Briggs' grave as the ocean pushed a light breeze through the air. She heard Blague and Eugene talking while on their way over.

Cherris turned around and hugged Eugene tightly, "Happy for the unexpected surprise. Welcome back. You were missed!" She said.

Eugene embraced her back.

Cherris turned to hug Blague, "I'm glad you're safe."

"Hah, you too. See? I didn't leave you too thin on protection," he said lightly, "Speaking of which, I have to address the civilians. I need to provide them with an update and express my condolences for the fallen fighters."

After a pause, they all turned to face Briggs' grave. The wind blew all of their hair back as they stood in the sunset.

"This win was for you, old friend," Blague said as he hit his chest and paid his respects.

Social Class Hierarchy

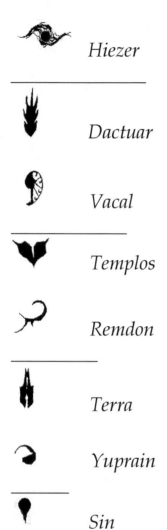

Hiezer

Dactuar

Vacal

Templos

Remdon

Terra

Yuprain

Sin

Rogue Movements

 Aura

 *Blague*

Acknowledgements

My sincerest thanks to the editor of Unearthed, Angela Loccisano, and to the cover artist, George Lovesy. I couldn't have done this without you.

Made in the USA
Charleston, SC
09 August 2016